THE RUEFUL RIVAL

"Oh my, Zachary, you have landed yourself with a real termagant, haven't you?" smiled Lady Foxx. "No wonder you are looking so woefully *harassed* these days. Poor thing, the trials you men must endure to secure your nurseries."

Samantha was still standing mutely, her bosom heaving in her agitation, but unable as yet to form a set-down sufficient to shutting Lady Foxx's face once and for all. The leering face of her rival crowding in on her set up a hum in her ears and caused her hand to reach out and clutch at the first thing to come to hand. That "thing" was an enormous strawberry tart oozing juice and topped with a large dollop of finely whipped cream. Before, as the lower classes might say, the cat could lick her ear, Samantha had shoved the tart smack into the grinning mouth of one Lady Lorinda Foxx!

Other Avon Books by
Kasey Michaels

THE BELLIGERENT MISS BOYNTON
THE TENACIOUS MISS TAMERLANE

THE RAMBUNCTIOUS LADY ROYSTON

KASEY MICHAELS

AVON
PUBLISHERS OF BARD, CAMELOT, DISCUS AND FLARE BOOKS

THE RAMBUNCTIOUS LADY ROYSTON is an original publication of Avon Books. This work has never before appeared in book form.

AVON BOOKS
A division of
The Hearst Corporation
959 Eighth Avenue
New York, New York 10019

Published by arrangement with the author
Library of Congress Catalog Card Number: 82-90480
ISBN: 0-380-81448-x

First Avon Printing, December, 1982

Printed in the U. S. A.

WFH 10 9 8 7 6 5 4 3 2 1

In remembrance of
Aunt Loretta's Fudge and
other lessons in Perspective.

Chapter One

IZZY, for the love of heaven, control yourself!" "I am in perfect control, Samantha. I only cried out because I felt a bit faint as I raised my eyes to the tip of the balloon," replied a vision in blue-sprigged muslin. "Do you really think it is safe? It looks prodigiously high to me. And don't call me Izzy," Miss Isabella Ardsley added with the resigned air of a person called upon to repeat a request innumerable times while knowing full well it would be ignored.

Miss Samantha Ardsley gritted her teeth and ground out, "You nitwit, the name is Samuel! You'll ruin everything yet, Izzy."

Miss Isabella turned her shocked face to her escort and whispered, "Do you think anyone heard? Perhaps I shall faint!"

"Do, and I'll leave you in the dirt, I swear it! Now behave yourself!"

Miss Samantha Ardsley (or was it Mister Samuel Ardsley?) took hold of her (or was it his?) sister's hand and led her to a nearby vacant bench. After depositing her upon the perch with no ceremony whatsoever, the questionable escort set off to spy out some sort of refreshment for the distraught girl. What madness, the young sprig of fashion thought, I should have known Izzy hasn't the starch for this intrigue.

Miss Samantha Ardsley—for in truth the well-dressed young gentleman was a young lady—allowed a small smile to light up one side of her face as she pushed her way towards a street vendor, thrusting boldly through the crush of young bucks to purchase a small flavored ice.

What would all these fine gentlemen think if they knew

who I really am? she asked herself. In a way she was glad her father had vetoed the visit to Green Park to see the balloon ascension; it was certainly more of a lark this way. Thank heaven she was able to hold the threat of Izzy's clandestine meeting with young Malcolm over her head, or she might never have talked Izzy into this delicious scheme. Oh, she could have donned her brother's clothes and come alone, as she had done before. But when Izzy caught her, one leg into Wally's outgrown breeches, there was nothing for it but to lug her missish older sister along. Experience had taught Samantha that the only way to keep Isabella's mouth firmly shut was to make her sister as guilty as herself.

It was such a bother being a female! Her brother Wallace was allowed the freedom of the city when he was home, and even Izzy had more leeway—considering she was already "Out," as the term went. But Samantha was just a few months past ten-and-seven, and resided in the city only because her father, Sir Stephen Ardsley, could not afford to keep the country house open just for her. Not that she was unhappy in London. Hadn't she already been to the Fives Court, The Tower, and even Covent Garden—all in the disguise of a country youth set loose in the city to acquire some town bronze?

Samantha harbored no secret desire to have been born a male. It was her impatience with the restrictions Society placed on young females and her envy of the freedom enjoyed by her brother and the rest of the masculine gender—a disparity she condemned as excessively unfair—that prompted her adoption of masculine attire. Oh, no, it would be irresponsible to dismiss Samantha as just another hoydenish tomboy.

She was just as predictably feminine as her demure older sister when it came to her weaknesses for the latest fashions, dancing till the wee hours at provincial balls, and excelling in most of the accepted female pursuits (excluding needlepoint, which she eschewed as an old lady's pastime). Horses, dogs, tree-climbing, and the like all had a part in her life, but they were not consuming passions.

No, Samantha's besetting sin—the failing that prompted her to don masculine clothing and poke about

London—was, quite simply, an unquenchable thirst for adventure. At almost predictable intervals she became overpowered by an inner voice urging her to explore, to discover, to experiment, to observe new things, and the by now familiar feelings of longing could no more be ignored than could a sharp splinter jabbing under one's tender skin.

And so, ever since her maiden aunt had decreed that Sir Stephen Ardsley's youngest daughter must begin to behave like a young lady and desist in her unescorted ramblings about the countryside, Samantha had simply taken her longings and her unorthodox method of indulging them underground. Her borrowed masculine attire gave her the freedom to pursue her penchant for adventure to the top of her bent; her secret was safe so long as the gods remained kind; and no one took it into his head to compare a certain slim, red-haired youth to the not-yet-Out Samantha Ardsley.

When it came time for the Ardsleys to come to town, Samantha's alter ego—in the form of Wally's discarded breeches—came right along with the baggage. There was so much to see and do in this great metropolis; Samantha's sojourns about the city thus far were seen by her to be in the way of tantalizing appetizers for the many fascinating discoveries yet to come.

Thanks to Daisy, her maid and sometime *confidante,* her excursions had been without incident thus far, but the balloon ascension was one treat she had almost missed. Poor Izzy! That girl had the backbone of a sea sponge. Samantha had better hurry back before the balloon went up, for Izzy would probably swoon at the simple sight of it.

But it was not so easy to thread through the crowd now that all were rooted where they stood. The men had climbed into the balloon, and amid the crush Samantha was finding it difficult to locate Isabella in the throng. She pushed and nudged, apologized, and bowed her way through the crowd only to pause at the sound of the *oohs* and *aahs* as the balloon slowly rose above the park. She stopped for a moment to watch its flight, but suddenly, out of the corner of her eye, she saw her sister standing now at the edge of the onlookers, rapidly losing color.

Samantha took one last wistful look at the balloon before making tracks for Isabella's side, arriving only a moment too late—for her sister was already reclining in an unconscious state in the arms of a very large man.

"Miss Ardsley, are you all right?" Samantha queried. Her voice had elevated to an octave a bit too high to sound very masculine, due more to her anger at missing the ascension rather than from any concern for the girl's welfare.

"Are you responsible for this female?"

The question was more of an accusation, and Samantha's head flew up to meet the speaker's face. Samantha was a tallish girl—one good reason for her ability to get away with wearing her brother's clothes—but this man made her feel a veritable dwarf. Eyes as dark as coals burned down on her out of a face that looked to be chiselled out of solid marble, though his skin was tanned as though he spent many hours in the sun. His hair was as black as his disconcertingly shrewd eyes, and slight streaks of grey marked his temples, adding not a whit to his age but making him look still more forbidding.

Even Samantha didn't have to look twice to know she was confronted with the notorious Zachary St. John, Earl of Royston. "Describe the Devil and you have likewise conjured up a likeness of Royston," the saying went. He was right, the wit who had made up those lines, thought Samantha; for truly it was Satan himself, glaring down at her in obvious disgust.

While Samantha was examining the Earl, he was returning her scrutiny. He saw before him a young blade, damned young by the lack of beard on his face—though you could never tell that for sure with a redhead. The lad was reasonably tall, but he certainly didn't look physically capable of holding up Miss Ardsley, who was small but no lightweight. Dresses reasonably well, even if he fails to fill his coat very neatly at the shoulders, thought his lordship; probably some young pup who's just recently shaken the mud of Yorkshire or Devon from his boots, as I don't remember seeing him about before this. None too overcrowded in his brainbox either; just look at those wide green eyes, gawking at me as if I were going to eat him in lieu of lunch.

"Well, sir? Are you dumb? I asked if you were escorting this unfortunate creature," he said at last, his voice booming like thunder in Samantha's ears.

"I—I, that is, I had gone to fetch her an ice." Samantha looked down at the paper cup with its melted contents and dashed it to the ground with a muttered oath. "I thank you for your kind intervention, my lord," Samantha tacked on when she belatedly remembered her assumed role, "but if you will, er, *pass* the lady to me, I shall take her off your hands."

"And do what with her? Toss her over your shoulder and march off like a Viking bearing a prize of battle?"

Samantha felt herself going beet-red, a habit she thought she had left behind in the country, as she retorted, "That is my concern, your lordship. Kindly unhand my—Miss Ardsley at once!"

Luckily, Miss Ardsley was at last showing signs of recovering from her swoon. The Earl led her to the bench she had (in Samantha's mind) so stupidly chosen to leave in the first place, and sat her down. Isabella stammered her apologies and thanks as her eyes met those of her rescuer, and she held out her hand to her sister.

Samantha took her hand and squeezed it unnecessarily hard in warning. Isabella threw her a darkling glance; she may have been only a female, but she certainly knew enough to be careful around the Earl of Royston. "I would wish to go back to Mount Street if you don't mind. I have an exceedingly painful head, I fear." There, she thought smugly, *that* should prove Samantha is not the only quick thinker in the family.

"Of course," came the reply from the Earl, before Samantha could utter a sound. "Do you wish this youth's company, or would you prefer I escort you in my curricle?" He shot a look at Samantha. "I can understand your feeling uneasy under his protection, as he has already failed you once this afternoon." He turned to Samantha. "Is *your* carriage nearby, Mr.—?"

Samantha quickly answered "Smythe," just as Isabella—suddenly and unfortunately displaying a heretofore carefully concealed flair for invention—supplied the alias of "Wright." The Earl raised his finely arched brows and turned from one to the other.

"Smythe-Wright," Samantha corrected with fervor. "Samuel Smythe-Wright. Your servant, and all that, my lord. And it is unnecessary for you to introduce yourself, for I would be a slowtop indeed if I did not recognize you, sir. Allow me to present Miss Isabella Ardsley, late of Ardsley Manor and—if I may be so bold—your arms, your lordship."

"Sam—!"

"Sam it is, all right!" Samantha almost shouted, to cut off her sister who was about to call her Samantha and land them both in the basket for sure. She quickly lowered her voice to its assumed huskiness. "Every one of my friends call me Sam, your lordship." Isabella would get the sharp side of Samantha's tongue once they were out of this; *if* they ever were out of this!

The Earl raised his quizzing glass to stare at the discomfited youth. "*I* shall call you Smythe-Wright," he supplied coldly, "and quite a bit more, if you don't get this unfortunate child to her carriage posthaste. We are attracting quite a crowd and I have a pressing engagement I shall be late in keeping if I cannot see a satisfactory conclusion to this mess immediately. Do I make myself clear, Smythe-Wright?"

Samantha felt the heat rush into her face again at the sound of Isabella's giggle. "Crystal, your lordship," she returned, boldly offering a stiff bow. "We arrived in a hack, which I allowed to leave. With this crush of people it will be impossible to find another with as much speed as you require. I suggest *you* return Miss Ardsley to the bosom of her family, as I am more than slightly bored with the chit and quite put out that she made me miss the ascension. Good day, my lord," Samantha fairly beamed as she favored him with a slight bow. "The pleasure has been *all* mine."

Isabella was completely dumbfounded at her sister's ungentlemanly behavior and gasped a *"Sam!"* before swooning once more in the Earl's arms—an unlooked-for aid that made a success of Samantha's unchivalrous abandonment. The Earl shot a look boding no good towards the youth's retreating back, but to pursue the young whelp and give him the sound thrashing he deserved he would have to leave the girl, which was quite impossible. "We'll meet again, Smythe-Wright," he called after Samantha as he balanced Isabella against his right side. "And you will rue the day you were born!"

Samantha turned with a wide grin and saluted the Earl smartly before vanishing into the crowd.

She took her sweet time getting home, and by the time she returned (through the back door Daisy always left unlatched for her) Isabella was only one short step away from complete hysterics.

"Where have you *been,* Samantha?" she demanded. "I have been out of my mind with worry, and Papa has been home for the last half hour. What if he had asked for you?"

Samantha hurriedly got out of her borrowed breeches and donned the muslin gown Daisy held out to her. She sat herself in front of the mirror and let down the burnished curls that had been pinned up to fit under her brother's curly-brimmed beaver. "Do not put yourself into a pet, Izzy. I am home safe and dry." She allowed a bit of a snicker to escape her lips. "Did you enjoy the Earl's company?"

"I most certainly did not! He frightens me right out of my wits! The worst of it is, he insists on calling upon me tomorrow because he wants more information on my 'escort.' He will tear a wide strip off your skin if ever he finds you out. What are we going to do? I cannot receive him alone; Aunt Loretta always falls asleep in the corner when we are entertaining guests. I know I shall end up blurting out the truth. Oh, I wish I were dead!" Isabella ended dramatically.

Samantha finished brushing her hair and turned to her distraught sister. "Never fear, Izzy. I landed us in this muddle and I shall get us out again. Both Miss Isabella *and* her schoolroom baby sister Samantha shall entertain the Earl tomorrow. And I dare him to get around *me!*"

Chapter Two

THE EARL OF ROYSTON, ma'am."

Miss Loretta Ardsley, Sir Stephen's middle-aged spinster sister (whose sole claim to beauty lay in her extremely long, black eyelashes, which were once the subject of a sonnet by some dull-witted swain who disappeared in a fortnight) placed a steadying hand to her throat and fluttered those once praised attributes at the forbidding form now darkening the doorway of the small salon.

"Your lordship, it is an honor, what a great honor indeed, to welcome you to our humble abode. Such condescension, I am sure," cooed the lady.

Samantha, sitting next to her sister on the small sofa, leaned towards her now to whisper, "Laying it on a bit too thick and rare, don't you think?"

Isabella threw her a look meant to squelch any further dangerous outbursts and raised her fan in an imitation of some envied debutante or other.

"La, yes, my lord," Isabella broke in as her aunt lost herself in inanities. "It is so very kind of you to call. Allow me to present to you my aunt, Miss Loretta Ardsley, and my young sister, who has come to bear me company for my time in the metropolis—Miss Samantha Ardsley."

The Earl bowed over each lady's hand in turn, pausing longest over Samantha's as he searched her features with a strange expression on his face.

"Charmed, I am sure, ladies."

Aunt Loretta rang for tea almost immediately, for lack of any other ideas to pass the time, and after serving it and trying to add her bit to the rather insipid polite conversation, she retreated to a corner where she quickly—and predictably—fell into a light doze.

At the sound of her slight snores the Earl carefully placed his teacup on the table and addressed his next words to Isabella. "Have you located the direction of our Mr. Smythe-Wright, madam?"

"I, er, that is, I—"

Samantha cut in quickly. "What my sister is trying to say is that Mr. Smythe-Wright is an old family friend and we do not wish to see him punished. You see, we grew up together and Samuel was always a rather simple soul, if you get my meaning. We have never quite held him responsible for his rather loose-screw starts. We regret any inconvenience to your lordship, but we wish the subject dropped."

His lordship chewed on his lip for a moment with what looked strongly like suppressed amusement, then rearranged his satanic features into an emotionless mask and informed Samantha stiffly, "I do not share your easy forgiveness, missy. I have been insulted and demand a chance to tear a strip from the dolt's hide."

"See, Samantha, I *told* you he would want—"

"Isabella," Samantha shut her off, "I do believe Aunt Loretta is being rude to our guest. Kindly wake her up."

Isabella colored prettily—she was a delightful, tiny blonde thing—and rose to do, as usual, just as her young sister bid her do. But she was stopped short by the Earl's next words.

"Do go and sit by your aunt's side, Miss Isabella. I wish a few private words with your, er, *sister.*"

Samantha's eyes commanded Isabella to stay where she was as Lord Royston's eyes demanded her departure and, sad to say, the Earl's look won out. With a defeated shrug of her shoulders, Isabella retired to the corner and sat watching her aunt's nostrils widen and contract as she continued to snooze on.

Samantha tensed and would have risen to quit the room had not the Earl's hand come down hard on her wrist. "I think not, my dear. I allowed you to run off yesterday, but I am not so encumbered today and would follow you immediately."

"Sir, I wish to go to my chambers."

"If you wish," he shrugged indifferently. "I am no stranger to a woman's *boudoir.*"

"How dare you!" Samantha bristled.

"Quite easily, *Mr. Smythe-Wright,* quite easily. I sincerely hope your father beat you often when you were a child."

Samantha searched his face and saw a glint of humor in his dark eyes. "Soundly, my lord, at least until he announced it a worthless expenditure of his energy. Now I am merely confined to my chambers whenever I am caught out, er, overstepping my boundaries."

The Earl threw back his head and laughed, his face completely transformed by this simple act. "Which is seldom, I wager—that you are caught out, I mean."

Isabella cringed in her chair at the sight of this huge man, who was feared by all in the *ton,* and clapped her dainty hands over her shell-like ears. Samantha did nothing of the sort. She threw back her own head and joined in the joke.

The Earl sobered first and returned his gaze to the girl facing him. "How old are you, Miss Ardsley?"

"I am ten-and-seven, my lord, with a birthday in two months. But I cannot make my come-out until Isabella is advantageously bracketed and off Papa's hands. My arrival on the scene before that time, according to my sire, would be enough to make any man of sense shy away from leg-shackling himself to a family with a bent towards madness," Samantha supplied candidly.

Isabella shrieked and ran out of the room when she heard her sister tell London's most eligible bachelor such a thing. Aunt Loretta roused for a moment from her nap, smiled in the general direction of the Earl, waved languidly, and returned to her dreams.

"I must apologize, my lord." Samantha said without a hint of remorse. "I should not have said that about my sister. Please disregard it completely."

The Earl sat back in his chair and considered the figure before him. She made a passable boy, but her figure was definitely enhanced by female fripperies. She was yet somewhat a child and still had some slight filling out to do, but she was the first girl whose head had ever come up to his shoulders. How he hated all these petite misses; he forever had a crick in his neck from bending down to hear their senseless chatter. Her eyes were very intriguing, too—green as emeralds and of a pleasing almond shape under those dark, winglike brows.

He surprised himself by asking, "How do you come by dark lashes and brows when your hair is copper?"

If Samantha found anything strange in this question she did not show it on her face. "My brows are like my mother's, I imagine, as she had the same coloring. She was Irish. And my hair is a common red, not copper."

"No, no, child. Red does not describe it at all. I stand by my description. You have a brother, I believe."

"Yes, my lord," she answered, then took a deep breath and added in a challenging voice, "Wallace is in his last year at Cambridge, much to his chagrin. He feels the time spent with his head between the pages of a book could be put to better use polishing the buttons on a Hussar uniform. My mother died when I was three. My father is a younger son who makes his living on a small estate in the country. This is our first trip to London, made only to present my sister to polite society. I no longer have a governess, although I put three of them through the hoops over the past ten years, causing the last to retire to her brother's parsonage not six months ago in a complete collapse. I ride extremely well, have a fair to middling command of the French language, hate needlework, loathe politics, break out in spots if I eat green beans, and my teeth are tolerably good," she concluded triumphantly. "Now, if there is nothing else you desire I would like to withdraw and check on my sister."

She made to rise, but at his firm "Sit down!" she fell back into her chair with a thump. "You are distressed, and rightly so, both by my questions and my manner. If I were a gentleman I feel sure I would be moved to apologize. But I am not, and besides, you must admit it is not every day that a man is confronted with a young girl with fire and spirit such as yours. I will thank you for your candor and will endeavor to return the courtesy."

"Don't burst a stitch on my account, your lordship, as I

find myself not in the least intrigued by your life story," Samantha returned sarcastically.

The Earl ignored this outburst and rose to stand behind his chair, forcing her to arch her neck as she looked into his face. "I am Zachary St. John, twelfth Earl of Royston, worth a good seventy thousand a year, and a bachelor of one-and-thirty years. I own three major estates—all large and productive—a townhouse in Mayfair, a hunting box in Scotland, and have a considerable stable. The St. John jewels are known as one of the best collections in the realm and I am the most eligible and elusive bachelor in the city.

"These are all minor things," he said, and then dismissed it all with a sweep of one strong, tanned hand. In a more serious tone he continued: "I have two major problems, and until today I had no way of solving either.

"The first is that I am bored. I can see that surprises you, but it is nevertheless true. I am bored to extinction with my life, my friends, my money, and my title. The second problem is that, at the advanced age of one-and-thirty—nearer two-and-thirty, actually—I have no heir. Until last year this lack did not bother me in the slightest, as I had a younger brother who I was more than happy to have succeed me when I finally am handed my notice to quit. Unfortunately, he was lost in the war."

"I am so sorry, your lordship," Samantha supplied, her tender heartstrings touched.

"Do not interrupt," he warned curtly. "As my friends, such as they are, will tell you, I am a very unlikeable man. I am hated or endured for my politics—depending upon your leanings—work and play hard as is my wont, and take what I desire when I see it. Yet, as I said, I am bored with my existence. In fact, the only emotion I have felt since the grief engendered by my brother's death was my extreme annoyance with you yesterday. Today you have amused me, my second voyage into this phenomenon called emotion in two days. I have astonished myself. I look at you and I am already assured you would never bore me, or at least not for some time. Therefore it would seem my first problem is solved.

"Strangely, solving the first problem also solves the second. I shall approach your father this afternoon for your hand. The wedding shall take place before the month is out. I like things to be neat, don't you?"

Samantha jumped to her feet. "You are out of your mind!" she accused shrilly.

"That had occurred to me, Sam." He started towards the door. "And close your mouth. It makes you look simple-minded; that is one thing I know you are not."

"My name is Samantha," she shouted at his retreating back. "And I wouldn't marry you if you came wrapped up in priceless gold chains and were next in line for the throne."

He turned towards her and smiled. "Really? I don't know of another woman in England who would cast me aside so quickly. I hope you never come to love me, for you would lose all your fire."

"There's scant chance of that eventuality. I loathe you! To put it in terms you should be able to comprehend, you are a conceited, pompous *ass!*"

"Good," he returned, not turning a hair. "You will give me lusty sons, *Sam.* That is really all I require."

Samantha sat down heavily and burst into tears.

"What? Tears? Oh, no, perhaps I have been too hasty. It appears you are just like any other female, resorting to weeping when things go wrong. I must have misjudged you."

Samantha picked up her aunt's sewing basket—the closest thing to hand—and aimed it at his head as if to throw it.

"Ah, I thought not. You have restored my faith in you, Sam. Do not forget to advise your father of my impending visit. I am assured he will arrange to be at home for me."

"I hate you!"

"And I feel nothing at all for you. Interesting, is it not? Good day, my dear."

All this commotion finally served to wake Aunt Loretta. "Oh, dear," she cried, rubbing at her eyes. "Has the Earl gone, then? I hope you made my apologies."

Samantha sent her aunt a withering look. "You are of about as much use as a chaperone as would be a stuffed owl. That odious man just proposed, and you slept through the whole thing!"

"Proposed? But where is Isabella? I must congratulate her! This is the *catch of the season,* I vow it is." Aunt Loretta hastily began gathering her shawls around her.

"He didn't propose to Izzy," Samantha said acidly. "It's me he wants."

Her aunt's agitated movements came to an abrupt halt. "But you are barely out of the schoolroom. Whatever can he want from you, Samantha dear?"

"Two things, Aunt," she told her dryly. "Entertainment and sons. It seems he sees me as a cross between a court jester and a brood mare. Isn't that romantic?" Samantha turned on her heel and left the room.

"Entertainment and sons?" her aunt repeated dully to the empty room. "I really mustn't stay up so late at night. The most interesting things seem to be happening in the daytime."

Chapter Three

IT did not surprise Samantha a whit that her father all but fell on the Earl's neck when he asked for Sir Stephen's troublesome younger daughter's hand in marriage. Neither tears nor threats could sway him from his stand that with this marriage their fortunes would be made. Isabella was certain to be snatched up almost immediately once her sister the Countess presented her to Society, and he and Loretta could retire at last to peace in the country. As for Wally: he had wanted to purchase a commission and surely his brother-in-law the Earl would be more than happy to be his patron. Oh, yes, it was a grand match!

There was only one slight problem: Samantha was being difficult, as only Samantha could be. She sulked in her room for hours on end, refusing to be fitted for the many gowns the Earl had ordered, and sometimes she disappeared from the house for hours on end with not even Daisy knowing her whereabouts. As the wedding day drew nearer, Sir Stephen was holding his breath for fear that the Earl would have second thoughts about the whole thing and cry off.

Samantha's treatment of the Earl was the worst part of the whole problem. She sat stiffly on the sofa when he called and refused to speak. Even when he pushed his ancestral betrothal ring—a dazzling diamond and ruby cluster supported by a magnificent gold setting—onto her slim finger, Samantha's only remark was that it was "gaudy."

Sir Stephen loved his daughter and would not have forced her to marry against her will, except that he felt sure the Earl would have a steadying influence on his rather high-flying child. Admittedly, the Earl had been a bit of a rakehell in his youth, but once he hit his thirtieth birthday he had calmed down considerably. He no longer kept more than one mistress at a time, and he had not dueled in at least six years—ever since the day he was almost forced to fly to America, when his opponent seemed mortally wounded. Luckily, the man had not died. The Earl was forgiven, but he had vowed to raise no weapons save his fists if ever challenged again.

Sir Stephen had sung his praises of the Earl to his daughter on several occasions, but he knew his words fell on deaf ears. As Sir Stephen watched his youngest daughter being handed into her *fiancé's* coach as they departed for a ball at Lady Brandyce's, he uttered a silent prayer that she would not antagonize the Earl overmuch tonight.

Only three more days and the two would be safely married. He raised his eyes to heaven and whispered, "I tried, Heather, I really did, but she has been too much for me. She needed a mother's guidance."

Meanwhile, in the coach, Samantha was keeping to her side of the plush seat and totally ignoring St. John. This was not easy as his presence, always intimidating, was in these close quarters almost overpowering. She stole a glance out from under her long, dark lashes, and decided he was a very handsome man in his evening dress. No fop, he. His simple clothes were well tailored and set off his strong body to advantage.

If only he weren't so old! she thought. He may not be a contemporary of Papa's, but he was certainly too ancient to understand the needs of a girl of seventeen. But Papa said I need the wisdom of an older man to keep me in line, she reminded herself. Bah! The man is almost a full fourteen years older than I, a veritable greybeard. *Lecher!* she accused silently, slanting a look full of outraged sensibilities in his direction.

The Earl was watching Samantha's face out of the corner of his eye. She was certainly giving him a thorough going over tonight! These past weeks had been quite a trial, with Samantha fighting him at every turn. She has taken me at my word: that is sure, he thought. I told her not to love me, and she shows no signs of falling for my fatal charms. Right now she looks like she could plunge a dagger into my chest with no compunction at all. Pretty chit, though. Even I am surprised at how well she turned out. Who said it took more than fine feathers to make a fine bird? No matter. I am anxious to see the St. John emeralds around that ivory neck.

"What are you thinking, Samantha?" he finally questioned, breaking the tense silence.

"You don't want to know, my lord." Samantha answered with a smirk.

"Ah, but I do, you secretive puss. I find I have a great need to know what goes on in that fiery head."

"Very well, my lord, as long as you remember you asked for it. I was just thinking that you are a lecherous old man."

The Earl appeared unmoved by her announcement and this upset Samantha no end. "Did you hear me, my lord? I said I think you *old*."

"I heard you, child. I am just trying to think of a way to convince you I am not quite that far along into my dotage. Perhaps I should alight from the coach and race you on foot to Lady Brandyce's," he suggested objectively. "No, I fear I am not dressed for it. A pity. Ah, well," he sighed, "there is nothing for it; this will have to do instead."

So saying, he slid his arms around her and brought his lips against hers in a crushing embrace that showed no concern for anything save his own pleasure.

Samantha tried in vain to push him away, but he was much too strong for her. His lips were bruising hers as his hand came up to force her jaws open. She could feel his heartbeat against her breast, and as his kiss deepened those beats increased to match the birdlike flutterings of her own heart. He cared not if she responded to his passion; this was merely an exercise in domination on his part, and she knew it.

Yet somewhere deep inside her a flame began to flicker and grow. She could feel her limbs dissolving against him and the experience was so pleasant she decided not to fight it. Only his sudden chuckle of amusement brought her back to her senses. Immediately she bit down hard on his probing tongue and tasted warm blood in her mouth. The

Earl jumped back and cursed shortly while reaching in his pocket for a handkerchief.

It was Samantha's turn to chuckle, and she forced herself to do it—though truly her heart wasn't in it. "Do forgive me," she purred sweetly. "You are not all that ancient, my lord. The 'lecherous,' however, I let stand."

The Earl sat silently for a few moments and then began to laugh softly. The laughter grew and grew until it filled the small coach and did not stop until he and Samantha had arrived at the ball.

He spent the entire evening by her side, refusing to have others dance with his betrothed—much to the consternation of the many acquaintances she had made in the three short weeks she had been making the social rounds with her *fiancé*. Since her new friends and the frolic of the light conversations with young members of the *ton*—both male and female—were her only amusement in coming to such affairs, she was mightily put out and took his action to be a form of punishment.

In that she was only partly right. It was true: the Earl did not wish to take the chance that Samantha might say something indiscreet about their engagement while she was in such an obvious temper, but he had another reason for staying so close by her side.

That other reason was the unexpected appearance of his latest mistress, Lady Lorinda Foxx. Although he had promised her that his affections (superficial as they might be) would still be hers, she was extremely jealous of Samantha. Lord Foxx was a fool (everyone knew it) but he was a fool encumbered with more money than he could spend in three lifetimes, which was precisely why Lorinda had married him.

The Earl had thought the dratted woman would understand that it was time he set up his nursery, but she had proved extremely irksome. There was no telling what she would say to Samantha had she the chance, and he had trouble enough without that particular complication.

Unfortunately for St. John, the lovely Lorinda spied Samantha alone later in the evening—when he was called away by Prinney, a request he could hardly deny. Samantha was sitting dejectedly at one side of the room, bored to distraction because no one seemed willing to dare the Earl's displeasure by approaching her after he had made it so very plain that he did not wish his betrothed to dance. However, every eye in the room was on Lorinda as she crossed the room to the girl and sat down beside her.

"Good evening, my dear," she said, smiling her condescension as she arranged the folds of her red-striped satin gown about her. "I am Lady Foxx. No doubt you have heard of me?"

Samantha took a long look at the raven-haired beauty. "I am sorry, madam, but I must confess I have not."

The older woman's eyebrows lifted for a moment in mock surprise. "How strange. Surely Zachary has mentioned me."

"I assure you, my lady, that the Earl has not spoken of you at all. Is there perhaps some special reason he should?" No, the Earl had *not* spoken of Lady Foxx, but Isabella *had*. Samantha decided to continue her pose of innocence nonetheless.

"I must offer you my congratulations on your upcoming nuptials, my dear," Lady Foxx said with honeyed sweetness.

"I believe your congratulations should be saved for the groom, my lady, and best wishes offered to me."

Lady Foxx was slightly taken aback by Samantha's bold answer, but she proceeded with the arrogance she used as part and parcel of her name and position. "Not so, my dear, for snagging such a catch as Zachary is a feat worthy of congratulations," she countered, slapping Samantha lightly on her folded hands with an ivory sticked fan. "Of course, we all *know* he is doing it simply to get himself an heir. But the St. John jewels should be ample compensation for becoming a breeding machine."

"M-e-o-o-w!" Samantha offered in her best imitation of their pet kitten, Muffet.

"What did you say, child?"

"I said *'meow,'* Lady Foxx. It is the sound a jealous feline makes. Please forgive me if I cannot imitate a vixen, as I believe a bitch *fox* is called."

"You impudent brat! How dare you insult me in that way!" the insulted lady fairly shrieked.

"I imagine I just chose it from the several ways you presented to me, my lady. It was really quite simple." Samantha told her in a so-demure voice.

"Nonetheless, it is true what I said about Zachary. He does not love you, you know."

"And for that I go down on my knees nightly and give thanks. It is sufficient that I bear him a son quickly so that he can return to your bed and the many others he has frequented. Perhaps then I can enjoy being a Countess. I too believe my new role in life has its compensations. I wish you well of the Earl, my lady, and hope you do not get trampled in the crowd of willing females once the great Royston calls to his light-skirts for comfort."

"Samantha! You will apologize at once!" She hadn't seen the Earl approaching but was not at all discomfited that he had overheard her.

"For what exactly should I apologize, your lordship?" she queried without a blink. "I did not see you come up and have no idea what you heard."

"It does not bear repeating, Samantha," the Earl said in an undertone. "Just apologize."

She was not imagining the glint of humor in his dark eyes. He was marrying her to be entertained: she had it from his own lips. She decided to see if he meant it. She turned to face the infuriated Lady Foxx and said in a clear voice, "I apologize for mewling in your presence and for using the term light-skirt in front of a woman who could have *no idea* what the words mean. I am sure you will forgive me for my feeble attempt at feline imitation, and if you ever desire a definition of the other please allow me to enlighten you. Oh, yes, and again, thank you for pointing out that the Earl is not in love with me. I imagine you speak from a like experience and are to be trusted to know his lordship sufficiently to make such a statement." She raised her rounded eyes to St. John and asked, "Is there anything I forgot?"

"Yes, scamp. You forgot that you have to ride home alone with *me.* You also forgot it is legal for a man to beat his wife. Your father's failing will not be mine." He turned and bowed over Lady Foxx's trembling hand. "My deepest apologies, Lady Foxx. I fear my bride-to-be had her first encounter with spirits tonight and was unprepared for its effect on the immature tongue. I shall definitely restrict the child to lemonade henceforth. May I call upon you tomorrow to reiterate my apologies?"

Lady Foxx smiled sweetly at the Earl, willing to overlook a multitude of sins if they were to gain her his company. "You are most welcome to come, but I fear my husband is still in Bath," she inserted smoothly.

"A pity, my lady," Royston told her calmly. "We shall miss him."

Samantha knew she didn't care a rap whether the Earl bedded the whole of London, but she was not about to sit idly by as he made his assignations in front of her. "I should like to retire, my lord, if you do not mind," she cut in coldly. "I was hungry earlier on, but I am afraid what I ingested upset my stomach. I never could abide *tarts.*" With an exaggerated curtsy to Lady Foxx, who had flushed livid with fury, Samantha started for the exit. The Earl was forced to follow after her.

Once in the carriage she turned on him with a fury. "So *that* is why you stayed by my side all evening playing the loving *fiancé.* You did not wish your latest flirt to come too near me. Did you think I could not handle the likes of her? Personally, I think I did rather well," she said randomly, before allowing her anger to take control again. "But do not imagine you can make arrangements to tumble your light-o-love in my presence. How dare you!"

The Earl was in no mood to answer her questions. "You stupid child! I leave you alone for two minutes and you succeed in insulting one of the most powerful hostesses in the city. How do you expect to be accepted in Society if you act the hoyden?"

Samantha shrugged her shoulders uncaringly. "I intend to be an *original.* I have no doubt Society will take all I have to give it once I am your Countess. After all, it tolerates you, don't it?"

"Why you little minx, I have a good mind to break the engagement and send you packing!"

"Do not hesitate on my account, sir. I welcome your retreat and long only to wave you on your way."

The Earl decided on a change of tactics. "Why did it bridle you so much when Lady Foxx teased you? I thought you didn't care for me. What difference if I have a romance or two, if I am discreet? Surely it would spare you my obviously unwanted embraces."

Samantha's expressive eyes flashed green fire in the darkness of the coach. "It is enough that I have to wed you. I refuse to do the civil by your sluts, no matter what their station." At his warning glance she added impishly, "Besides, you said I entertained you. Were you entertained tonight?"

The Earl found himself caught between a need to strangle the child for her ill manners and a desire to laugh at Lorinda's discomfiture at the hands of a young chit supposedly green as grass. After all, the child had handled herself brilliantly in a thrust and parry with one of the most sophisticated women in London. He found himself slightly proud of the minx, and try as he would he could not keep a stern face. "I missed the part about the cat, child. Why on earth did you meow?"

Samantha relented and told him exactly what had transpired before he came on the scene. He chuckled appreciatively and declared, "We shall stand the entire *haut ton* on its respective ear, my pet. I congratulate you. I feel almost young again."

"Nonsense. You are a greybeard. I am only marrying you to amuse you in your declining years."

"For that, and to bear me sons. Do not forget *that* Samantha," he said with a returning note of gravity.

He moved closer to her and whispered a short apology in her ear for his earlier treatment. "I am much better at lovemaking than that kiss demonstrated. Would you like me to give you an example?"

"I believe I can live with my interest until after our marriage, my lord."

"That is another thing. My name is Zachary. When are you going to use it?"

Samantha looked over at him and tried to fit the face with the name. He looked younger when he smiled—as he was smiling now—younger and less forbidding. She had to admit to herself again that he was a handsome man, a very handsome man. "I will do my best, Z-Zachary."

His smile widened and he returned, "And I shall continue to call you my Sam. But only in private. I feel it would not be understood in public."

"Thank you, my l—, I mean, Zachary."

He tilted her chin up with his hand and studied her face for a few moments. "You are a pretty child, Sam. I shall enjoy bedding you." With that he lowered his mouth to hers and gave her a slow tender kiss.

Samantha did not sleep well that night.

Chapter Four

MUCH AS Samantha had hoped (and even, as time was fast running out, prayed) for another earthquake or Great Fire to strike the city, or for the Thames to overrun its banks and wash London downstream, her wedding day dawned disgustingly dry and bright and devoid of any such opportune calamity.

Even Mother Nature was on Royston's side. After one heart-sinking peek through the curtains at the rising sun, Samantha crawled back into her bed and pulled the covers up over her eyes.

Daisy entered with her mistress's morning chocolate and a cheery, "Good morning, Miss Sammy," only to make an abrupt exit moments later, the china cup and its contents only just missing her head as she hastily pulled the door shut behind her. "Well, I never!" she exclaimed as she beat her hasty retreat.

An hour later Aunt Loretta scratched timidly at her niece's door before tiptoeing in (carefully avoiding the dried chocolate and splintered crockery). Reluctantly she approached the lump of covers on the bed. "Samantha," she croaked in a fearful whisper. "Samantha, my pet, the hour grows late."

"The hour can grow *whiskers* for all I care," came the muffled retort from beneath the coverlet. And then, as if it were an afterthought, came a garbled declaration, "Go away, Aunt Loretta, I'm never getting up again. I shall just stay here. The Earl can stand at the church until cobwebs run from his miserable carcass or he drops dead, infant-chasing lecher that he is."

Aunt Loretta stifled a weary sigh. It wasn't that she was not extremely agitated by this latest start of her brother's youngest child. It was just that the thought of racking her brains for an argument designed to budge Samantha from her quilted satin hidey-hole was very fatiguing. Over the years she had spent under her brother's roof she had tried everything from pleas to threats, bribes to punishments, dire warnings of bogey men and even—as a last resort—appeals to sweet reason. None of these ploys had ever resulted in even one small success, and she was loathe to expend any undue energy only to be met with another failure.

"Have it your way then, Sammy dear. You always do," she advised her niece calmly. "Frankly," she added for no good reason she could think of, "I believe the Earl well out of it, if you must know. You'd never make more than a mediocre Countess in any event, what with being so cowardly and all."

After all the years and all the failures, Aunt Loretta had unconsciously hit upon the one way sure to get a reaction from Samantha: she had issued her a challenge. The bedcovers exploded into the air as a flame-topped jangle of arms and legs kicked and swatted its way out from under the coverlet and scrambled to its knees in the center of the bed.

"*Mediocre,* is it, Aunt?" the tousle-haired creature sneered as she bounced up and down on her knees in a fine temper, in her fury straining more than one seam in her lawn nightgown. "I'll have you know I'd make a damned good Countess. No! Better than good. I'd make a *great* Countess! Get Daisy in here at once and in an hour I'll show you a Countess fit to beat the Dutch!"

Aunt Loretta, chagrined that it had taken till the last day of her chaperonage to discover the way to gain her niece's cooperation, left the room muttering, "When you will she won't, when you won't she will." But finding the pondering of any problem too fatiguing for words, she promptly expelled her vexation in a prodigiously satisfying yawn and took herself off to rest on her *chaise longue* until it came time to dress for the ceremony.

The bride and her party were late arriving at the church, but not because Samantha had dawdled. Indeed, she had been gowned and coiffured and champing at the bit long before anyone else was even half-dressed. But the marriage of the Earl of Royston was, because of his wide acquaintance and due to his improbable choice of bride, an event to pique the interest of even the most jaded of persons. The roadway in front of the church was therefore clogged with a line of carriages that successfully blocked passage of the bridal coach for a full half hour.

At long last the organist pounded out an entrance hymn and an endless parade of bridesmaids inched its way with babylike teeterings down the long aisle. As they went, the bridesmaids cast their eyes about, flirting and simpering and generally behaving in a way that prompted the Earl to wish the floor would open and swallow the lot of them. The ridiculous spectacle served also to prompt his bride to inform her maid of honor, Isabella, that all this farradiddle was making her teeth ache.

Isabella—a hopeless romantic doomed to living with a family that seemed to harbor not a jot of sensibility—followed at the tag end of the bridesmaids, her angelic face alternately displaying trembling smiles, maidenly blushes, and affecting quiverings of her full cherry-red lower lip as she fought down her emotions. This last was a very effective touch, producing a jewellike tear or two that announced to one and all that she truly loved her dear sister (even if that same younger sister *had* beaten her to the altar).

From his assigned place at the foot of the altar, Zachary St. John observed all this display of pomp with a jaundiced eye. His groomsmen may have been content to stand at their ease and appraise the bridesmaids for a likely candidate for a dalliance behind the shrubbery during the reception, but the Earl of Royston was mightily bored by the whole affair. He was, furthermore, unlikely to conceal his disinterest from the acutely observant *ton*, on the watch for any titillating *on dit* the ceremony might produce.

And so it was that the cream of London Society was privileged to see the coldly austere Earl in a rare moment of animation, when at last his eyes spied out a vision in white silk patterned with *peau de soie* lace as Samantha floated down the aisle on her father's arm. She was tall enough to carry off the heavily embroidered gown, which trailed a good six feet behind her—exactly the same distance as did her *peau de soie* veil, which fell from her seed-pearl encrusted cap. The cap rested lightly on Samantha's artlessly casual (but in truth painstakingly arranged) burnished curls, which framed a face of much the same creamy ivory shade as the bride's gown. The only colors to be seen, other than Samantha's copper hair, were the mauve of the orchids she carried and the sparkling sea-green splashes of her almond-shaped eyes. The choice of bride may have been a shock to Society, but everyone was forced to agree that the girl's beauty went a long way toward making sense of Royston's haste to get her shackled.

While the Earl watched Samantha and the guests watched the Earl, the end of the aisle was reached and Sir Stephen placed his daughter's ice-cold hand into Royston's warm one. Quietly he wished them happy.

As they turned to face the minister the Earl whispered sarcastically, "And are you happy, my dear?" to which his "dear," her face hidden from all but Royston and the minister, promptly responded by crossing her eyes and sticking out her tongue.

It was some moments before the astonished clergyman regained his solemnity sufficiently to begin the ceremony, never really recovering from his shock as the Earl's shoulder's persisted in shaking in silent mirth for the entirety of the service.

Hours later, at the reception held at the Earl's townhouse, the dinner over and the dancing in full swing, Zachary and Samantha St. John—the Earl and Countess of Royston—found themselves at table, alone together for the first time since they had joined their fates together.

"Well, my pretty prankster," his lordship drawled intimately, "the time has come to ask a question that has been on my mind the whole afternoon. Was the sight of that pretty pink tongue an attempt at protesting to the last moment that you would prove an unworthy Countess, an expression of distaste directed at yours truly, or—and I sincerely hope this last was the case—a tantalizing preview of the delights I shall taste and explore later this night at my leisure? I must say I would rather you forego the eye-crossing, however, as the sight puts me strangely in mind of a tutor I had in my youth. It was ever so fatiguing, you understand, trying to look the man square in the eye."

During the course of this speech Samantha's green eyes had narrowed to slits and her full mouth had pinched itself into an angry pucker. As her sister, brother, father, maid, or Aunt Loretta could have pointed out, that well-known expression was a warning any prudent person was quick to heed—and one which any person sincerely committed to self-preservation avoided provoking at all costs.

The Earl, already slightly familiar with that particular storm warning, yet unafraid, merely leaned back in his chair, folded his arms (Isabella, if she were present, would have suggested safety would be better served by clapping them about his ears rather than placing them in that negligent manner across his chest), and waited patiently for the storm to break about his head. Ah, having this volatile, unpredictable child about was going to go a long way towards relieving the monotony of being surrounded by brainless ladies and dull-dog men. He sincerely hoped it might also blunt the raw edges of his pain over the loss of his beloved younger brother.

But ho! What was this? It had been a full minute since he had facetiously baited his new bride, and although her armed-for-battle visage showed no signs of softening she had not retaliated in any of the several ways her husband had suspected. Those ways, of course, ran the gamut from a verbal retort to an all-out physical assault on his person.

The Earl smiled, "Pardon my poor humor, Sam, but—er—cat got your *tongue?* I ask this *tongue*-in-cheek, of course," he concluded with a chuckle, extremely well pleased with himself.

At last Samantha roused from her silent contemplation. "Firstly, my lord husband, unless you are admiring of the appellation Zack—and unassuming enough handle that has served many a coal-heaver, swineherd, and chimney sweep for a lifetime, you would be advised to dismiss from your vocabulary any shortening of my name that you so unkindly employ to mock rather than as a term of affection." She could see her thrust had hit home as her husband visibly flinched at her idea of a proper nickname for Zachary.

"Furthermore," she continued, the bit firmly between her teeth after her initial victory, "the face I made at the altar was meant to convey a message obviously too far removed from both the gutter and your most consuming interest, your own doubtful consequence, to penetrate your limited understanding. I was merely," she explained carelessly, examining the neatly-rounded fingernails of her right hand, "giving my first performance as official Royston court jester, trying to dispel some of the suffocating pomposity I was sure was as painful to you as it was to me." Samantha allowed a slight smile to curl the corners of her mouth. "If I am not mistaken, I succeeded fairly well."

The Earl smiled back at his wife. "That you did, you mischievous brat. My mood lightened considerably at the sight, and once I spied out the gape-mouthed astonishment of the worthy minister and tried to visualize his swooning dead away if you had dared to embellish your monkeyshines by plugging up your ears with your thumbs and waving your fingers at him, I was hard pressed not to plunk myself down on the altar steps and howl."

The last of Samantha's anger had all but disappeared. "The thought had occurred to me, but I refrained in deference to my Aunt Loretta's prediction that I will be a dismal flop as a Countess."

The newlyweds chatted on in complete charity with each other for a few more minutes. Then Aunt Loretta's "*pssst!*" called Samantha to her side, and that unnaturally animated woman dragged her niece off to a small room and endeavored to explain the responsibilities of the marriage bed. Considering the woman was a spinster, she could speak only from hearsay rather than experience, and that—plus an abhorrence of the murkier details—kept her instruction on a largely vague and uninformative level.

Samantha remembered her husband's earlier reference to the coming night and ingenuously asked her aunt to explain exactly what use a *tongue* might be put during this mysterious ritual between men and women. This merely prompted her flustered aunt to suddenly recall pressing business elsewhere—supervising the display of wedding gifts or some such thing.

I'll bet Lady Foxx could tell me what I need to know, Samantha thought grudgingly. Ah, well, the bargain was entertainment and heirs. The first part of the bargain seemed easy enough to keep, as she appeared to amuse Zachary even when she wasn't applying herself to the project.

But the second part might prove a bit more difficult.

When Isabella entered the room in search of her sister—who should even now be upstairs changing into travelling clothes—she found her leaning over a table, peering into the glass hung above it and scrutinizing her stuck-out tongue.

"Sammy, whatever are you about?" Isabella exclaimed, almost startling her sister into biting off that same tongue.

"Izzy," Samantha ventured, once she had recovered her composure, "Do you know anything more to the point about the begetting of heirs than Aunt Loretta's mumblings about squeezing your eyes shut and thinking of England?"

Isabella blushed hotly. "Perhaps if you asked questions on, er, specific areas of doubt, I could attempt to help you," she offered weakly.

Striking a belligerent attitude of hands on hips and tapping one satin-clad foot in agitation, Samantha demanded, "What does my tongue have to do with it?"

The elder, unmarried sister tottered weakly to a nearby chair and sank into it in an attitude of complete bafflement. "Your *tongue?*" Isabella gasped.

Samantha perched herself gingerly on the edge of a facing chair and nodded vigorously. "Yes, you ninny, my *tongue.* Zachary was most particular about it."

"I was always under the impression the center of interest was considerably *lower* on the anatomy," Isabella mused almost to herself, silently vowing to pump her maid, Maude, as soon as the opportunity presented itself. "Perhaps it would be best if your husband explained, Sammy, as he is the one who brought it up in the first place," she suggested at last.

Samantha considered this idea for a moment, nodded

her head in the affirmative, and abruptly charged her sister with lolly-gagging. Time was a-wasting; the groom was being forced to cool his heels until his bride was dressed to travel.

As Isabella led the way up the back staircase to the room already containing Samantha's newly-purchased wardrobe—a chamber adjoining the Earl's—Samantha's mind was humming along at a frantic pace. Soon the time for questions would be over and the moment of reckoning at hand. Ah, well, at Zachary's advanced age he most probably would content himself with only one or two heirs (meaning, to her naive mind, just one or two trips to her bedchamber), and spend the remainder of his nighttime hours engaged in that restorative agent so necessary to the elderly—sleep.

So thinking, Samantha began her wedding night prepared to endure with good grace the ministrations of her new husband as well as its presumed consequences: the production of a miniature St. John, probably male, however long that sort of thing took. In exchange, she would enjoy the honor and privilege (not to mention the enlarged personal freedom) that went hand-in-glove with her new rank and believed her life just might be reasonably all round tolerable after all.

It was only when she and Zachary were alone in his great travelling coach on the way to Margate—where his private yacht, *Sea Devil*, was moored—that she began to have some misgivings.

He was so very *big*, her husband, and so very formidable. He had been honest enough to tell her he had no feelings towards her, but did that mean he would seek his "pleasure"—or so she had heard the procedure called—without regard to her very natural apprehensions? Aunt Loretta didn't come right out and say so, but Samantha had the suspicion the next few hours of her honeymoon might just prove physically uncomfortable. She peeked at the Earl from under her long, dark lashes and tried to imagine his muscled body in relationship with her own slender figure and decided that thinking of England wouldn't help her a jot. Unconsciously, she shrank into the corner of the carriage.

"What's the problem, wife?" Zachary queried from his side of the carriage. He was very much at his ease now that all that wedding ceremony foolishness was behind him, and he was looking forward to the next few hours with considerable enthusiasm. "You aren't about to—heaven forbid—become ill from the motion of the carriage?"

"Don't alarm yourself, husband," said Samantha in a sharp, if somewhat forced, reply. "If I begin to feel unwell I promise to warn you in plenty of time for the coachman to halt, so I can hide away out of sight and sound whilst I cast up my accounts. At the moment, I am happy to say, I am enjoying the usual robust health associated with those of tender years. It is I who should be asking you—who are older and more prone to upsets of the liver and the like—if you are not ailing after the fatiguing exertions of the day and would perhaps be in want of a warm shawl about your shoulders and a restorative draught to sip on until your man can tuck you up in bed with a hot brick at your toes."

The Earl's laughter cut through the air like a pistol shot. "Just when I think you have emptied your budget of slurs and aspersions highlighting the difference in our ages—a topic that over the weeks has established itself as your major grievance among the many you hold against me—you come up with yet another insulting little barb."

Samantha thanked the darkness for hiding her shamed blush as Zachary went on in a more serious tone. "The only reason I have not taken you over my knee to spank some of that insolence out of you is that I have been patiently biding my time until the day I could prove once and for all how very far removed from my dotage I really am. Tonight, my dear tormentor, you will see for yourself just which of the two of us will be the first to plead exhaustion. I'll wager you a crown to a penny-piece it shan't be I that cries *enough!*"

Royston, with his steel-edged joviality, confirmed Samantha's worst fears. In his bid to prove himself the stronger, Zachary would have scant concern for his young bride's inexperience in the ways of the marriage bed. Why had she allowed Aunt Loretta's taunts to goad her into setting out to prove herself a creditable Countess? If only the dratted woman had not saved her "little talk" till *after* the ceremony, Samantha would have gladly endured the embarrassment of a last minute halt to the wedding. That way she would not be in such a pickle now. Ah, well, Samantha scolded herself: it did no good to cry over spilled milk. She was married. She might as well put a good face on it and make the best of things.

"You go on and on about your plans to humble me, Zachary, but I have found that barking dogs rarely bite," Samantha finally taunted back.

"Ah, but again I find myself forced to correct you. I most certainly *do* bite, Samantha," he chuckled, "as you shall yet discover."

As if it were ordained, the carriage hit a depression in the road just then and Samantha was abruptly jolted out of her corner and into her husband's quickly outstretched arms. Before she could pull away he had lowered his head to the whiteness of her slender neck and with his lips traced a moist path up to her exposed ear lobe. There he nuzzled for a moment before giving the velvety skin a gentle nip. "Mmm," he whispered. "Just as I thought. Delicious!"

Samantha, her blood on fire with an emotion she refused to recognize as anything but righteous anger, scrubbed roughly at her neck with her gloved hand and hastily scooted back to her own corner of the coach. "Perhaps you could have the coachman fetch you a soupbone to gnaw on at the next posting inn we pass, if you are so sharp set as to be reduced to cannibalism by the rumblings of your stomach," she reproved scathingly.

St. John chuckled. "I admit to a near ravenous appetite, my sweet, but have no fear for me, please. I have every intention of satisfying my hunger—just as soon as we are aboard the *Sea Devil.*"

"And I hope you choke!" Samantha bit out before turning her head to the window and the pitch-black countryside whizzing past as the carriage rumbled on. The remainder of the journey was passed in silence, the atmosphere inside the carriage so charged with emotion the very air fairly crackled.

Chapter Five

IT WAS passably pleasing as yacht cabins went: well-appointed and designed to give every possible comfort. There was, however, an encroaching lowness of the ceiling that generated the "caught like a rat in a trap" uneasiness so prevalent among landlubbers. This was enhanced by the knowledge that the view from the minuscule portholes included the sight of white-tipped waves lapping greedily against the hull, not two feet below those fragile glass barriers.

But when it became apparent that the single piece of furniture in those same quarters (well, at least in Samantha's opinion the only one that positively screamed out to be noticed) was an ornately carved, draped, and dauntingly *huge* four-poster bed absolutely smothered under burgundy and cream striped satin and a score or more artfully positioned pillows (she giddily imagined for a moment that the immense mattress had been brought aboard *enceinte* and then pupped), the term "claustrophobic" developed whole new worlds of meaning for the young bride.

No matter how earnestly she commanded her eyes to avoid the bizarre structure, they seemed possessed of a will of their own and persisted in straying in the direction of that ludicrously out-of-place contraption. Her treacherous mind, meanwhile, taking no notice whatever of her pounding heart and damp palms, insisted upon presenting a vision of Lord Royston propped up amidst the prolific pillows and their litters (by now Samantha's fertile brain had decided the first generation pillows had themselves matured and begun to whelp). She could even conjure up a maroon dressing gown, heavily frogged and braided, wrapped negligently about his person as St. John calmly accepted a peeled grape from one nubile young nymph while a whole covey of other supple beauties outdid each other in frenetic dances meant to capture his lordship's favor.

"*Yeech!*" Samantha declared inelegantly, wrinkling her nose and curling her upper lip. She allowed her facial features full indulgence in hoydenism as a reward for enduring an entire day of being schooled into ladylike insipidity. "The man is depraved, totally beyond the pale. All that is lacking are barkers, a bearded lady or some other touted freak, and a juggling act. He would then have all the makings for a mediocre travelling circus. Truly a case of arrested development if ever I saw one, for if this—this—*bed* is any indication of the man's lifestyle it's no wonder polite Society bores him to flinders. He would be better served to shun all but greenheads and peep-o-day boys who get their jollies setting up coffins in front of house doors or pelting each other with oranges in Drury Lane Theatre squabbling over who's to take the newest young actress under his protective wing."

Samantha shook her red tresses in disgust (loosing what was left of her pins and sending her long locks cascading down her back in a tangled riot of liquid fire). "E-gads!" she exclaimed to the empty room. "I may have promised to do my best to keep him from being bored to death, and I may have been constrained to agree to provide him with an heir, but there is a limit to what I shall endure. And this," she told herself as she cast an evil eye at the satin-bedecked monstrosity that had so incensed her, "*this* is definitely *it!*"

There was the sound of a single pair of hands clapping before St. John's sarcastic "*Bravo!*" caused Samantha to whirl about. Her long hair lagged along behind her as she turned but speedily caught up and even passed her before doubling back to wind itself around her face, turning her look of affronted dignity into a comical tangle of features glaring balefully at her tormentor from between a living—as well as a livid—haze of red.

Samantha impatiently raked her fingers through her hair, pushing it away from her face with a total lack of concern for her feminine appearance, and directed an awed gaze upon her newly-acquired husband. While she had been spending her time since descending to her cabin in pointless procrastination, the Earl had obviously used the interim to wash away the stains of travel. His long, lean frame was now clad in moroccan slippers, slim black pantaloons, an impressive frogged and quilted midnight-blue dressing gown and—to add just a touch of dash—a snowy-white silk cravat was draped negligently about his tanned neck. Samantha pulled herself hastily together. "My, my," she smiled wickedly, then shrilled in her best imitation of the type of females she had observed in one of the seedier streets of London: "Ain't ye jist the eel's eyebrows, guv'nor? Coo-ee, but them be fine duds, real prime goods, I wager. Musta laid down 'alf a crown easy to the rag and bone man in Piccadilly for hoity-toity gear the likes of that."

St. John merely chuckled and advanced further into the cabin, his hooded eyes assessing his bride—who was still clad in her travelling cloak. "I hesitate to point out the obvious, but you have not yet changed, Sam. Have you a chill, or perhaps even a trifling attack of *cold feet,* my dear?"

Now Samantha may have possessed a fine spirit, but she was still little more than a child, and her rapidly slipping façade of bravado—if the evidence presented by her over-bright eyes and quivering chin were reliable clues—was visible to her husband. He began to have second thoughts about his decision to travel without his valet or an abigail for his wife. At the time it had seemed that the fewer people wandering about on board, the more comfortable it would be for Samantha, but perhaps a female in the form of some adored and ancient family retainer would not have come amiss. His lordship's eyes shifted to the mound of baggage still sitting untouched on the cabin floor, and he asked if Samantha would not object to some assistance—an offer that was hastily turned aside by a vigorous shake of one flame-topped head. Considering himself dismissed, St. John excused himself with some farradiddle about speaking to the captain and quit the room, an amused smile hovering about his lips.

Samantha waited just until the door was closed before diving toward the nearest case and drawing out her Aunt

Loretta's conception of all that a wedding night *toilette* should be: yards and yards of shimmering white silk that, once donned, had the curious effect of making Samantha look totally naked. Within minutes she was burrowed deep in the cavernous bed and tucked up to her chin in striped satin bedspread. That the burgundy clashed badly with her hair bothered her not a whit.

After cooling his heels on deck for nearly an hour, watching the yacht's progress over the water, the Earl descended once more to the main cabin, opened the door, and began jauntily: "I am returned, my bride. Are you ready—?" Whatever he was about to say the world is destined never to know, for at that moment a loud gong somewhere above his head set up an imperious clanging and his sentence was left forever dangling.

"What in the name of all that's holy is that?" Samantha shrieked from her cocoon.

Her only answer was Zachary's sharply bitten out "Damn my eyes!"—and she was once again alone. She remained immobile for a few short moments, long enough to hear the sound of many running feet on the deck and the thunder of male voices—St. John's among them—as orders were barked and "aye-aye's" shouted back. Samantha threw back the bedspread and was perched on top of the blankets, her nightgown covered by a dark green velvet dressing gown, by the time the Earl reappeared.

His face was a study in controlled nonchalance as he told her with a sigh: "Well, pet, it seems we have a spot of trouble in the galley. The late supper I had planned for us is ruined quite beyond reclamation."

Samantha wrinkled her brow in consternation. "All this tow-row for a ruined supper? What happened to it?"

St. John shrugged his shoulders regretfully. "It burned."

"The *entire* supper?" Samantha asked, testing the air with her nose and catching a whiff of odd-smelling smoke. "How?"

The Earl allowed himself a rueful smile. "Sparks from the passageway, I imagine. One of the men tripped and dropped a lantern. It seems we—or at least you, my dear—must abandon ship." He held out one steady hand. "My lady?"

So matter-of-factly did the Earl inform her of the fire that Samantha herself almost accepted the threatened catastrophe as a trifling event. So blandly toned, masterfully polite, and calmly convincing was the Earl's directive that she abandon ship that Samantha held out her hand almost as if St. John were about to lead her into a country dance. Almost.

But not quite. Oh, no. Before her automatically bestowed hand could be taken into his possession, Samantha jerked it back as if she had just encountered a white-hot poker. Wrapping both arms tightly around a velvet pillow she privately thought to be the pick of the litter, she exclaimed gleefully, her words tumbling over themselves in her excitement, "A fire, Zachary? A real, honest to goodness, smoking, crackling fire! Oh, how splendid. I always did so want to fight a *real* fire. Not just a puny blaze, like when a spark from our parlor fireplace started the hearth rug on fire and I dumped the vase of Michaelmas daisies—there was water in the vase of course, but I guess you know that—anyway, I dumped it all over where the rug was smoldering, and *pffft!* the thing was done. The smoke afterwards was quite horrible, but Aunt Loretta—who was dozing not three feet from the fire—never so much as twitched an eyebrow." Samantha's face looked thoughtful for a moment. "I never could understand quite how Aunt Loretta came to be such a sound, and one could almost say, quite *dedicated* sleeper. Papa says Aunt Loretta's body functions on only two levels: slow and stop."

As Royston began to mumble to himself through clenched teeth and shift his body as if he were about to lunge onto the bed to drag his wife up onto deck by brute force, Samantha abruptly dismissed any thoughts of her aunt and turned on the offensive. "Zachary, I refuse to abandon ship like some cowardly rat scurrying down the anchor chain." Fears of the sea were lost in her thirst for adventure and she tilted her chin defiantly. "We will fight this fire together."

"In a pig's eye we will, missy," St. John growled, as he

dove for one of his wife's dramatically outflung arms. Samantha had already anticipated his move, and was yards from the bed and halfway to the already open cabin door before the Earl recovered sufficiently to intercept her.

"You are going to go up on deck with me and allow me to assist you into the boat I have waiting. You are not—I repeat, *not*—so much as even to be allowed a glimpse of the fire," he bit out succinctly, as his coal dark eyes tried to bore a hole in her defiance. "Not only is your presence not wanted, it is not needed, for the last thing the crew should have to concern themselves with right now are the hoydenish proclivities of an immature, sensation-seeking, irresponsible brat who would probably only succeed in hampering their efforts and losing me my yacht. *Is that clear?*" he ended, punctuating each word with firm shakes of the strong tanned hand that held Samantha's upper arm.

She directed a long, cool stare down at the offending hand, then raised her head to impale Zachary with a full dose of her potent emerald-green eyes—showing him, he thought randomly, just how truly fitted she was to be his Countess. Her face, indeed her entire tall, slim form, was etched in lines of outraged dignity, her expression a virtual *pot pourri* of angelic innocence, injured sensibilities, shocked disbelief, and a well-defined, all-over glazing of superior disdain or even contempt. But it was within those emerald eyes that the Earl found the true center of the storm that he could almost feel building up rapidly inside Samantha, for her eyes showed one emotion he could readily understand—that overpowering desire for adventure, the chance to dare the fates and even risk life and limb, just to see if it were possible. He had felt the same when he jumped his first six-bar fence, milled down his first man, broke the faro bank at Lady Devonshire's and—yes, even then—when he pinked his man in his first duel. Samantha's expression brought it all back to him: those mad, frantic days of his grasstime, when any excuse was good enough to send him racing neck-or-nothing into adventure.

Slowly, St. John relaxed his grip on his wife's arm, saying almost kindly, "Poor infant, you really do so want to go play with the fire, don't you? Ah, but I must tell you, sweetings, much as I feel for your frustration, it is beyond the question. Perhaps some other time, preferably on dry land and with a convenient escape route nearby, I will set you a fire and allow you to exercise your whim to the limit. But for now," and all traces of humor left his countenance, "you will do as I say."

"But—"

"No more, Samantha," the Earl commanded in a voice that would brook no denial.

"But my clothes, all my beautiful new clothes! What if they were to burn? I must take them with me. Please," she pleaded with uncustomary humbleness. Samantha may have been guilty of an unladylike interest in subjects and activities more common to the masculine gender, but deep down she was still—after all was said and done—very much a female.

St. John had sprung for a monstrously expensive and plentiful *trousseau* for his bride, and Samantha—loving every stitch of it—had brought the entirety of her new wardrobe along on her honeymoon. She was proud of her finery; it was as outrageous as its owner, who happily was also probably the only female in the entirety of the British Isles with the face, figure, style, and downright devil-take-the-hindmost attitude able to carry off such unusual styles and colors as she had chosen. There was no way she would sit idly by in a leaky old scow while her major (and, to date, only) fringe benefit went up in smoke!

By now the sounds reaching them from the passageway far at the stern end of the ship—as well as the few ominous-looking, thin trails of smoke that snaked past them into the cabin—had effectively banished any of the Earl's fond reminiscences of his exploits in his salad days, and Samantha's latest, purely feminine argument did not cause his conscience one single qualm. Clothing could be replaced. This red-haired termagant could not be, and he had a most particular reason for making sure not one hair of her head—or one pillow of that inviting bed behind her—were so much as slightly singed.

Grabbing the soft flesh of Samantha's upper arm in a viselike grip, St. John leaned over and snatched up a huge-brimmed poke-bonnet, profusely trimmed in blue grosgrain ribbon and several long, curling feathers, and jammed it down tightly on her untidy head.

"There," he proclaimed wickedly. "Unless I am in error, a possibility so remote it fairly boggles the mind as I am considered to be well versed in such things as feminine fripperies—having over the years found myself paying down the blunt for so many of the overpriced things—this particular creation is a *cap à la Charlotte Corday.* She, poor unfortunate thing, so favored this particular style that she chose to wear it in the tumbril on her way through the streets of Paris to her fatal *rendezvous* with *Madame Guillotine.* Just the right touch, my dear, for your sojourn in the boat *that awaits you now.*" As he was finishing his sentence he bent over, grabbed Samantha around the back of her knees, and hauled her up and over his shoulder from where she rained down ineffectual punches onto his broad back and mouthed blistering—if somewhat muddled—curses that only made her husband laugh out loud.

Samantha was unceremoniously dumped into the small jolly boat, and the crewman saddled with the task of keeping milady out of the fracas immediately rowed off until a good thirty feet of water separated the two crafts. Once Samantha regained her breath she sat ramrod stiff on the plank seat, her breast rising and falling mightily in righteous indignation, her hands knitted together tightly in her lap, and her eyes engaged in trying to pierce the moonless dark night for some sign of how things now stood on the *Sea Devil.* For a moment she felt a pang of guilt over her headstrong behavior, for it had kept Zachary away from the scene of the fire for precious minutes when his leadership abilities could have been well employed. But, she shrugged, it was after all just for a small moment. Mostly she was making rapid mental plans as to how she could threaten, cajole, bribe or even flirtatiously maneuver the loyal crewman into returning to the yacht. Finally—although it was really only a matter of some five or ten minutes later—Samantha got what she believed to be a near divine inspiration.

First she pried the misshapen *Corday* off her head and tossed that particular piece of ill judgment as far out into the ocean as she could. She would never have bought the dratted thing if she had known the ridiculous woman it was named for had actually had the poor taste to wear a straw hat on a head destined, in the very near future, to be plunked entirely into yet another straw container. Yet, she thought upon reflection, it would have been a rare sight to see a disembodied head all rigged out in ribbons and feathers and fancy tuck bows.

Samantha giggled, but quickly sobered and began sliding open the dozen or so buttons of her dressing gown. With the absence of the moon, all the bemused crewman actually saw was a hint of white silk and the glimpse of one well-turned slim bare ankle as Samantha abruptly shed her dressing gown, stood, and dived neatly over the side.

Her tomboy ways had come to her aid, for Samantha swam like the proverbial fish—even with the folds of her nightgown tangling slightly about her legs. She was quickly situated alongside the yacht and, locating the rope ladder she had seen earlier when she first came aboard, she made short work of her climb to the deck.

Once aboard it was a simple matter to dash to the cabin and throw her travelling cape over her wet clinging nightgown and, disregarding both her bare feet and her dripping hair, she raced off in the general direction of the fire.

It was a scene that would send most young ladies into gracefully executed swoons, but to Samantha it was a sight to inspire poetry. Orange-tongued flames licked hungrily at the walls and ceiling of the galley but although the passageway—the initial site of the blaze—was obviously soot-darkened and even charred in places, there was no sign of fire there anymore.

No, all efforts were now being directed towards beating down the flames that had already inflicted considerable damage on the left side of the compartment and were now threatening to burst out of control entirely. It was easy to spot Zachary's tall figure in the center of the group of black-faced, tattered men, his calm and authoritative voice issuing crisp, clear commands that urged his crew to keep beating at the fire with their water-soaked blankets.

Samantha hot-footed back to the main cabin and yanked

the offensive burgundy bedspread onto the floor with one mighty heave, sending three (by now) generations of pillows spinning into the air. Then, using the nail scissors from her reticule, she cut into the fabric until she had enough of a handhold to be able to tear the spread into two ragged parts. That done, she went on deck and plunged the material into a nearby water barrel before running back to the galley, clutching the soggy bundle to her breast.

For a considerable time, perhaps even a quarter hour, Samantha swung her impromptu fire-beater with all the gusto of her young muscles. Her hair was soon dreadfully tangled, and bits of ash and splinters of charred wood nested there in abundance. Her face became as black as the others; so did her bare feet and uncovered arms. On the whole, it could be said that Samantha was having the time of her young life—and when the last sparks in her little area of concentration could no longer elude her flailing bedspread, she was more than a teeny bit pleased with her accomplishment.

Then Zachary saw her. A second later Zachary saw red—the crimson hot heat of anger. He advanced on his bride with menace in his eyes, eager to take her out of sight and sound of his crew so he could box her smoke-begrimed ears, when Samantha pointed out in an amused voice:

"Zachary, you are black as pitch from your head to your toes. If the *haut ton* could see you now, they would surely be convinced you were not just in league with the devil, but were, in truth, old Fire-and-Brimstone himself! Oh, and Zachary, if your Lady Foxx could just have a moment's sight of you with half your one eyebrow all but singed off and your hair all spikey and out of order, she would run so fast the whole Quorn couldn't catch her!"

The crew melted discreetly away, especially Samantha's supposed bodyguard—who had considered rowing back to Margate and disappearing out of the reach of the Earl's punishment, but who had decided instead to come back and fight the fire and then hopefully hide himself away below decks until his lordship got so occupied with his honeymoon he forgot the crewman's existence. Samantha and

Zachary were left alone among the debris of the destroyed galley.

St. John glared at his wife for some moments as she met his gaze stare for stare, and slowly he began to see the humor in the situation. Samantha looked like a chimney sweep after a long hard day, and if she was correct, he looked no better. "Madam," he told her, "as Cervantes said, 'the pot calls the kettle black.' "

Samantha looked down at her damp and dirty cape and examined her grimy hands and feet before looking up at her husband and bursting into laughter—laughter into which he quickly joined. In between chortles Samantha explained her impromptu swim, which St. John applauded as quite inventive. And even he found humor in her admission of destroying a very costly bedspread for the freely admitted, twofold purpose of fighting the fire and ridding herself of such an offensive article.

At last physical discomfort overtook their pleasure, and each went off to await steaming hip baths and a necessarily light cold supper, made up from supplies kept in storage separate from the galley. Samantha was so exhausted by the time she crawled onto the right side of the mattress—the side she had arbitrarily chosen for herself—that she was asleep moments after her damp (but *clean*) head touched the pillow. If St. John wished to consummate the marriage this night, he would have a mightier task *rousing* his bride than ever he would have *arousing* her.

Chapter Six

WHEN Samantha woke the next morning and turned in the bed, she saw St. John was sound asleep beside her.

She lay quietly for a few minutes, studying the dozing Earl. He slept on his stomach, and as she inspected his bare back—down to where the sheets covered him at the waist—she noticed he slept without nightclothes, much to her consternation since she too preferred to sleep in the nude before marriage intervened. St. John's head was turned towards the middle of the bed, so that she had a clear view of his full lips—slightly relaxed now in sleep—as well as his dark, slightly curled, unruly thatch of hair, and the long sweep of his curving black eyelashes, which all joined together to give him the look of a much younger, more approachable man. Even his singed eyebrow looked innocent.

Samantha sniffed. So much for appearances; the man didn't have a kind bone in his body. If he did—she told herself as she remounted her favorite hobby horse and started in to ride—he wouldn't have maneuvered me into this marriage against all my wishes. Arrogant, self-centered, toplofty, selfish, domineering *old coot!* she screamed silently, her sleep-flushed face and tangled curls looking curiously at odds when combined with a pair of narrowed green eyes and a cherry-red bottom lip that was at the moment jutting forward in an unmistakable pout.

Such was the vision of contradictory impressions to meet his lordship's eyes when he awoke with the eerie feeling that someone was staring at him. He was not accustomed to sharing a bed—at least not for an entire night—and he was at first pleasantly surprised with the sight of his new bride. That glorious, long red hair, looking as if it possessed a life of its own, licked like living flames (he winced slightly at the thought of flames and fire) over the pillow and down about Samantha's shoulders. Her clear skin and pleasing, slight shape beneath the covers went a long way towards convincing the Earl that there were indeed benefits other than the obligatory heir to be derived from sharing a bed with this complicated child. But then, as his sleep-fogged mind cleared, his brain took in the mulish expression on his bride's expressive face. "Are you going to tell me I snore?" he asked quietly.

"What? Oh, Zachary, you are awake," Samantha said, startled out of her reverie. "I do not know whether or not you snore, as I slept quite soundly, thank you, not that you asked," she informed him pithily. She could not tell him she had been staring at him while he slept, just like a cat eyeing a strange dog just come into the yard, so she changed the subject. "I was just lying here trying to decide where this ridiculous bed came from and, to be even more curious, *why* you or anyone would wish such a bizarre thing in your possession."

There! That was a reasonably intelligent question, if one considered that it came from a young girl lying in a strange bed beside a comparative stranger. And, if she but admitted it, she was a girl scared half out of her wits.

St. John turned onto his back, plumped up his pillow, and crossed his arms behind his head. "That, my inquisitive and impolite child—as well-behaved young misses do not go about casting stones at another's taste—is a long story. Do you wish to hear it?"

Samantha wished she were home in Mount Street sipping her morning chocolate, but as she was reluctant to crawl out from under the covers with Zachary there to see her indecently *décolleté* nightgown (another of Aunt Loretta's little surprises), and the alternative of her husband climbing from his side of the bed in the raw was even less appealing, she settled herself and said she would like above all things to hear the tale. Under the covers, she crossed her fingers on the lie and then pressed her empty stomach and silently implored it not to growl.

"Very well," the Earl nodded, with the air of a tutor about to impart the morning's lesson. "It seems that one James Graham, an undoubted quack but a man with an undeniable ability to attract the desperate, opened his 'Temple of Health and of Hymen.' " (The Earl stole a peep at Samantha, but her only reaction was one of interest. Ah, he mused, how lamentably innocent she is. At times even *I* believe I am depraved.) "Graham's first Temple was opened in 1783 in the Adelphi, but he moved up in the world, thanks to the beneficence of his grateful patrons, and was eventually located in prestigious Pall Mall. It was said he was the Emperor of the Quacks, and although honest physicians condemned him his establishment flourished for many years."

Samantha was truly interested now, no longer needing to counterfeit her curiosity, and she sat up crosslegged in the bed—the better to see the storyteller—heedless of the fetching picture she presented.

Zachary sent a regretful eye over the soft body so close to his and continued with his tale. "Graham's most touted, and no doubt most financially rewarding invention was that of a stupendous 'Celestial Bed.' Inside a chamber guarded by two gigantic porters, any married couple possessing the ludicrous sum required as payment by friend Graham could spend one heavenly night in this magical bed, thus obtaining an instant, guaranteed cure for infertility." He shot another look at Samantha and her blush told him she was at least educated on this one point: bed was the place to begin if one was to go about setting up one's nursery.

"Graham's Celestial Bed was all the rage for some years," the Earl continued, "until his Goddess of Health, a *dear* friend of his, took a chill one day and died. It was a well-known fact that the Goddess made a practice of sleeping in the miraculous Celestial Bed on the nights it was not needed by some hopeful couple, and the rumor was soon bruited about that the bed's damp sheets had hastened the lady to her final resting place. With the bed no longer an attraction, Graham gathered his profits and disappeared. And the bed—" St. John trailed off, giving an eloquent shrug of his broad shoulders.

"*This* is the Celestial Bed!" Samantha cried, torn between repugnance and the thrill of it all.

At last Zachary dropped his instructional tone and gave his wife a grin. "Alas, my child, I have no idea of the whereabouts of the infamous object. But it was an interesting story, was it not? I hesitated to tell the truth, as it is far less dramatic. Actually, my father bought this particular contraption from some dethroned prince or other, and I do fear built the *Sea Devil* around it. Like a ship in a bottle, the bed's presence in this tiny cabin defies all logic, but I am afraid if I have it dismantled the entire vessel will fall apart. I will change the hangings, however, now that you have already destroyed the bedspread. Besides, I cannot abide having my wife clash with the color scheme," he finished jovially.

Samantha did not, after a few moments reflection, take umbrage at the Earl's teasing with his preposterous story and only mused, "A *real* prince?"

"Bona fide blue blood," his lordship assured her.

Samantha raised her eyes and assessed the heavy canopy, its posts carved and gilded over every inch of wood. "The mind boggles. I did not know royalty could be so vulgar."

St. John threw back his head and laughed. "My dear, as you go on you will learn that rank and position are considered ample excuses—yea, even downright *demands*—for frequent displays of vulgarity. I submit in evidence our own Florizel, the Prince of Wales."

Samantha looked puzzled for a moment and then, her mind conjuring up an image of the flamboyant prince as she had seen him one day in Hyde Park, she joined in the laughter.

This air of *bonhomie* lasted throughout the day—already mutually agreed to be their last day aboard because of the damage to the galley—and it was only as the satinwood table in the cabin was set for an obvious *diner à deux* that she began to feel apprehensive. By dawn the next day they would be back in Margate, their honeymoon officially over, so tonight would surely be the night St. John would claim her as his own.

The Earl sensed Samantha's tenseness and went out of his way to be a charming dinner companion, keeping the chatter and the wine flowing freely throughout the meal. Indeed, Samantha was so relaxed that, when Zachary remarked on her creamy complexion and how it was set to glowing from the candlelight, she blurted out her misgivings about the value of freckles on a Countess's nose and cheeks.

"I have tried a freckle removal recipe of strawberries crushed in green grape juice and a quantity of ass's milk, but I fear it is much the same as Mr. Graham's cures—a bucketful of promise backed by only a thimbleful of results. So if you can learn to tolerate the horrid, spotty things, I'd appreciate it, as I can't abide going to bed with bits of strawberry clinging to my cheeks."

St. John manfully hid his amusement at this ingenuous disclosure and proclaimed that he for one would cast neither aspersions upon nor attempt to eradicate such an entrancing sprinkling of golden dust.

This and a multitude of other compliments, when added to the unaccustomed quantity of wine she had sipped from glasses that were mysteriously refilled from the bottom every time she took a swallow, combined to throw Samantha into such a mood of congeniality that she quite forgot her intention of yawning prodigiously throughout the meal and then pleading fatigue and the need of an uneventful night. In addition to her unconscious tippling, she had attacked her dinner with all the efficiency of a practiced trencherman so that she could not complain of a headache or unsettled stomach with any real confidence of being believed.

As the sun dipped below the horizon and the stars began to twinkle in the darkened sky, Samantha was left with no choice but to prepare for bed and the inevitable granting of Zachary's husbandly rights. But she was determined to win at least one small battle and dragged out the time required for her *toilette* as long as possible, demanding a hip bath be brought to the cabin and then soaking in it so long she feared her fingers and toes would be wrinkled for a fortnight. If nothing else, she would make one thing clear:

the St. Johns might be going to bed together sometime this night, but Samantha St. John alone would set the hour.

Outside, the wind—which had been blowing fresh all day—began to increase in intensity as Samantha dressed in another *négligée* of her aunt's choosing: this one in a flattering sea-foam green rather than the virginal white of the other two she had already worn (even Aunt Loretta was acknowledging the disappearance of her niece's innocence), but no less revealing in its cut. Samantha had blithely left the choosing of her nightwear to Aunt Loretta—what with the pressure of an entire *trousseau* to gather in a little under a month—but then she had not then been aware of any latent lascivious streak in her spinster relative's character. As Samantha stood scowling at her reflection in the long mirror cunningly hung inside the closet door, the wind suddenly gusted, causing a bit of water from the hip bath to splash onto the carpet.

St. John—once again outfitted for a casual evening in a tobacco brown banian (a friend had sent it from India) and leather slippers (vanity may have prompted the change in his appearance, but weighing more heavily was the strong smell of smoke that still clung to his other garments) —sized up the situation as soon as he came into the main cabin. He rang for someone to remove the tub, now a miniature sea complete with white-tipped waves Samantha was regarding with a fixed stare, and poured out a glass of burgundy for himself and some ratafia for his bride.

A wave rocked the yacht just as Samantha took the glass, and some of the liquid spilled onto her hand. She looked about for a napkin and, finding none, proceeded to daintily lick the moisture from her fingers. Before she was half done Zachary, his wife's naive sensuality stirring him into action, took up those same fingers and—looking intently into Samantha's oddly saucer-wide eyes—completed the job with the tip of his own tongue, licking slowly down the sides of her fingers and tracing a pattern in her palm.

So *that* is what the tongue is used for, Samantha concluded silently: first her neck and ear, now her fingers. She could imagine the sensation could be quite pleasant if the technique was employed in any number of ways, in a variety of places, none of which she could imagine at the moment. I should be dissolving into strong hysterics, she recollected mistily as she watched Zachary's mouth blaze a trail of kisses from her palm to the sensitive pulse in her wrist.

A proper lady would at least put up a show of reluctance when presented with such a situation, she scolded herself, as St. John showed all signs of repeating his ministrations on her other, ratafia-free hand. My family is right, Samantha decided with an indistinct nod of her head. I *am* a truly shameless creature, allowing Zachary to kiss my fingers, my wrist, and oh! I never knew men enjoyed nuzzling the crook of a woman's elbow. How utterly delicious!

Samantha closed her eyes just as another wave tipped the floor of the cabin sufficiently to propel her into the Earl's arms. She allowed her head to droop against his muscular chest and decided her strange feeling of lightheadedness came from the butterfly kisses Zachary was now bestowing on her neck and one exposed shoulder. She opened her eyes and the room tilted precariously, then refused to come clearly into focus. This phenomenon also seemed to have an unfortunate effect on her stomach, so she squeezed her eyes tightly shut—a dizzying maneuver that caused her to lose her balance completely.

St. John thought his bride was perhaps a bit tipsy from the wine. But, being a good seaman himself, he ignored the effect the heavy seas might be having on someone unaccustomed to close acquaintance with either liquid, scooped Samantha up, and deposited her gently on the turned-down sheets of the immense bed.

Samantha was nothing if not honest. She looked up at her romantically eager husband and said, "I think I may be a bit drunk."

"Just a trifle up in the world, my pet. That is all," his lordship assured her, then smiled a very intimate smile as he removed his robe and lowered himself beside her. "It might even lend a bit of *cachet* to the proceedings."

The object of this assurance would dearly have liked to believe it, but her stomach had already taken control of the situation from her hands. All at once Samantha's eyes widened, their deep green showing darkly against her suddenly ashen cheeks, and she sprang clumsily from the bed to run to the basin set on its stand in the corner. There she cast up her accounts, over and over again, while St. John held a cool wet cloth to her perspiring brow.

"It—it's the boat, Zachary. It *will* keep moving," she wailed piteously.

At long last the Earl escorted his wan bride back to the bed, tucked her in up to her chin, and left her to rest. Some three hours and several trips to the basin later his lordship allowed reluctantly that the seas were a bit rough if one was unused to spring storms in the Channel, but assured Samantha that there was no danger of the *Sea Devil* going to the bottom.

Samantha opened one bleary eye and glared at her husband balefully. "In that case, my hopes are quite cut up. I had been comforting myself with the thought of a quick and painless death by drowning to rid me of this misery." Samantha was many things, but she was not a good patient. Like many normally healthy people, she considered illness to be a personal insult. When really under the weather—as she was now—she was easily convinced that her malady was sure to prove fatal.

"Tch, tch, Sam! Such a craven, cowardly way for my little spitfire to talk. I thought you were made of sterner stuff."

His lordship was teasing, of course, and very commendable it was of him, too, considering how drastically his plans for the evening had been altered. But Samantha was in no mood for friendly raillery.

"Why not be a good little demon and run along outside and amuse yourself? Maybe you can find a crewman, on his hands and knees working on the decks, and give him a kick in the pants. Better yet, you jolly ghoul, why not tie a length of rope, one end to your waist and the other to a large rock, and jump overboard for a swim?" She rolled back onto her side, drew her legs up in a fetal position as if to guard her tender stomach and slurred sleepily, "Off you go now, mate. Give my regards to all the little fishies."

St. John did leave, chuckling beneath his breath, but he returned off and on during the remainder of the night to check on his wife—who was not once aware of his presence.

The next morning, when Samantha finally awoke clear-eyed and even a little hungry, the Earl learned that Samantha was unaware of more than just the passage of the night. Ah, the resiliency of youth! he thought, watching her as she alternately munched on dry toast and sipped sweet tea. Then Samantha recalled aloud how everything about the previous evening after the observation of that miniature tempest in her hip bath was a total blank. In all seriousness she asked Zachary if she had been much of a bother.

The smile left the Earl's face. It was unbelievable! Lord Royston had employed some of his most proven-effective techniques on this unfledged girl, with what he thought were remarkably encouraging results. Now here was that selfsame female, baldly proclaiming that what he thought had been a highly successful prelude to complete intimacy had in reality impressed her so little that a few glasses of wine and some slight seasickness could erase the entire episode from her mind.

From her vantage point, sitting crosslegged in the middle of the bed looking across at St. John as he lounged elegantly in a leather-stuffed chair near the first porthole, Samantha could see that the man was not best pleased about something.

"Then I was a nuisance," she wailed. "Oh, Zachary, I know I am an *absolute pig* when I'm sick. Aunt Loretta and Izzy say they'd rather nurse a bear with a sore paw than me, but I promise you I hardly ever get sick, honestly." With a touch of her usual spirit she added, "Besides, you were the one with the brilliant idea of having our honeymoon on this bloody boat. How was I to know I've not the makings of a sailor? I've never been on the water before—unless you count Smithdon's Fish Pond, in a rowboat, which I certainly don't because that water is clear as glass and only three feet deep most of the time."

St. John, his chin and mouth nearly buried in his cravat as he sat slumped in his chair, told her ruefully, "You weren't seasick, sweetings, or at least you probably wouldn't have been except for my stumbling stupidity. What you were, infant, was drunk."

Wrinkling her brow, Samantha pondered this information for a few moments before clapping her hands together in glee. "How utterly famous! I've always wanted to be drunk," she cried happily. "Thank you, Zachary. If you allow me to become bosky it must mean you consider me an adult, for everyone knows how freely the spirits flow in Society."

St. John mumbled something nasty into his neckcloth.

"So, anyway, Zachary, what *did* happen last night? Is there anything I should know?" she questioned seriously.

How was he to answer a loaded question like that? Did he tell her nothing happened and take time to regroup his forces before planning another, less alcoholic, assault on her senses? Or did he tell her they had graduated from compliments and hand-kissing to pleasurable cuddling and neck-nibbling—procedures that appeared to have been mutually edifying—and had even progressed to the point of actually sharing the same bed for some few fleeting moments before Fate interrupted in the form of a sick belly? Would she believe it? Who would? Even he had trouble recognizing the so-willing girl in his arms last night as the same young miss whose greatest pleasure in life was slashing him to ribbons with her sharp tongue.

Ah, well. It was early days yet. There was time and enough for everything to come round once they were back in London.

"I assure you, my dear invalid," the Earl said at last, "nothing occurred last night that is of any lasting importance to either of us. Let us just say we had been spending a reasonably civil hour together when suddenly you took ill. And as there is bound to be another evening later today after the sun goes down—and another tomorrow, and another the day after that, and so on—I doubt the loss of one insignificant night shall weigh too heavily in the long run."

With those words Royston rose and quit the cabin, going out into the air to pace the deck and rough out the next moves in his assault plan, while back in the cabin a thoroughly miffed Samantha was wrinkling up her nose and doing a creditable imitation of St. John's tone as she parroted, "And another the day after that, and so on and so on. Bah!

"Fusty old crow, condescending to me like I'm still in leading-strings." She cocked her elbows on her crossed knees, and plunking her chin down into her cupped hands stared intently into space. "*Something* went on in here last night, I'd bet my pearl-and-sapphire bracelet on it, and whatever it was it has set old Zach well up into the tree-tops. I wonder if, when I vomited—or shot the cat as Wally says—I missed the bowl and got . . . no, I'd remember that. Then again, maybe he tried to kiss me and *that's* when I shot the . . . no, even I wouldn't do anything that awful. I hope. I guess I'll just have to forget it like wise old Solomon said I should, but if I don't know what happened last night, how am I supposed to prepare myself for tonight? Frankly, I wish he'd just do whatever it is he's bent on doing and get it over with. All this to-ing and fro-ing is becoming a strain."

She raised one hand to twirl a burnished curl idly around her index finger. "Marriage," she scoffed. "Given my druthers, I'd rather not bother with the business, thank you!"

Meanwhile, leaning heavily against his forearms as he stood at the rail looking out at the approaching coastline, Zachary St. John was thinking, "Marriage, an institution created by sadists to be indulged in only by morons, masochists, and peers with entailed estates. Blast the institution to blazes! Who needs it?"

Shortly before noon, with the *Sea Devil* in the capable hands of a local ship's carpenter, Royston's crested coach (followed again by a second smaller coach containing Samantha's copious luggage) was on the main turnpike to London. Whatever awaited the newlywed couple in that metropolis could not possibly be so unsettling and counterproductive as what befell them on the *Sea Devil*. Fate could not be so fickle, so perverse, so mischievously disruptive as to dip its meddling fingers into the affairs of the Earl and Countess of Royston again after leading them such a merry chase, almost from the moment they met.

It couldn't.

Could it?

Chapter Seven

CARSTAIRS, the so-proper St. John butler, stepped a foot into the room, cleared his throat, and undertook to announce in his best stentorian tones: "Miss Loretta Ardsley and Miss Isabella Ards—." That was as far as he got before the new mistress of the sedate Royston Mansion in Portman Square cut him off by pithily pointing out that marriage had not so unhinged her ladyship or distorted her eyesight as to necessitate the promptings of a third party in order for her to recognize members of her own family—now foolishly being made to cool their heels out in the draughty hallway.

Samantha then clapped her hands imperiously and made shooing motions in the direction of the insulted and valued family retainer before flinging her arms out wide and wheeling about in front of these same awestruck relations (now officially admitted to the Countess's presence), demanding their honest opinion of her new morning-at-home *toilette.*

"Well," she asked impishly, plucking at her *décolleté* neckline, "what do you think? I have at least a dozen others in my chambers you've yet to see as they've just come this morning. Confess now, can you ever in your life recall seeing such a magnificent ensemble?"

The two gape-jawed females could only wag their heads in speechless denial as their wide-eyed stares drank in the sight before them. The newest Countess of Royston had truly outdone herself.

Oh, the materials that made up her gown were not so extraordinary in themselves. But when incorporated as they were into the Circassian wrapper Samantha wore, with its rather daring palest-peach lace bodice and long, flaring sleeves, fashioned of that same lace in alternate stripes with the moss-green, soft muslin cloth that made up the slim wrap-skirt that clung from just beneath the bodice to end just above the carpet, the result was decidedly unsettling. The illusion (or carefully engineered delusion, depending on the proclivity of the observer) of Samantha's being clothed *only* in wisps of moss-green muslin was momentary but it served its purpose, as evidenced by Aunt Loretta's muffled gasp, Isabella's involuntary gulp, and—lastly, as well as predictably—Samantha's triumphant crow of laughter.

"I have dazzled you both, no doubt," Samantha pursued happily.

Isabella, subsiding daintily into a nearby chair, was the first to find her tongue. "Sammy, that gown is outrageous! Whatever did the Earl say? Surely he won't allow you to appear in *public* looking, er, looking—" Isabella struggled to search out a ladylike way to express the inexpressible and ended weakly, "looking—like *that*!"

"A pox on his lordship," Samantha returned airily, her green eyes—made even brighter by her gown—dancing about playfully as she showed all the signs of a delighted child who has somehow escaped her nanny. "Besides," she twinkled, "my new husband may be many things, but he is definitely not such a sober-sides as to cut up stiff over his wife's choice of gown. At times, you know, Izzy, I almost begin to believe old Zachary somewhat human."

Knowing any suggestion that Samantha's future might be endured more comfortably if she endeavored to speak a bit more respectfully about and to her new husband would be laughed away, Aunt Loretta contented herself with complaining that all this watching of her niece as she flitted about the room was "most prodigiously fatiguing," and the aunt withdrew from the conversation to take up residence on a faraway sofa that looked a good spot for a short restorative nap. Within moments, her head was nodding.

"Good," Samantha pronounced, as her aunt's chin took up familiar acquaintance with the top of her pouter-pigeon breast, "now we can get down to cases. I imagine," she put forth baldly, "you are champing at the bit wondering why we are back in town so soon."

Isabella shelved any missish disclaimers that it was none of her business as she had been on pins and needles with curiosity ever since her sister's note had come round to Mount Street that morning, demanding her presence in Portman Square within the hour. "I admit it, Sammy, I am utterly shameless," she urged her sister on eagerly. "Please tell me *All!* Why are you here? What happened on your honeymoon? Where is Lord Royston?" Her agitated questions tumbled upon each other.

Samantha smiled a singularly suggestive smile, guaranteed to pique Izzy's interest to the limit. "Firstly, to answer your questions in the order they were presented, I am here because—if you'll but turn your mind to a certain ceremony that took place in Hanover Square some three days ago—I live here.

"Secondly, nothing and everything, or should I say everything but *one particular thing,* happened on that atrocious, oversized scow Zachary calls a yacht.

"Finally, I haven't the foggiest notion of the current whereabouts of my esteemed lord and master—not, never fear, that I shall go into a sad decline over his absence. In actual fact, the man could be in Jericho for all I should ever miss his odious presence."

Isabella's insides tingled deliciously as her virginal mind made a speedy inventory of the many and varied passages in her collection of Minerva Press novels depicting the plight of Young Innocence once in the clutches of Evil. "Was he such a brute?" she shuddered, quite fascinated.

Samantha moved slowly across the room to a cream striped-satin sofa, took up a reclining position with her feet tucked up on the cushion, draped one arm dramatically along its curved wooden back, pressed her other hand to her breast, tilted her head back against the side cushion, closed her eyes, and gave a soulful sigh. She maintained this pose, and her silence, until several furtive peeks at Isabella from beneath her effectively fluttering eyelids told her the girl promised to be a suitably responsive audience. Slowly she returned her head to an upright position, only to stare off into the middle distance as yet another deep sigh escaped her so far maddeningly silent lips. She was hard pressed not to laugh out loud, but willed herself to maintain her air of the aggrieved innocent.

In desperation, Isabella was forced to position herself on the floor beside Samantha—the pupil kneeling attentively at the fountain of knowledge. "Sammy. Sammy!" she pleaded earnestly. "Speak to me, dear sister, you must! Oh, how like you to laugh and joke and put up a brave front before others, but you have allowed me a glimpse of a hidden sadness, a secret despair, that is the direct result of some event on that yacht. You can tell me, dear Sammy, and even if it means telling all to Papa so that he agrees to return you to Mount Street and the bosom of your family, I will do so gladly for you, my sweet baby sister."

Isabella thought she could see some slight alteration in her sister's expression, a certain tightening of the lips as if to keep them from trembling, before the shutters were lowered once more over those vacantly staring emerald eyes. "The yacht, Samantha," Isabella prodded encouragingly, "I feel the roots of your anguish lie there. Tell me about the yacht. What was it like?"

With great effort, Samantha's lips trembled and then parted, and her voice—in a weak, ear-straining whisper—said the one word: "*Bordello!*"

Isabella's so far limited but longing-to-be-expanded knowledge of the interaction between men and women in delicate situations was given a nasty jolt. Samantha had, with but a single word, pricked her sister's romantic vision of true love—hand-holding, tender kisses, and, in time to come, cuddly, chubby-cheeked children on her knee. She had always known that between the romantic interlude and the cherubic babies there lay a grey area she did not entirely comprehend.

Now, upon the hearing of one short word, that grey area became blindingly illuminated. Wives provided the same service as opera dancers and other fashionable (and not so fashionable) impures, but to be *treated* no better than one of the muslin company was an indignity no wife should be forced to endure. What if *her* husband, when she married (if, she adjusted frantically, she ever married), was as lacking in respect for the tender sensibilities that true ladies possess in such high degree?

But this was not the time to indulge in selfish concerns, for if Isabella interpreted Samantha's description correctly, the poor girl had been imprisoned for two days (and *nights!*) aboard a floating house of ill repute.

The object of all this solicitude had, for the past few minutes, been close to choking on her suppressed mirth while watching so many disparate emotions on her sister's face. The poor dear must by now have me fighting to retain my unsullied innocence while Zachary sets scene after scene of wild debauchery in order to entrap me, Samantha decided happily. Perhaps she even envisions the brute becoming violent when he cannot bend me to his depraved will. Samantha had described the yacht as a bordello because of that so-outlandish bed, of course, and—as was her inclination—to see how much of a clunker of a tale her sister could be made to swallow. It appeared that Isabella had a healthy appetite for Sin.

"Samantha," Isabella at last commiserated sadly, "how totally *awful* for you," earnestly striving to hide that small, pleasurable titillation that can so easily be felt when the object of such base attack (as her sister must have been) is anyone other than oneself.

It was the sight of Isabella's respectability doing battle with her baser female instincts (and losing, sorry to say) that at last overpowered Samantha's control of her "tragedy queen" countenance. "*Awful*, dear, sweet, *concerned* big sister?" Samantha challenged with a hint of laughter in her once again strong, clear voice. She reached out and placed an admonishing finger on the tip of Isabella's tilt-tipped nose. "Not nearly so awful as your fevered little brain imagined it, if that maidenly blush is to be taken as evidence of your penny-dreadful version of my so-unfortunate debauchment. Confess, Izzy: you had me all but sold into the white slave trade, didn't you?"

For a moment Isabella had remained at Samantha's feet, too stunned to react. Now she jumped up, and—in a move that expressed her degree of agitation more clearly than could any words—reached down and soundly boxed her sister's ears.

The two might have come to blows had it not been for Samantha's desire to keep her new gown out of harm's way and Isabella's belated recollection of her own consequence as a London debutante. They cried friends and as a peace offering Samantha described her honeymoon in elaborate detail—holding back nothing but her inexplicable (and, at times, almost wanton) reaction to her husband's attempts at lovemaking. Instead she centered her recitation on the infamous royal bed and its magically multiplying cushions, a stirring re-enactment of her role in dousing the blaze that threatened the ship, and a disturbingly graphic description of her bout of seasickness-*cum*-drunkenness.

Isabella cut this last bit short with an entreaty to Samantha to bring her story up to the present, including knowledge of the newlyweds' first night under the same roof on dry land—and the reason (just a teeny bit lurid, she hoped) that her sister seemed so thoroughly out of patience with St. John this very morning. "Hurry, do, for Aunt Loretta has already had one nap after breakfast and we cannot depend upon her sleeping much longer. Besides, you know as well as I that no matter how lost in slumber she may appear, her stomach wakes her within one minute of mealtime without fail."

So Samantha told Isabella of the events of the previous evening, sadly disappointing events that they were, being solely that his bride—exhausted from a long day's travel—was carried into the mansion fast asleep in her husband's arms. She remembered nothing more until she awakened to find herself all alone in a strange bed and was handed her morning chocolate and a note that read: "I have gone out. We are engaged for Lord Frazer's this evening. Plan accordingly. Z."

Really! thought Isabella, who had more experience in the care and feeding of her sister's volatile personality than she felt she either wanted or needed. If this is how the Earl intends to deal with Sammy, it's a long and stormy path he has chosen to trod. The surest way to set Samantha off hell-bent on mischief is to attempt to order her about like some child. Add to that his cavalier abandonment of his bride their first day back in London (and Samantha at her most dangerous when alone and feeling bored), and it seemed to Isabella that the man must harbor a death wish.

To pass the time before luncheon (and while waiting for Aunt Loretta to rise from her slumbers), Isabella decided to occupy Samantha's mind with thoughts of the latest fashions, and Samantha happily expanded on her plan to become a trend-setter in the fashionable world. "I wish to become an *original*," she told her sister candidly.

Her sister, experiencing one of her increasingly common flashes of independent judgment, declared, "But my dearest sister, you already *are*."

Samantha merely nodded, accepting this judgment not as praise but as a simple statement of fact. After all, she was not so naive as to be unaware of her talents, nor so hungry for adulation that she bothered to protest prettily her sister's words—an open invitation to Isabella to heap even more flattery on Samantha's head after each half-hearted disclaimer. No, she had scant time for such self-serving maneuvers, no more time than she had for portrayals of false modesty when she was tolerably well pleased with her appearance and brainpower. Some people—probably those less blessed—would call her vain or arrogant, but if she were guilty of anything it would have to be, as ever, her unsettling tendency to speak her mind with refreshing, if startling, candor.

And so it was no surprise that Samantha merely agreed with her sister's assessment of her probable establishment as an *"original"* of the *ton* before adding, attacking her subject realistically, "It is not enough to just stand out from the rest of the sheep. I must be their acknowledged leader—of the females at least, for a start. If I were, for example, to proclaim sackcloth and ashes all the rage, I would not be happy until Almack's was a sea of grubby-looking debutantes moving through a country dance while nobly ignoring an almost unbearable desire to relieve the discomfort of their rough garments by indulging in a veritable orgy of scratching."

Isabella's giggles went a long way towards lifting the dampening mood that had threatened to overwhelm Samantha during their discussion of Zachary—and the perplexing attitude of disinterest he had maintained ever since his so odiously condescending replies to her request to refresh her memory concerning the events of their last night aboard the *Sea Devil.*

She had only just begun to believe there was a slight glimmer of hope that theirs could be an amiable, if not romantic, union before he had abruptly poured cold water all over her budding optimism. The journey from Margate had been an exercise in self-discipline as St. John remained motionless in his corner of the coach, hour after tedious hour—so very off-putting with his eyes hidden beneath the forward tilt of his curly-brimmed beaver hat.

How she had longed to knock the lean pantaloon-encased leg supporting his relaxed frame from its place—propped against the facing seat—and see him tumble to the floor in an ungainly heap. For a few brief mad moments, she was even tempted to take target practice at the tassel swinging just above and to the right of Royston's head with one of the carriage pistols just to see how well he could continue to pretend he was unaware of her existence. In the end she had done nothing—nothing, that is, but sit and glare at the tip of one of his aristocratic ears, thinking dire thoughts until on the outskirts of London fatigue at last claimed her.

Samantha brought herself back to her surroundings with a slight shake and tried to catch the tail end of her sister's question. "Isn't the dowager Countess due to arrive in town fairly soon, Samantha? I must say I would be dreading a visit from my husband's sole surviving relative—although I imagine that, as the Earl's grandmother, the good lady must be pretty well up in years and very frail."

"Izzy," her sister said blightingly, as she settled herself more comfortably in her chair, "it's a wonder you ever dare to set a foot out of bed, given the number of fears you harbor in your mind. Why on earth should the prospect of meeting Zachary's ancient grandmother overset me, let alone *you?*"

"Well, really, Sammy," Isabella argued defensively, "she *is* the dowager. What if she don't like you?"

Samantha shook her head disbelievingly and laughed, "A great whacking lot of good that would do her, Izzy. What would you have her do? Order St. John to seek a divorce?"

"Not a divorce, Sammy," Isabella blushed. "An *annulment.* Unless you aren't telling *all* about your honeymoon."

Samantha busied herself with the sleeve of her gown. "No, it was a near-run thing, I admit. But you are right, Izzy, at least for now. An annulment would serve just as well. Do you propose to let the dowager in on our little secret?" Isabella's fiery cheeks were her only answer, so Samantha went on to point out the fact that—if the dowager was too delicate to face travelling from the country over the muddy spring roads, even to be present for her only grandson's nuptials—it was likely many months yet before the St. Johns were blessed with the woman's presence. "By then I'll probably be with child, if Zachary has any say in the matter, and the question won't even arise."

"It has been dry this last week and more," her sister pointed out anxiously.

"Is that a fact? Have you turned weather-watcher then, Isabella? How droll," Samantha chided. "Really, Izzy, all this fuss about one timid old lady. I can handle the dowager with both hands tied behind my back. After all—"

"Ahem. Madam," cut in Carstairs, who had stepped inside the room.

"If you're about to tell me luncheon is served, man, I'll eat when it suits *me,* not you," Samantha cut him off shortly—slightly drunk with her new power and more than ready to establish herself as mistress of the household. Turning back to her sister, she went on as if there had been no interruption: "After all, Izzy, even if the old tabby takes it into her head to cut up stiff at me, do you think me unable to send her to the rightabout directly?" she finished smugly.

Isabella, whose chair faced the doorway, could see the

butler was obviously in the throes of some serious dilemma. "*Ahem!* My lady, if you *please—*" he began in strangled tones.

"Now see here, Carstairs," Samantha began, only to stop when she noticed the color leaving her sister's face. As her back had been to the door, Samantha slowly turned her head to see what had sent Isabella's eyes to near popping from her head and was greeted by the sight of a hand-wringing, cringing Carstairs, who was vainly striving to keep a truly magestic looking *grande dame* from fully entering the room.

Realizing the futility of his efforts, he gathered about him the rags of his respectability, pumped up his chest and announced: "The Dowager Countess of Royston, madam," whirled smartly on his heel, and quit the room for the kitchens and an alcoholic restorative.

Chapter Eight

ALL THE COMMOTION had served to rouse Aunt Loretta, who proceeded to yawn, stretch, inquire if luncheon was served, and—on being told it was not—sink gracefully back into dreamland.

"And what," the dowager demanded in a deep voice that set the Sèvres vase on the mantelpiece to jiggling, "is *that?*"

Whilst Aunt Loretta was performing her only party trick, Samantha had taken the time to rise and face the dowager, doing a quick inventory of her ladyship at the same time. Egad, she thought, the woman must be six feet tall if she's an inch, and built more along the lines of a village blacksmith than a peeress of the realm. All in all, quite an imposing figure, decked out as it was in deep purple draperies, the whole topped off by a veritable bush of hair that was incongruously snow-white on the crown and sides and coal-black at the back. Zachary's hair will look like that one day, Samantha thought to no purpose. Then she shook herself mentally and, valiantly blocking the dowager's view of the rapidly wilting Isabella, told her newest relative, "*That*, as you put it, is our *dear* Aunt Loretta—chaperon, companion, and mentor of our formative years."

"*Hummph!*" snorted her ladyship. "Preserve me from dotty, middle-aged ape leaders. So that's all the resistance Zachary had to overcome in his rush to rob the cradle. I don't count yer father, of course: the man most likely drooled all down St. John's best waistcoat in his ecstasy over the match. We Roystons are quite plump in the pocket, besides being able to trace our line back to the

Domesday Book," the dowager concluded, as she settled herself into a nearby chair.

"And so modest with it all, too," Samantha fairly purred, as she retook her own seat.

Oh, dear, Isabella groaned inwardly. I knew Sammy would cause a scene the moment I laid eyes on the dowager. I just knew it. Drat Sammy and her quick tongue! Will she never learn to keep her thoughts to herself? Look at the two of them, she thought as she sank deeply into her chair, eyeing each other like birds of prey sizing up their quarry. She dragged her eyes from the two staring adversaries to search out Aunt Loretta, who was still deep in dreamland and promising to be of no more help than a brass doorstop once the feathers started to fly. If there was only one thing about her aunt that could be depended upon, it was that she could not be depended upon at all.

The dowager was the first to break the tense silence that followed Samantha's irreverent remark. "So," she cackled, slowly eyeing Samantha up and down as if she were a bit of goods on a shelf, "this is the best my grandson could come up with, heh? A spoiled chit dressed up like a Bartholemew baby, trying to ape her betters but unable to do more than come off looking for all the world like a brass-faced light-skirt, and with the manners of an orange girl at Drury Lane to boot. What a sorry state the St. John name has come to, if a creature like you is to be the mother of the next generation. Tell me, gel," she added insultingly, "is that by some sordid chance the real reason for all this unseeming haste to get to the altar? Are you in fact already breeding a bastard for Zachary?"

Samantha didn't bat an eye as she replied in bored tones: "Frankly, *madam,* when it comes to motherhood—and especially when it comes to mingling my bloodline with that of the so-blue St. John strain—the prospect of that delicate condition leaves me totally unmoved."

"And besides," Isabella said, as she found herself staunchly supporting her sister (who didn't seem in the least need of any help, but blood is thicker than water), "my aunt and I happen to think Sammy's gown is slap up to the echo." At a piercing glance from the dowager Isabella subsided, mortified past all bearing for having inadvertently succumbed to one of Wally's cant expressions in her agitation.

"There is no need for you to set yourself up as a martyr in my cause, Izzy, but thank you anyway," Samantha soothed.

The dowager took a moment to assess Isabella—this fluffy kitten who had so unexpectedly shown her claws—and chanced idly, "This must be the debutante. I had wondered why Royston passed you by for a younger sister, but now I can see his reasoning. He would have devoured you with one gulp and had enough appetite left for half the opera company. But you're a fair enough beauty," she added condescendingly. "If you can remember to keep your mouth shut and your expression blank, I imagine you will take well enough in this inane circus we call Society."

Isabella didn't know whether to thank the dowager or demand an apology, her kittenish courage not extending to any great lengths, so she merely nodded and busied herself with the buttons on her gloves.

Thankfully, Carstairs picked that moment to bring in the tea tray, thinking it to be the lesser of two evils since her ladyship had not rung to tell him to set another cover for luncheon as was her plain duty. He did not place so little value upon his skin that he could ignore the demand for refreshment the dowager had issued upon her arrival, no matter how his mistress might choose to ignore common good manners (not that he could find it in himself to blame her for her lapse).

The three ladies (the insubstantial nibblings a tea tray normally held were not enough to rouse Aunt Loretta) maintained a tense silence until Carstairs made his bowing exit, but he was still within earshot when Samantha chose to take umbrage at the dowager's cutting remarks about Isabella.

"It is more than plain that you are up in the boughs over the belated delivery of our wedding invitation, caused—so my husband says—by the muddy roads to the south," she supplied in such a way as to let her audience know she was merely retelling an obvious fib made up to hand out to anyone at the wedding who inquired as to the dowager's whereabouts. "But that," she said, her voice stiffening perceptively, "does not give you the right to speak vulgarly to or about my sister!" Samantha charged in righteous indignation.

Once again the dowager eyed the girl who dared to take her on in a battle of wills. "My dear child," she imparted mockingly, "don't you know that vulgarity is just one of the many privileges of age, and—although I am convinced your sister there is no more or less than any of the charming, vacant-faced nitwits that abound throughout London—you, gel, I am forced to admit, are fast on your way to becoming a bit of a tartar. It is only my generation—the few of us that are left aboveground—that retain any sense of individuality or spark of spunk at all. But I seem to sense a bit of kindred spirit in you."

"If I believed that, madam, I would promptly ring for Carstairs to bring me a knife—which he would doubtless deliver with solemn pomp, the blade borne on a silver tray and cushioned by a lace napkin—and I would proceed to slice my throat," Samantha retorted with some asperity. She had already admitted to Isabella her desire to be an *original*, but if she had thought her natural high spirits and frankness of speech would with age degenerate into obstinacy and hurtful sarcasm she would have to rethink her plans.

If, on the other hand, moderation was to be Samantha's new motto, her resolution was never to see the light of day. For just then the dowager raised her quizzing glass, a gold-rimmed circle that had until this moment been dangling from its black riband just below that awesome bosom, and proceeded to inspect her surroundings to see if her grandson had kept so much as one stick of the furniture that had been her choice when she reigned supreme in Portman Square. He had not.

Almost immediately Samantha's eyes lit with admiration for at least one of the dowager's affectations. Isabella saw the look and squirmed in her chair; she knew that gleam in her sister's eye of old, and would have wagered her pin money for the next quarter that Samantha would be sporting a quizzing glass of her own before the week was out. Her sister's impish wink in her direction confirmed her worst fears.

But the dowager Countess was wrong when she prophesied Samantha would someday be very like herself, Isabella decided loyally. Anyone who knew how endlessly kind the girl could be to those less fortunate than herself would with clear conscience promptly swear Samantha didn't have a mean bone in her body. As to the rest—the spark of spunk the dowager spoke of her possessing, along with the definite air of an excessively unique individual—oh, yes, Isabella concurred grudgingly. The dowager had hit the nail right on the head that time, though even she, at least on such short acquaintance, could not imagine the depth and breadth and highth of Samantha's vibrant personality.

But she must pay attention. The dowager was speaking again, and by the sound of things she was rushing blindly in where angels fear to tread—to quote Alexander Pope, a poet best loved by the older generations but one seemingly not on the dowager's list of favorites.

"Enough of this verbal jousting, pleasant though it may be," the dowager was saying. "The time has come for me, the head of the family, to lay out a few pertinent facts. Since your family don't have the good grace to leave us to speak in privacy—by the way, are you *quite* sure that lump in the corner, the one that doesn't answer when you call her Aunt Loretta, has not silently slipped over to the other side? Ha!" she chortled merrily. "And if she had, how ever could you tell?"

"I don't care a button what you say of me, my lady, but you will refrain from tearing up my relatives or, for that matter, my friends, once I am out in Society—either to my face or behind our backs. Have I made myself sufficiently clear, madam?" proclaimed Samantha with countesslike dignity, not in the least penitent for having spoken so to Zachary's grandmother. It was a dignity only slightly impaired by the mulish expression on her face and the whiteness of her knuckles as they clutched the chair arms, as if she was just barely managing to hold herself back from making a direct physical assault on the woman who had so blatantly insulted her kin.

She felt as if she had been caught out in a blizzard in her nightdress, unaware of and unprepared for the unexpected appearance of this bizarre woman and the vicious attack that she launched within moments of her arrival. Drat Zachary and his vague explanation that: "Grandmother is a bit of a dragon and we never did get on. I left her invitation too late in order to avoid a scene before the wedding, but I shall put it abroad that the wet weather delayed her removal from Dorset. Once we are married she'll not have any choice but to bow to the fact gracefully, in public that is. In private I'm afraid we'll have to put up with at least one small scene. Like I said, the old girl's a trifle overbearing."

Trust Zachary to understate the case, Samantha seethed helplessly. And trust him too, to disappear the single time I could be passably pleased to have his company. Standing alone against the force of the dowager's anger was much like trying to light a candle in the wind. Every time you think you have struck a spark, another gust comes along to snuff it out. And the dowager was like a strong blast of wind, sweeping onto the scene and creating turmoil with each fresh gust of air she sets whistling past my ears.

What a brimstone of a female! Samantha marveled. If Wellington had a hundred more like her, the war would have been over a good three years earlier. The portion of the enemy she and her pattern-copies could not slay with a look would soon take to their heels at the sound of her booming voice, which would rattle their brains and jangle their nerves until they broke ranks and ran for their lives.

"Now that we have dealt with the preliminaries, and I have laid down a few ground rules," Samantha at last offered charitably, "you may proceed with whatever it is you came to say. I can tell you will not budge from that chair until you have emptied your budget of grievances. I regret my rash remarks, if only because they set you off on another tangent, thus delaying the stating of the true purpose of your visit sooner, and freeing you to push on to your destination with all deliberate speed. I would, of course," she added with disarming sweetness, "beg you to stay in Portman Square with us, but I know you don't wish to intrude on newlyweds still officially on their honeymoon." *There,* Samantha thought smugly. That should serve to put a spoke in her wheel!

The dowager had been more than a little surprised with Zachary's choice of bride. Oh, yes, the chit's extreme youth was a shock— but then many a man pandered to his ego by opting for a *jeune fille* who would worship her worldly-wise husband and be content to be molded like soft clay, to conform to his every desire. But this girl was more than just youthful. She was pretty—beautiful, actually—and would be even more stunning once she matured. But she was also intelligent, witty, self-confident, and a person of strong principles. Zachary had chosen himself a rare handful. The dowager, if she could only allow herself to relax her belligerent attitude a bit, could almost find herself liking Samantha, but she had worn her protective armor of cold pride too long. She would not know how to begin to change at this late date.

She would settle for a grudging admiration for the girl's great spirit. She could not know that Samantha was similarly crediting the dowager with a like admiration; tempered, of course, by Samantha's distaste for the old lady's obnoxious airs of snobbery.

With their dissections of one another's character and motives completed—much to the relief of Isabella, who had been holding her breath for so long in the charged atmosphere of the quiet room that she was beginning to feel giddy—the dowager at long last came to the point. "I have travelled here from Dorset, as you say, not planning to stop with you but only to make a brief visit before continuing on to an acquaintance of mine near Richmond. Since my grandson so feared my reaction to his plans that he felt he needs must hide them from me—stuck in the back of beyond as I am—until such time as the deed was done and my wishes in the matter were no longer worth a tinker's damn, I felt it my duty to the Royston ancestors to travel to London and assess the amount of damage Zachary has done the family escutcheon.

"So far I would be willing to say your sister, at least, has shown some sort of genteel education, so I imagine you too have been taught at least the rudiments. However, my young hoyden, your veneer of sophistication seems dangerously thin, as you do not seem to have yet mastered your temper or your tongue. To go abroad in Society one needs both a broad back and a thick skin, figuratively of course; if those physical descriptions were actually to fit you all the poise in the world couldn't get you accepted into the *ton*. Beauty is one path of entry, as is money—as long as there is plenty of it and not a farthing of it smelling of the shop. Beauty you have, wealth you acquired through marriage. But," she warned authoritatively, "you will not be able to conduct yourself in Society with the propriety demanded of a Royston if today's example of your volatile temper—just one of your many shortcomings—is to be used as a judge."

Samantha searched her brain wildly for a suitable setdown, but then realized any such retaliation would only confirm her to be a hotheaded nuisance who could not be trusted to behave with any consistency or ever be allowed to run tame in Society for fear she would totally disgrace herself with some impetuous word or deed. All Samantha could do (while Isabella tried vainly to disappear so as to not be witness to her sister's humiliation) was to sit and stare in stupefaction, her composure a total shambles.

The dowager recognized her advantage and decided to enlarge on her victory. "But let us not dwell only on your own consequence, my dear," she instructed Samantha. "You must also consider your husband's reputation for discretion, finesse, and all-over general air of *savoir-faire*. His standing in the *ton* is impeccable, but even one so firmly entrenched as he cannot remain unblemished if his wife continually makes herself a figure of fun." Here the dowager directed a long, dispassionate stare in the direction of Samantha's peach lace bodice. "Trial that he may be to me, Zachary is my sole remaining grandson, and I am really quite excessively fond of him."

The dowager's last statements served to snap Samantha out of her stupor. Her ladyship had been over-anxious for a quick capitulation, and made a tactical error by underestimating her youthful adversary. Zachary St. John was the author of more scandal than she, his wife, could generate in three lifetimes, and—if it was prudent to give a thought or two to her plans for her own success in Society—it was absolutely ludicrous to believe she could do anything to St. John's reputation that he hadn't thought of and already done to himself, twice! Samantha's Irish blood tingled in her veins as she brought up her previously bowed head, stared the dowager straight in her coal-black eyes, and drawled with heavy sarcasm: "Fond of Zachary are you, madam? Well, that makes *one* of us."

Isabella had to sit on her hands to restrain the impulse to applaud Samantha's brilliant recovery.

The dowager was clearly astounded. She had assumed the match was as much the chit's idea as her grandson's. Could this girl actually be such a blockhead that she didn't appreciate the honor that had been bestowed upon her? From Samantha's mulish expression it was clear she did not. "How dare you look down your nose at the Royston name?" she fairly shrieked. "I'll have you know, missy, that—"

"Here, here, now, we can't have this," came a cheerful voice from the doorway. The Earl of Royston, once silence was restored, sauntered casually into the room to kiss first his wife's forehead, then the dowager's cheek, and lastly Isabella's trembling fingers. Aunt Loretta he chose not to disturb. "Ladies, ladies, I beg you," he continued, once he had seated himself in a chair he pulled up alongside that of his wife's (clasping her hand in a loverlike fashion that hid both her attempts to withdraw from his grasp and the tightness of his grip). "It is too nice a day for dramatic confrontations, don't you agree? Samantha, pet, your hand is quite warm; surely you are not overdressed?" he questioned as he leered at her revealing *décolletage*.

Leaving Samantha to seethe silently, mentally devising a suitably painful way of murdering her husband, St. John then favored Isabella with a flattering fulsome declaration that he had never before seen her in quite such good looks: not that she was not always a miracle of feminine perfection, but the unusually rosy flush on her cheeks—which seemed to come and go like shy rosebuds—was simply too, too enchanting.

Finally, never for an instant allowing even an inkling of his distaste for the project to be visible to the ladies, he addressed his grandmother. "I hope you and Samantha have had a comfortable chat in my absence, getting to know one another and trotting out all my past sins to cluck over as you rehash the follies committed in my misspent youth?"

"We have not had time for mawkish reminiscences, even if I could lay my mind to dredging up a past best left to lie undisturbed and unlamented. It is your wedding, an event you preferred to accomplish in my absence, that occupied our conversation this past half-hour," his grandmother contradicted bitterly. "That and an exhibition of disgraceful manners, with—most noticeably—an utter disregard for civility, my rank, and natural Christian charity displayed by your," and this last was said with a sneer, "*wife.*"

"Samantha!" St. John admonished in mock astonishment. "Have you been a naughty puss? Pining for your darling husband, no doubt, and taking out your sour mood on our guest. For shame, Samantha." A white-hot poker right through his gullet, Samantha decided, that's how I'll do the deed. No, she quickly adjusted, that's too quick. It must be gradual, a lingering death. Maybe a slow-acting poison in his port? she speculated gleefully.

"Your wife was not pining for your presence, grandson," the dowager put in nastily. "The total opposite is more like it. I cannot make myself understand what you can see in a willful, spoiled nursery brat with no background and even less conduct, who—besides being totally lacking in the rightful appreciation of the prestige of the St. John name—has made no pains to conceal her dislike of you personally. Look!" she commanded. "Look at the gel's face! It's a clear reflection of her feelings. She don't like you, grandson. That should be obvious, even to you. A blind man could read that face. I cannot understand why you married her!"

"Lord, madam, why should you?" St. John shot back cheerfully. "Only a woman would have to ask such a question. Any man could tell you right off why I married Samantha. A blind man could see why, grandmother, provided he had not lost his sense of touch along with his eyesight."

Isabella giggled behind her gloves while Samantha discarded slow-acting poison and dredged her memory concerning racks, thumbscrews, iron maidens, and the like. She was not the only person to be displeased by the Earl's flippant answer, but the dowager's anger took a startlingly different direction. "Go on, damn your eyes! Make a joke of everything, as usual. Life is just one long silly Drury Lane farce to you, isn't it? Even as a child you used your wits to get you out of trouble, while poor Robin—who hadn't your devious mind—was made to pay the penalty for your folly over and over again. My poor, poor Robin," the dowager lamented in a carrying voice. "He worshiped the ground you walked on, and lived only to follow your every lead—even when it meant going off to war in an attempt to match your foolish show of bravado."

"Now, Grandmother, let's not rake up old hurts. I'm sorry if my silly banter upset you, truly I am, but let us not get into a discussion about Robin today. It's my honeymoon!"

But the old lady was not to be denied. As Isabella and Samantha looked on in stunned silence, the dowager rose to her imposing height and pointed a long nail accusingly at her grandson. "You killed him, you know. You and your devil-take-the-hindmost attitude, your complete arrogance and sick perverted sense of humor *murdered my Robin!*"

The room was silent as each of its occupants wondered how this radical shift had come about, swinging from a discussion of Zachary's poor judgment in treating the dowager's complaints as a joke to this emotion-charged accusation of fratricide.

"Grandmother, sit down please. You're overset," St. John reasoned calmly, holding onto his temper with remarkable control—although Samantha's fingers were near to breaking as his grip on them tightened like a vise. "I thought we had this all out a year ago, when Robin was reported killed. Whether it was to follow my lead or not, Robin was army mad ever since he was out of short coats and you know it. The second son is expected to go into the army, but I would not have bought Robin his colors if he had not pleaded, truly *pleaded* with me to do so. He would have gone whether I had served or not."

Slowly, insidiously, something began to grow in Samantha's breast. She had only heard Royston speak of his brother twice, but each time his face and voice had betrayed deep emotion. How dare this woman, whether she had raised them both or not, presume to find fault with Zachary's decision to fulfill his younger brother's greatest wish? And hadn't Zachary himself spent three long years risking life and limb for his country? Surely he did not laugh his way through the battle at Salamanca, or the disastrous march to the winter quarters at Ciudad Rodrigo —when a Horse Guards quartermaster's incompetence left the column without food for four long days! Samantha's father had taught her enough of the ways of war to give her a healthy admiration for anyone who served in Spain, and the dowager should be proud of her grandson.

"How dare you," she heard herself saying, as she jumped to her feet. "How *dare* you presume to belittle my husband's motives for volunteering to serve on the Peninsula? Zachary told me he was with Wellington for three years—three long, hard years—and no man does such a thing lightly. If Robin chose to admire his brother, I say he could have done worse than to emulate him by joining the army."

Isabella was weeping softly into her handkerchief now, uncaring if she was seen. St. John rose slowly and placed an arm around his wife's slim shoulders. "You need not defend me, sweetings, though I am honored that you do," he said sincerely, as he observed Samantha's high color and the agitated heaving of her bosom. "Grandmother and I have never been known to agree on anything, except perhaps our love for Robin. It is possible, knowing the true horror of war firsthand, I should have tried harder to sway Robin from his determination."

"Ah!" the dowager cried victoriously. "You admit it, then!"

"I'd admit to setting the Great Fire if it would put period to this distasteful discussion," St. John agreed dryly. "You have upset my wife, and I cannot allow you to remain here further if you will not agree to desist in your accusations." Privately, though he abhorred his grandmother's vile timing almost as much as he was sickened by her refusal to be shaken from the idea that he was responsible for Robin's death, St. John was inwardly elated by his bride's vehement defense of his honor. Perhaps she was softening towards him at last.

A flurry of movement from his grandmother signaled her gathering herself for departure, a leave-taking that he wished had been more pleasant, but he knew how slim the chance was for a reconciliation any time soon. Well, he mused, at least I can be thankful that she's a strong old curmudgeon. With her hate to feed on, she should live another twenty years just to spite me. Perhaps twenty years is soon enough to hope for some sign of forgiveness. He couldn't really say he loved his grandmother—who had had scant time for him even in his youth, showering all her love on Robin—but he did respect the woman, and he fretted about her abnormal grief over Robin's death. He could even, if pushed, have grown to love her a little now that he was a grown man, but the woman made any overtures impossible. St. John sighed, and Samantha slid one peach-and-green-clad arm about his waist.

"I'm leaving, Royston," the dowager said, "leaving and consigning you and your infant bride to your fate. I had entertained the idea of handling your wife's entrance into Society, lending her my countenance as it were, but I refuse to be a part of what is sure to be the social disaster of the century. Farewell. You shall not be bothered with my presence for some time," she prophesied profoundly.

Samantha glared at her, and did not hesitate before proclaiming with great feeling, "And *that*, my dear madam, suits me to a cow's thumb."

"Oh, Sammy," Isabella exclaimed once the dowager had stomped from the room in high dudgeon, "how utterly famous of you to come to the Earl's defense like that. I should never have behaved so bravely. Never in my life have I been so overset by anyone as I was by the dowager. She was, er, rather unique, don't you think?"

Samantha soothed her agitated sister while St. John followed his grandmother outside, where she grudgingly allowed him to hand her up into her large, old-fashioned travelling coach. "You know, Zachary," she said at the last, "that wife of yours surely knows her way around a nice sharp dig. I don't remember the last time anyone bested me in an exchange of set-downs. She may even have prompted me to think a bit more on Robin's determination to go to war. You know, son," she whispered hoarsely, "we are all we've got left now. Maybe it's time we start to get to know one another. Who knows? We might even find we can tolerate each other."

"I'd like that, Grandmother," St. John replied earnestly, giving the old lady's hand a firm squeeze.

"Perhaps—perhaps I have been too hasty. Perhaps I should postpone my journey and stay on with you a few days," she mused mistily.

"Grandmother, unless you wish a total breach in our relationship, you will hie your carcass off posthaste," the Earl contradicted vigorously. "Madam, lest it has slipped your mind, I am on my honeymoon."

The dowager cackled, her humor and her vigor seemingly restored. "And a prime bit of fight and fire you chose for a bride. A monkey to a copper penny she'll have you at her feet on a leash before the year is out. I can tell you, Zachary, if I weren't so damned jealous of her beauty, youth and spirit, I could find it in my heart to really like that gel. She reminds me a bit of myself in my salad days."

"So that explains why I was so immediately drawn to the creature," Royston said with a wink, as he gifted his grandmother with a spontaneous—rather than a dutiful—kiss, admonished her to resist the temptation to order the coachman to spring the horses (as was her custom), and waved the dowager on her way.

As the Earl was remounting the steps, Isabella and Aunt Loretta were just beginning their descent. The excitement of the morning had prompted Isabella to forego lunch in favor of a quiet meal at home, and she was in the act of soothing her aunt's distress over missing out on luncheon at an Earl's table.

"But, Isabella," her aunt complained, "I don't understand your haste. I could vow we have not stopped above a half-hour with Samantha, and her invitation *did* include luncheon. I distinctly remember it."

Royston suppressed a grin as he helped the ladies into their carriage, which had just pulled around front, and comforted Aunt Loretta somewhat by extending a dinner invitation for the following week. Isabella smiled her thanks and Royston signaled the driver to move off, just as Aunt Loretta was innocently asking Isabella if anything exciting had happened while she had been taking her "little rest."

When St. John re-entered the main salon, it was to find his wife pacing the floor restlessly, her hands clenched into angry fists and her mouth moving in quiet fury.

" 'Lend me her countenance,' she said," Samantha muttered angrily. "As if I need to be taken under her wing, so she can parade me about at every insipid Venetian breakfast and choral concert in town, showing me off as her *protégée*—like a pet monkey. It's beyond everything wonderful that I was able to restrain myself from doing her grave bodily harm."

"Now, now, pet," the Earl reasoned shrewdly, "you succeeded in routing her quite beautifully, and without any loss of blood. Actually, Grandmother unbent sufficiently in the end to pay you some fulsome compliments, words of praise I hesitate to repeat else they turn your head."

Samantha allowed herself to be slightly mollified. "I thank her for her kind words, but that doesn't erase the fact that she is a particularly overbearing person."

Royston chuckled. "And you, of course, are full to overflowing with all the first-rate virtues. As a matter of fact, I always felt you reminded me of someone—and at last I think I have placed the resemblance. Not physically, of course, but in many other ways you remind me a great deal of Grandmother before her grief for Robin turned her so bitter.

"No, no, infant," he pleaded, holding his hands in front of his face as Samantha looked about to deliver him a solid facer, "I mean that as a compliment, truly."

Shaking her head in disbelief Samantha asked, "How can you be so casual about it all? That woman stood right in this room not ten minutes past, and baldly accused you of murder. Aren't you the least bit angry? I vow I was so incensed for you I barely remember what I said to her."

While in the midst of removing an infinitesimal speck of lint from the sleeve of his coat, Royston answered quietly, "To be perfectly honest about it, I was about to give vent to a few thoughts of my own when, lo and behold, my wife gallantly stepped into the breach in my defense. If I have not thanked you before, I do so now."

Samantha was not satisfied. She was mystified by the depth of her outrage over the dowager's insulting remarks about her husband, and she was having great difficulty bringing her emotions under control. "But Zachary—" she began one more time—only to be cut off in mid-harangue by the bruising pressure of Zachary's lips against her half-open mouth.

She stood stock-still while his mouth softened and coaxed her own stiff lips into the first glimmerings of response. He had already placed his hands on her shoulders, and soon she felt her own hands moving with an independence she could but marvel at. Finally her nerveless fingers encountered and clutched at Zachary's muscular chest.

An involuntary moan escaped her when he at last drew away, to look down at her bemused face with what she considered to be an expression of insufferable smugness. She dropped her hands as if she had just encountered a hot coal, stepped rapidly back a pace or two, and charged indignantly: "And just what was that particular exercise meant to prove?"

St. John's answer was anything but soothing. He had kissed her, he said, because he was still feeling angry over the set-to with his grandmother.

"Well, that smacks of a singularly stupid brand of reasoning," Samantha railed back at him indignantly.

"Oh, I don't agree. As the kiss is now concluded and my anger is considerably abated, your insulting remark concerning my logic is quite superfluous. Events, my dear, speak for themselves."

"If that's so, then your logic is only half true. *My* anger is no less heated than before your vicious assault on my person," Samantha told him testily.

St. John stroked his chin, clucked his tongue, and commiserated, "That really is too bad. May I suggest we repeat the process, concentrating our efforts entirely in your direction?"

She backed up another pace. "Do, and I'll scream," she

warned. "Carstairs may expire of a severe case of injured sensibilities, but let that be on your own head."

In answer the Earl shrugged, turned, and strolled towards the door. As he was about to pass through the doorway he hesitated and threw back over his shoulder, "It is a pity, actually. You have denied what could well have been an extremely interesting experiment."

Not appearing the least bit upset, he then quit the room, leaving behind a fuming Samantha who could not decide whether she was angry that he had kissed her at all or, perversely, even angrier that he had abandoned his second attempt so readily. Eventually, she decided it would be prudent not to delve too deeply into the matter and took herself off for her belated luncheon.

Chapter Nine

IN THE END, Lord and Lady Frazer were to be denied the presence of the St. Johns at their select little affair (no less than three hundred of their closest friends) that evening, thereby robbing Lady Frazer of the social *coup* of the Season. It was a sad deprivation for which her esteemed husband would pay dearly, in the form of numerous dressmaker's bills and other bouts of expensive *récompense* that would only serve to lower his dear wife's high flight of hysteria by a degree or two. Poor Lord Frazer!

But his tribulations paled in the face of the puzzle set before Royston when confronted with a message from Samantha, presented to him by the stammering maid, Daisy, informing him that Lady Royston was ill and already in bed with a warm brick at her toes.

"P-powerful ill, she be, too, m'lord," Daisy ad-libbed loyally.

"My goodness," St. John returned in suitably concerned tones, although his attitude of relaxation—positioned as he was in a leather wing chair, one leg crossed negligently over his other knee, his hands facing each other, splayed fingertips touching—seemed oddly at variance with his words: "Do you think then, dear woman, that she'll last the night?"

Daisy had the goodness to blush and supply her opinion that her ladyship was in no grave danger of being put to bed with a shovel.

"Oh, bless you, woman," his lordship thanked her. "How you console my mind. But wait." He held up a restraining hand as Daisy was about to take her hasty exit. "I would consider it a kindness if you would inform her ladyship that I shall make it a special point to check on her personally before I retire. No, no," he shook his head as Daisy launched into a garbled protest, "I assure you, Daisy, it is no imposition. Her ladyship would, I am persuaded, be devastated, simply *devastated*, if I—her husband of only a few days—should be so remiss as to not make her health my prime concern." St. John's smile, which he permitted to replace his serious frown of husbandly solicitude once Daisy had curtsied awkwardly and sped from the room as if the Devil himself was on her heels, was distinctly evil.

His aura of husbandly distress already discarded, he now contemplated a suitable punishment for his prevaricating bride (who was at that very moment pacing her bedchamber roundly cursing her insufferable husband).

That Lord Royston had a fair inkling of his wife's thoughts went a long way toward keeping a smile on his face all through his evening toilette, presided over by no less than his valet, two honored footmen, and the majestic countenance of Carstairs himself in the role of general overseer. Standing before his shaving table—a deceptively plain mahogany affair that had only moments before been miraculously transformed into a dressing stand by means of secret drawers, catches and levers, and complete with a large mirror that had been raised by means of a spring latch—he surveyed the results of his labors amid his servants' hushed murmurs of awed appreciation.

He silently agreed with their opinion that he looked "fair top-o-the-trees" in his full-length maroon silk dressing gown, casually draped neck scarf, and moroccan slippers. The silvery wings at his temples accented his carefully pomaded black curls and—yes, he complimented himself silently—he was right to have endured the offices of Carstairs as the august butler himself had deigned to shave him for the second time that day. He looked, he chuckled quietly, ready for *anything*.

Royston was sure Samantha had heard the bustle of preparation taking place this past half hour in the dressing room beside the main bedchamber. He wondered what he would find once he opened the connecting door—his bride cowering nervously under the bedcovers, perhaps?

He shook his head. No. Lying in wait, possibly—but never cowering in terror. With studied nonchalance, he dismissed his attendants and walked purposefully toward the door that stood between him and his "ailing" wife. One well-defined eyebrow rose in slight surprise to find the door unlocked as he stepped into the darkened room, where the only illumination came from a small brace of candles reflected in the mirror behind the Hepplewhite dresser.

"Samantha?" he called softly, as his eyes fought to grow accustomed to the dimness. A prickle of apprehension touched lightly between his shoulder blades, and he was careful to keep his back to the wall as he turned his seeking eyes from side to side. It didn't hurt to be a bit prudent when dealing with one such as Samantha: there was no telling what sort of rig she was running.

Finally, when she felt his nerves to be sufficiently stretched, Samantha stepped out of the darkness of the far corner of the chamber and addressed her husband. "Good evening, Zachary."

The sudden sound, after long moments spent in eerie silence, would have caused many a man to give a start, or flinch, or in some other way give evidence of some slight agitation. But St. John, not being just *any* man, merely turned slowly in the direction from whence his wife's voice came, returned her polite greeting, and proceeded to devour her visually from beneath his casually lowered eyelids.

Samantha's choice of nightwear this evening was enough to set even so jaded a palate as Royston's to watering, as it consisted of a cunningly simple gown and outer robe done in emerald-green shot silk—a material that hugged every one of Samantha's several delectable curves and angles and shimmered and changed color with her every movement, her every breath. Her long auburn hair, unbound and tumbling about her shoulders, seemed to move with a life of its own, and Samantha's eyes sparkled as they took in Zachary's reaction to her appearance.

She decided this was not the time to quibble over her earlier story of indisposition. She felt St. John would oblige her by not teasing her with her fib if she didn't mention it, and so proceeded directly to the next step of her plan.

"You like my gown, Zachary?" she asked as she languidly lifted one hand to push back an errant curl. It was a move calculated to inflame her husband's senses, or those of any other male, provided he had eyes in his head and numbered not five years more than Methuselah.

"Imp," Zachary returned with a grin, "if you knew but half of what the sight of you in that particular gown puts me in mind of, you would run screaming from this room in terror."

"T-terror, my lord?" Samantha queried.

St. John began to move in his wife's direction. "Not terror, perhaps that is too strong a word. Substitute instead the word anticipation, and, knowing your love of adventure as I do, change the course of your flight from *away* from me to—"

"You flatter yourself, sir," Samantha interrupted hastily, retreating a step. "Let me tell you something, Zachary—"

St. John advanced another pace. "Tell me anything you want, puss," he soothed, not completely hiding the gleam in his eye.

When it became obvious that just one more step would bring him face to face with her, Samantha's show of bravado wilted and she scampered out of reach behind a nearby chair. "Oh, this isn't going at all as I'd planned," she wailed pettishly.

"And how was that, my sweet?" Royston asked gently, controlling his unsteady heartbeat and shallow breathing with superhuman effort. He looked about the chamber distractedly.

A drink. That's what he needed, what they both needed: a good, stiff drink. While Samantha sidled around to perch on the edge of the chair, her wide eyes never leaving her husband's form, he walked to the bell-pull and summoned a servant who fetched some brandy.

Samantha eyed the snifter warily when Zachary offered it. "Are you sure this is a good idea, my lord? We both remember my last association with spirits."

St. John assured her, "Nonsense, pet, it was the storm. You were perfectly sober."

"I was *not.* I was *ape!*" Samantha giggled, but she took the snifter anyway and held it between her ice-cold hands. "I guess you are wondering a bit about, er, my appearance tonight."

St. John pulled up a footstool and folded his long frame to sit at his wife's feet. "Not unduly, Samantha. I will say that your choice of nightwear is, as ever, most pleasing."

Samantha started, nearly spilling her brandy as she set it on the floor beside St. John's drained snifter, and corrected him: "Oh, this gown was not my choice, Zachary. Aunt Loretta chose all my nightwear. You'd think she was supplying me with a *trousseau* for a sheik's harem. Really, that woman can at times be so obtuse."

"Yes," Royston returned amicably, "and the rest of the time she is unconscious. But we must strive to forget your aunt, as we are, I do believe, gathered together here tonight for something other than polite conversation."

Samantha did not much care for the gleam in Royston's eye as he rose, raising her up with him by simply holding her shoulders in his grip as he came to his feet. She spoke quickly. "Zachary, I know I said I would honor our agreement and all that. No." She held out a hand when she saw he was going to speak. "I know it is highly unfair of me to break my word this way, but—I just don't think I can go through with this!"

Zachary leaned down and began to nibble on Samantha's shoulder. "Nonsense, imp. You were *made* for this. Think of it, if you must, as another little *adventure.*"

As his lips began a trail of kisses up her neck to a tender place just behind her ear, Samantha said again, but with less conviction this time, "I can't go through with it."

"Ah, my dearest goose," Zachary crooned as his tongue traced the hills and valleys of Samantha's ear, "you fill me with dismay."

Oh, such pleasant sensations were coursing through Samantha's body, sensations she felt were vaguely familiar. "Izzy said you could seek an annulment," she gasped, as her arms wound around his neck.

"And I thought your sister to be a sensible puss," Zachary soothed, tightening his hold on Samantha's silk-clad body.

She gave it one last shot. Pulling her head back, she turned her face to look into her husband's smoldering eyes. "Izzy is *so*—" she got out before Zachary sighed and said, "Oh, do shut up, Sam," and laid claim to her lips.

Sam did as she was bid.

Long moments later, Zachary raised his head, smiled, and mused, "One could almost believe one hears the swell of an angelic chorus."

Samantha, deep under the spell cast by Zachary's wandering hands and persuasive lips, smiled back at him and rallied: "Randy old goat!"—before she became much too pleasantly occupied to say anything at all.

Chapter Ten

THERE WOULD BE no annulment. When the Earl and Countess of Royston at long last became aware of their surroundings, and their need for bodily sustenance of a bit more mundane but equally demanding sort than that craving they had repeatedly sought to satisfy throughout the long, delicious night, it was well past noon of a new day.

Daisy, accompanied by one favored footman pushing a serving cart, was allowed to enter the bedchamber long enough to arrange two place settings on the small table in front of the center window and gather up the candle stubs of the night before. But when she made so free as to cluck her tongue, no more than two or three times, at the insufferably smug expression worn by that red-headed child of the Devil whom she, that most devoted of maids, had tossed and turned the whole night fretting over, she was curtly dismissed by the Earl himself.

He had not deemed it necessary to remove himself from the bed before Daisy entered, and his face, as she swore to Cook once back belowstairs, wore a pronounced look of cheerful debauchery (although Daisy put it more bluntly: "There 'e sat, lookin' fer all the world like the cat wot caught up the canary. Disgustin', that's wot it were, downright disgustin'!").

After Daisy's departure, speeded on her way as she was by Royston's admonition that he and her ladyship be disturbed for nothing less than a heavenly visitation, the at-long-last truly honeymooning couple succeeded in emptying the serving cart of every edible crumb—St. John handfeeding his wife dainty trifles and Samantha unselfconsciously nuzzling his fingertips whenever the opportunity arose.

After a time they discussed the dowager's visit of the day before, and while Samantha once more referred to the old lady's cross-questioning and rude remarks, she objected less strenuously than before as she found it hard to summon up much ill-feeling for anyone in the entire world while in her present mood.

"Your grandmother pointed out, Zachary, what an exemplary catch you are," she told him happily. "In addition to your illustrious name, she listed your financial situation as sufficient inducement for me to have trapped you into marriage. I knew, of course, that you weren't pockets-to-let or any such thing, but are you really *that* well-lined with brass?" Samantha asked, as she sipped delicately at her sherry.

St. John wiped his lips on a snow-white napkin before replying, "I am in no danger of being slapped into debtors' prison, pet. In fact, to be totally truthful, I am quite odiously wealthy. Does that, by some typically illogical twist of your unpredictable mind, upset you? If so, I shall beggar myself at the earliest opportunity."

Samantha's laughter was natural and unaffected. "Don't be a goose, Zachary. Although I am sure many, many people manage to be quite happy without money, I am equally persuaded just as many more are quite miserable. I did not, as you well know, marry you for your well-lined pockets, but as long as we are so, er, *comfortably* situated, I see no compulsion to fret over it. I would not even have brought it up had your grandmother not all but labelled me a scheming fortune-hunter."

Leaning back comfortably in his chair, St. John observed: "Grandmother can be a bit of a tartar at times."

Samantha then launched into a quite creditable (and only slightly exaggerated) imitation of the dowager's behavior of the previous afternoon—including the lady's insinuation that Samantha had seduced her grandson and was already with child, along with an almost word-for-word recital of the woman's reaction to Aunt Loretta—all of which had Zachary wiping tears of mirth from the corners of his eyes. Samantha's concluding rendition of the dowager's chagrin at finding the place stiff with relatives of the bride only days after the wedding almost finished him off completely.

"I am certain she thought I was soon to be bringing in Ardsleys by the cartload, planning to have them all sponging off you throughout eternity," she ended cheerfully.

For a little while longer the couple, feeling quite comfortable in each other's presence, talked of this and that, sipping from their wine glasses and sometimes touching hands across the table. It was only when St. John suggested some suitable activities to fill his wife's daytime hours that Samantha took exception to her husband's words.

"Other than your suggestions concerning a drive to Richmond—which I shall undertake just as soon as your grandmother has returned to the country—and taking Isabella and Aunt Loretta to view the maze at Hampton Court, I cannot begin to express my total lack of enthusiasm for the activities you have just outlined," Samantha told him in a distressingly matter-of-fact voice. "Leaving cards on morning calls, daily forays to Bond Street, restorative naps in the afternoon, and posturing at five in the Park Promenade with a passel of fashionable fribbles all seem, to me at least, sure roads to an early demise due to terminal boredom." At the sight of St. John's expressive eyebrows, raised in mock incredulity, she challenged, "Well, what do *you* do to fill the day?"

St. John was not taking Samantha's outburst as lightly as he wished her to believe. Even this early in their relationship he knew that his young wife's view of life was not limited to the usual feminine pursuits. Oh, no: Samantha's interests were as many and as varied as there were hours in the day, and if he wasn't capable of channelling her unusually inquisitive mind and—equally unnerving—her penchant for indulging that mind to the utmost whenever the mood struck her, there was no telling what sort of scrapes she would land them in each time he turned his back. But what could he do, this model mate, blessed as he was with endless understanding, overflowing with husbandly concern, endowed with a forgiving nature, and blessed with a remarkable sense of fair play that told him a person's sex should not arbitrarily preclude enjoyment of most of the good things in life?

He permitted himself—or, at least, a part of himself—to view Samantha's antics with indulgence. But he also, quite predictably, harbored his fair share of fondness for another of his personality traits—less charitable, perhaps, but eminently understandable—the desire for self-preservation. When the silent warring back and forth between all his commendable attributes and his single selfish (but, to be fair, excessively *human*) inclination that—if St. John's personal balance sheet was to be used as a guide—was the only blot on an otherwise spotless record nominating him for eventual sainthood, the result was as certain as if it had been preordained. Self-preservation won hands down.

And so, as St. John prattled with childlike innocence about his diversions—checking to see what was on the boards at Tatt's, passing a pleasant hour or two shooting billiards at the Royal Saloon, or even sauntering off arm-in-arm with comrades to the caricature shop for an inspection of the latest prints—he was all the while skillfully maneuvering his starry-eyed bride in the direction of their rumpled bed.

"Ah, my dearest rebel, what a pretty dance you've led me," he said, skillfully changing the subject as Samantha lay back against the pillows and smilingly invited him to join her on the bed.

"I am so terribly sorry, my lord, to have been such a slow-top. If I had only placed as much faith in your boasts as you seemed to do, perhaps we would have come to—um—an *agreement* earlier, and saved me many an anxious hour into the bargain," Samantha remonstrated mildly, making bold to caress St. John's bare shoulders. The last of her shyness had disappeared hours ago with the realization that she loved this husband of hers who had, with such gentleness and consideration, changed her from an untried girl into a woman.

As yet no words of love had passed their lips, but already they were more comfortable with each other. This shared intimacy, if only a half-loaf, was immeasurably better, in Samantha's mind, than no bread at all.

Zachary read the unspoken message he saw so clearly registered in Samantha's expressive eyes: the girl believed herself to be in love. It was only natural, for given her youth and inexperience she could not fail to view what they had shared in the most romantic of lights. Only the passage of time would reveal if she truly loved him: he was not vain enough to disregard the possibility that his wife's feelings for him were only a temporary infatuation.

He was older, wiser. He knew the exact depth and permanency of his involvement with his beautiful and ardent young wife, but it would not do to share this knowledge with her just yet. There were many variations of self-preservation, and carefully concealing his emotions—their intensity or their superficiality—beneath a veneer of irreverent nonsense was one way to defend himself.

Keeping Samantha too occupied to leave much time for indulging in mad starts or adventures was another. The solution to this particular dilemma had been reached, with typical male logic, halfway along the short journey from dining table to marital bed.

"Ah, dearest imp, I did warn you of my ravenous appetite for you," he reminded her softly, as she cuddled against his chest, and as she giggled at the not-so-distant memory, he called upon that centuries-old formula for subduing willful wives. He would give her a child.

But not even pursuing such a worthwhile (not to mention pleasant) project as securing the St. John inheritance for yet another generation could be allowed to occupy *all* of the Roystons' time. Morning of the next day found St. John conferring with a few of his fellow peers at the Ministry—and his wife at home and at loose ends.

Indulging in a leisurely breakfast in bed and a refreshing tub before the warm fireplace (all the while grinning like a confirmed lunatic at the openly disapproving Daisy), Samantha relived the last two nights in her mind and thanked her lucky stars St. John had not tiptoed any longer around the inevitable bedding of his wife. Oh, yes, she sighed inwardly, sinking down into the tub of bubbles:

being a Countess, especially Zachary's countess, was quite lovely after all!

Before setting off with Daisy for a shopping tour of Bond Street, Samantha gave a cursory inspection of the imposing assortment of white cards on the library table. Invitations bearing the names of London's best-known hostesses appeared in profusion; and Samantha flirted with the idea of tossing them all up into the air and gracing with her presence only those balls, routs, and other activities whose cards were fortunate enough to land right-side up. She dismissed the notion as overly capricious and decided to leave the decision making up to her husband. She chose instead to trip happily out to her waiting carriage, with Daisy huffing and puffing in an effort to keep up with her mistress, who would not hesitate to leave her behind.

It was in a small shop tucked behind Albemarle Street that she at last discovered the establishment of a French *émigré* named Bertrand. Before the enraptured man she put a plan that would be her first step in becoming an *"original"* (a plan the ambitious Frenchman was quick to see would also go a long way toward making his fortune).

Bertrand's shop was devoted to the manufacture, maintenance, and repair of umbrellas. After a good rain, his shop was knee-deep in gentlemen requesting he press and refold their immense, ugly Robinsons (so-called by the French after the famous Crusoe umbrella). But the increase in popularity of the umbrella had resulted in the establishment of no less than sixty-three umbrella shops by this year of 1815, and Bertrand had yet to make much of an impact on the local buyers. Perhaps this was because his first love, women's parasols, had never gained the popularity among the rich London ladies that it had in France.

"Ah, madame," he crooned reminiscently to Samantha, "and such parasols as I made in Paris!" He kissed his fingertips. *"Magnifique!"*

As Samantha listened, entranced, Bertrand went on to catalogue some of his better efforts—creations wrought of India muslin, Mechlin lace, colored crêpe, damasked satin, checked silk, and other materials—all trimmed and accented to the tastes and whims of his feminine patrons.

And the handles! Lovely turned handles containing telescopes, stilettos, secret compartments for *billet doux,* any special design madame required.

Samantha was so excited she could scarcely contain herself. And when Bertrand lovingly produced some of his creations for her personal inspection, it was all she could do not to jump up and down, clapping her hands in glee. By the time Daisy succeeded in dragging her away, Samantha had purchased no less than half-a-dozen of Bertrand's finest creations and ordered a dozen more, each to be made up in materials she would forward immediately.

After a solitary luncheon, Samantha tried to curb the restlessness brought on by her exciting morning. It was, however, an exercise doomed to failure from the moment she discovered an old London guidebook in her husband's library. "A man who saunters about the capital with pockets on the outside of his coats deserves no pity," read the warning against pickpockets inside the guide's cover. And as if that bit of delicious nonsense were not enough to set Samantha off searching for Wally's breeches, a sampling of a few of the descriptions of parts of the city hitherto unexplored by the adventurous lady succeeded in turning the trick.

She made her escape from Portman Square with ridiculous ease, and a friendly jarvey welcomed her aboard his broken-down hackney for the ride to her first stop: The Field of the Forty Steps, behind Montagu House. Both Samantha and the jarvey, who had not heard the legend, climbed down to search the ground for the spot where, years before, a young lady had watched two men duel for her hand in marriage. The guidebook pointed out that no grass had ever again sprouted where the woman had stood. After several minutes spent in fruitless investigation, Samantha and her driver were agreed the guidebook had either been in error or the young woman's scene of shame had at last succumbed to a persistent English gardener.

By way of easing his temporary employer's disappointment, the jarvey was happy to halt his hackney in the middle of King Street, begging his customer's pardon, to point out the Duke of Wellington and ask if he wouldn't like to see "our Arthur" crossing the road.

Samantha voiced her approval of the scheme and as coaches, carriages, and tradesmen's carts backed up along the street, she called out three impetuous cheers to the great Iron Duke as he crossed behind a young crossings sweeper, doffing his hat indulgently at the young gentleman in the hackney.

Samantha's next stop was Ludgate Hill, and the house where Daniel Lambert—who had exhibited himself for a time years before in Piccadilly as the self-proclaimed fattest man on earth—had died in 1809 and his 739-pound frame was loaded inside a coffin constructed of 112 feet of elm wood. One entire window and part of a door had to be removed to get old Daniel out of his house, she told the jarvey, and in the end his nine-foot-four inch girth had to be rolled into the grave, as no one could lift him. Samantha, viewing the house and mentally removing the window and door, was as suitably impressed as any young gentleman fresh from the country could be.

The delighted jarvey—partly in jubilation over the whopping tip his customer was bound to bestow upon him and partly because he was enjoying himself—urged his horse on to the summit of Fish Street Hill and the Monument, a Doric column 202 feet high, commemorating the Great Fire of 1666. Samantha read aloud from St. John's guidebook the history of the Monument, and the jarvey learned it was said to be, if laid on its side, "the exact distance from the shop in Pudding Lane where the fire began." Both jarvey and customer climbed the 311-step spiral staircase leading to the balcony and a fine view of the city—and that's when the trouble started.

Samantha's strong eyes could see beyond the dome of St. Paul's to Smithfield and the hodgepodge of tents, riding machines, and animal pens that made up Bartholomew Fair. She fairly dragged the jarvey back down the 311 steps in her haste to explore the famous Fair.

The jarvey, who had been fleeced more than once by the thieves of Bartholomew's, hastily pocketed his fare and a generous tip and hied his horse off with a warning to the young gentleman to guard his purse.

But Samantha hadn't forgotten the warning in the guidebook. She patted the plump purse that she had tucked snugly into her waistcoat and was quickly swallowed up in the crowd.

The first thing she did was to satisfy her hunger pangs (for she was certainly sharp-set—a possible result of having lived mainly on love and sherry for the best part of two days) with a plate of spiced beef and some miniature sausages that had been fried over a saucepan filled with hot coals. Although there were cloth-covered tables and ample forks and knives nearby, she noticed that most of the stall's customers—either by choice or due to lack of familiarity with the accepted utilization of such niceties—were putting their fingers to good use. Slopping up sausages and huge chunks of beef with their grimy paws, they then wiped their chins, chest fronts, and greasy hands with the handy tablecloths. When more than one of her fellow diners remarked on the *la-de-da* tadpole sitting easy as you please before one of the tables, slicing a tiny bit of sausage and daintily putting it in his yapper before starting on to slice another bitty piece—"just like one of them namby-pamby lords that calls themselves our betters," one rather large man in a somewhat strong-smelling leather jerkin leered menacingly—Samantha quietly laid aside her cutlery. She picked up a fat sausage, ripped off a healthy portion with her teeth and, as she chewed opened-mouthed, favored her fellows with a broad smile and broader wink. Some thirty minutes, eight hearty backslaps, and two mugs of ale (pressed upon her by her newfound friends) later, she was once again jostling along with the crowds, eager to see as much as she could in the time she had left.

She watched skeptically as a learned horse read the mind of "a woman in the audience" and declared it was her greatest wish to be married. There were at least two score and five women looking on, but the horse did not choose to single out the woman in question because of the delicacy of her desires.

A man standing near Samantha yelled out, "If the woman be Mazie Leaky, it's not wishin' as much as needin' a 'usband she be—seein' as 'ow she's clear full blown and near to whelpin'. Be there any man 'ere to 'elp puir Mazie and play Da ta 'er kiddey, eh, mates?" The man laughed heartily at his own joke and, encouraged by the mirthful appreciation of his own fellows, would have said more. He was interrupted by the arrival on the scene of one very irate and very pregnant female, who hesitated not a moment before swinging a slop-bucket (she had been carrying it from a nearby stall to the common sewer at the end of the pathway when she heard her name being called out) and loosing its offensive-smelling contents over the jokester's head.

" 'Ow's that, ya bastardly gullion? An iffen that don't mum yer clack, Oi ken gift ya wid a wherrit across the chops wid this 'ere bucket," the woman (whom Samantha supposed to be Mazie) screeched triumphantly, as the forever-fickle crowd applauded her assault as heartily as it had her tormentor.

As the scene before her was distasteful as well as distressing to her sense of smell, Samantha pushed her way out of the knot of thrill-seeking spectators, now goading Mazie on to more inventive punishments while just as eagerly urging her dripping, stinking adversary to give her "wot for." She spent the next hour viewing a puppet-show enacting the Queen of Sheba's visit to King Solomon and a bloodthirsty rendition of the plight of Daniel in the lion's den.

She rode the up-and-down, a mechanical marvel that raised her person, once it was positioned in a swinging seat, above the heads of the fairgoers. From that vantage-point she could see the animal pens that made Bartholomew Fair the principal live horse-and-cattle market in the city.

She did not linger at the wrestling or cudgelling exhibitions, but found herself fascinated by the pugilist who would take on all comers, offering the prize of a shiny guinea to anyone who lasted five minutes in the ring. Three strapping young country lads stepped into the ring, and three strapping young country lads were carried out again before the boxer's eyes lit on Samantha and he issued his challenge once again.

Samantha retreated hastily, only to be approached by another person interested in her body—this time not with the intention of breaking all her bones, but instead with the stated promise to take the peach-faced young cub aside and, after just a paltry sum had changed hands, transform the unfledged boy into a *man.* With a barely suppressed shudder at the painted face and black-toothed grinning mouth, Samantha turned and fairly ran back towards the tamer sights of the puppet-show booth, as the two-penny whore's echoing, cackling laughter sent a chill down her spine.

Buying a ticket for the play—*Medly of Mirth and Sorrow,* with the added feature on the bill being a rendition of *The Mad Lover*—just about to begin, Samantha was more than happy to lose herself in the crowd for the duration of the show. Midway through the first act she was weeping copious tears into her handkerchief at the plight of the heroine, who was beset by all manner of travail and degradation, until the final act. The arrival of the promised mirth set her to chortling as heartily as her benchmates in the airless tent, tears of glee replacing those of sympathetic suffering until Samantha's spirits were quite restored. She was soon eager to walk the grounds in search of more entertainment.

An hour later, munching on a gilded gingerbread that had capped a snack of five fat oysters served up on shells as huge as tea saucers, she stood at her ease, now picking her teeth with a long blade of grass in imitation of the men around her, watching one daring man ingesting broken glass while his partner gingerly swallowed a ball of fire. In her free hand she held a square wicker cage containing two white mice. She had won it as a prize for wagering sixpence she could best a stall-holder who had vowed she couldn't outlast him in a grinning match. Tucked under her arm was a small sack containing a fine, gaudy necklace of Bristol diamonds for Daisy that had cost just three *s.* six *d.*

She might have escaped the coming calamity had she not at that moment spied out of the corner of her eye Lady Lorinda Foxx, delicately picking her way through the crowd while leaning heavily on the arm of—none other than Zachary St. John. Samantha stood transfixed, the gingerbread boy dangling from her mouth as she stared in disbelief, until—without warning—she was whirled about on her heels by two sets of racing bodies, each running across the fair grounds towards each other from opposing directions. Yelling and screaming fit to wake the dead, they mowed their way through the crowd. By the time the two forces had exchanged places, many a gold watch, pearl necklace, and fat purse had disappeared, never to be seen again.

Amid the bustle of fainting women, cursing men, and crying children, Samantha stood alone, silent and unmoving, unfeeling and unseeing, as she—buffeted physically only moments after receiving a stunning blow of a vastly different but equally debilitating sort that had set up an agonizing throbbing in the area of her heart—succumbed to the lure of that soothing retreat from reality that often accompanies a sudden shock to the system.

Zachary and Lady Foxx, *together!* Samantha's confused brain acknowledged the sight mournfully. Zachary and that pretentious hussy. *Her* Zachary! Didn't the last few days mean anything to him, hadn't they changed anything for him? Could he be so unfeeling as to get up from his marriage bed and go directly into the arms of another woman? Had he just been doing his duty by the St. John name, and—preferring to secure his objective as speedily as possible—enacted that prolonged display of husbandly ardor, only to have the distasteful chore over and done with in a single go? Feeling his bride must surely by now be carrying the heir to the Royston title and lands, was he now celebrating his happy release from the clinging arms of his wearisome wife?

A single tear escaped down one ashen cheek, the only sign that the ramrod stiff figure of the young gentleman was in reality a living person and not a statue.

I loved him, she screamed silently. And worse yet, I almost *told* him I loved him. Thank the Lord for that at least: I stopped short of making a *complete* fool of myself.

But it was so wonderful, she warred with herself, and he was so magnificently kind. No, more than that, he acted as though *he too* enjoyed our little honeymoon, as he called it. He has got to be either the best actor or the greatest liar in all the British Isles. Or else—*or else*—he is a creature completely without honor: bankrupt of soul, devoid of any finer feelings, and an out-and-out cad into the bargain. He was, perhaps, an insensitive Casanova, taking his pleasure where he found it and caring not a whit for the hearts he trampled along the way!

The single tear dried, and no new moisture appeared on Samantha's cheeks. From the numbness of shock she had plodded to the land of disbelief and denial, traveled onward to initial despair, pushed doggedly ahead through a mire of self-pity, and at last reached the crossroads that awaited her. At first jolt it seemed there were two possibilities left to her: one, gracious acceptance of a thing she could not change; the other, making the most of the crumbs she was offered.

But Samantha was not one to take the road to a dinner of humblepie. Oh, no!

How dare he trifle with my affections! she thought, as her temper flared. Just who does he think he is anyway?

Samantha regained control of her emotions again, and examined her storm-tossed person. She then checked on the two mice (who seemed none the worse for wear) and the gingerbread boy (now missing one gilded leg, but much to her chagrin still stuck firmly between her teeth) before gritting out a garbled: "They took Daisy's Bristol diamonds!"

A young man standing nearby overheard the outburst but dismissed the stolen bauble as being no great loss. He suggested a check of the gentleman's purse might be more to the point. Predictably enough the purse—and with it all of Samantha's money—was gone.

"I had thought as much," said the extremely neat but rather shabbily-dressed man, who introduced himself simply as Robert. "It is an old trick, I fear, but a profitable one. At an agreed-upon signal, two gangs of thieves rush through the crowd at great speed, relieving their victims of any valuables as they stampede past. It's a good job they didn't fancy your waistcoat, for I've seen them all but strip a person when they put their minds to it."

Samantha, fighting a maidenly blush, introduced herself as Samuel Smythe-Wright—a name she had begun to fancy—and the two talked together for a few minutes, pondering the dilemma of how Samantha could return to

Portman Square when she had no money to engage another hackney.

"I would be pleased to loan you the money," Robert told her sorrowfully, "but I am not in such plump currant myself just now."

That had already been made plain to Samantha by his dress, but it did not mean she wasn't favorably impressed by the young man. His manner was extremely pleasant, almost as pleasing as his dark good looks—except for a certain thinness of face and pallorous complexion, which hinted he had recently been ill—and it did not occur to her that she was being too familiar with a complete stranger.

After some discussion, during which Samantha's personal pain somewhat inhibited her normally quick-thinking brain, it was decided that Samantha would hire a hackney anyway and have Carstairs's pay the driver after she reached Portman Square. She took her new friend up as far as Conduit Street, and arrived home just as dusk was falling to astound the Royston butler with her bizarre appearance and the gift of the cage of mice (by now christened Sheba and Daniel).

In exchange for Carstairs's silence, she agreed he could dispose of Sheba and Daniel any way he desired—short of serving them up to the kitchen cat—but if a single hint of her late arrival, peculiar dress, or probable misconduct (considering she was now a Countess) reached St. John's ears she would make it a point to personally guarantee that the care and feeding of the mice (or their replacements) would be made solely the butler's own responsibility. Carstairs bristled, saying he was sure he knew his place, and no threats—however ridiculous—were necessary to secure his silence. If the Countess did not wish his lordship to be aware of her, er, *attachment* to masculine attire, far be it from he, a loyal servant, to countermand her wishes.

"Piffle!" said Samantha, and she loped off, taking the stairs two at a time.

It was a nasty trick to play on Carstairs, leaving him standing in the hall with his white-gloved hand holding the wicker cage aloft as if it contained the Crown jewels,

Samantha confided to Daisy as she shed her breeches. But it was an unavoidable effect of her afternoon's activities.

"He should just be thankful I didn't bring home that monkey I fancied," she declared, thereby vindicating herself somewhat—for she had suffered much this day herself.

She turned her mind (reluctantly if the truth be known) to the evening ahead and the knowledge that she would soon be forced into her husband's company. She had as yet no clear-cut picture of the method her revenge would take. Never allowing her resolve to falter for a second—for anger sustained is tears denied—she decided to wait out the events of the evening and then, as her father was apt to say, play her cards as they lay.

Chapter Eleven

HE WAS etched in black from his sleek ebony locks to his shiny patent evening pumps, throwing his white-on-white satin waistcoat, perfectly matched shirt-points, and snowy cravat (always in the first stare, but tonight—ah—*la triomphe!*) into stark relief. Sapphires twinkled at his cuffs and on his fingers; one even winked out from among the folds of his cravat. As he raised his quizzing glass from where it dangled negligently at the bottom of the black riband tied around his neck, he looked every inch an Earl (and every inch a devilishly handsome disciple of his namesake, fair fit to lure unsuspecting maidens to everlasting damnation—or so thought Samantha as she descended the broad staircase).

In contrast to St. John's funereal black (which even Samantha could not in clear conscience find the least depressing—unless one could count the unmistakable involuntary leaping of her heart at the sight of him as a reaction to be mourned), his wife was a vision in angelic palest ivory. Her gown was fashioned in an off-the-shoulder style, with a falling tucker of lace extending to a length of six inches over the upper arms, low bodice, and low-scooped back. Her tiny waist was molded, rather than tightly fitted or allowed to hang loose in the French manner, and the slightly belled skirt widened as it neared the back to end in a demure *demi-traîne.* Seemingly random scatterings of lace on the skirt, repeating the pattern of the tucker, were dusted with sequin-backed seed pearls, so that her every movement was accompanied by sparkles of reflected light. Elbow-length French kid gloves, diamond-studded clips on her white satin shoes and—in a surprising but quite flattering diversion from the fashion of piling oneself with all the precious jewels one can possibly wear and still be able to stand erect—she had for her only ornaments a huge gold ring with an onyx center surrounded by diamonds, which she wore over her gloves, and a black velvet ribbon wound snugly around her neck and tied in a delicate bow at her nape.

Her hair, always a glorious burst of color, seemed to have been piled almost negligently on the top of her head. Errant but fetching curls were allowed to tumble about her slender neck, with one artlessly casual-looking ringlet falling front over her shoulder to rest on her creamy expanse of exposed skin. This tousled look had taken Daisy over an hour (and frequent recourse to sips of her secret store of medicinal spirits) to achieve, but the result was well worth the effort.

Samantha looked ravishing. Royston, suitably impressed, was about to cross the wide foyer to tell her just how truly beautiful she was, when from behind a fold in her gown Samantha produced a most ridiculous, impractical, incongruous, and totally extraordinary contraption, which in any other instance he would have been quick to recognize as some demented form of sunshade. The long stem, intricately carved handle, and spines of the creation were of finest ivory, and satin streamers hung fetchingly from an eyelet-hole about a quarter of the way up the center shaft. The shade itself (for by now Samantha had opened the thing and perched it perkily on her shoulder) was an eight-gored circle half the size of an ordinary sunshade (meaning one built for the practical purpose of shielding the owner from the sun's harmful rays), and it was decorated in the same manner as Samantha's gown: lace, pearls, sequins, and all.

"What in bloody blazes is *that?*" St. John got out at last, stunned into inelegance.

"Do you like it?" Samantha asked coyly. "It's a parasol, of course, and it is to be—for the moment, at least—my trademark. I have ordered parasols for every costume, every event—indeed, for every hour of the day or night!" she ended triumphantly, twirling the parasol between her fingers.

Royston, once more under control, allowed but one eyebrow to arch and strictly schooled his willful features, which longed to break into a grin. "Am I to deduce that one of these, er, *parasols* is to become our bed companion? I fear, my dear, I must object. While I have no oppositon to you creating a, shall we call it, *personal signature* for yourself in fashionable circles, I am obliged to dig in my heels and deny any such contraption between my sheets. But think: I could toss in my sleep and be impaled, or—worse yet—I could, in a drowsy haze, mistake its stem for the figure of my wife and the heir to Royston Manor would be a half-breed—part man, part umbrella—and with a carved ivory handle for a nose. Good god, girl, consider the consequences!"

While two footmen choked on their rising hilarity, and Carstairs stood looking very smug and all too sure of his superiority, Samantha fought to bring down her rising temper by counting to ten and ten again. When at last the Earl had done with his juvenile jokes she looked him square in his laughing black eyes, smiled sweetly, and asked, "Are you amused, my lord?"

St. John threw back his head and roared, causing the footmen (who had together served ten years in Portman Square without hearing his lordship laugh in just such an unrestrained manner) to gape open-mouthed at each other, while Carstairs had the decency to grimace (he had never been known to actually *smile*) indulgently in her ladyship's direction.

As Daisy descended the stairs to lay a high-collared white velvet cape lined in black satin over her mistress's bare shoulders, St. John raised Samantha's gloved hand and bestowed a brief kiss on the bare flesh just below the pearl button that held the glove at the underside of her slim wrist. She tolerated the salute with equanimity, and moved regally across the hall toward the open front door.

The normally short drive to Park Lane was made interminable by the line of carriages waiting to disgorge their passengers, and the curved marble staircase leading to their hosts' reception line and ballroom was a positive crush of bodies. As they slowly worked their way up the stairs—Samantha clinging doggedly to her unfurled parasol, and gaining for herself not a few sidelong glances—the

Earl regaled her with tales of the more memorable squeezes of past Seasons, where it was not that rare for a delicate female to be extracted from the *mêlée* almost entirely *in naturabilis,* forced to cower in a dark alcove until a petticoat or other covering could be found. Indeed, he told her, at Carlton House, scene of many an overpopulated affair, the servants were known to gather up shoes and other articles of clothing in huge hogsheads the next morning.

Samantha was diverted, as she was intended to be, but she did not allow her resolve to weaken by so much as a hair. After all, how dare he go on as if everything were just peachy-dandy when he had spent the afternoon in the company of that odious female!

Zachary felt the tension in his young bride and dismissed it as an attack of nerves over her first public appearance as Lady Royston. He had no personal qualms, he soothed himself rationally, for after all, this business of keeping a woman happy was really quite simple. All one had to do was delight them in bed. That, plus a goodly supply of pin money and some tame amusements, were more than ample occupations for any female. If he was not entirely convinced this particular logic quite described Samantha's own recipe for happiness, he eased his mind with the thought of that shadowy Royston heir waiting just now in the wings—a sure seal on his wife's tendency towards the outrageous.

Oh, yes, he commended himself, you have done well in your choice of bride. She is beautiful, intelligent, witty, refreshingly honest, unexpectedly loyal, well-behaved when she chooses to be, and in time she will make an admirable mother. That he had fallen more than a little in love with the child was just an unexpected bonus. But it would be unwise, he reminded himself, to let his emotions get the upper hand. To allow himself to become mawkishly romantic at his age, and over such a slip of a girl, could prove embarrassing.

Not that I couldn't bring her to heel any time I chose, he pointed out to himself silently. But Samantha was an unpredictable creature, and the love he had seen burning in her emerald eyes not four-and-twenty hours ago had been remarkable by its absence this evening.

It wouldn't do to build fantasies in the sky. Samantha was just a child—a precocious, unpredictable, rambunctious child—and he, the older and wiser of the pair, would have to be the one depended upon to keep a clear head. Even if she did smell like spring sunshine. Even if she was the most beautiful woman in all England. Even if she did possess the charm of a dozen sea sirens, the body of a Greek goddess, the courage of a warrior, and the heart of an angel. Even if—oh, what was the use? He hadn't thought of it, hadn't planned for it, hadn't even *wanted* it. But there it was: he loved the girl.

So deeply was St. John embroiled in conversation with himself that he had twice to be brought to attention by his host who was trying in vain to welcome him.

The amenities over, Samantha's intrigued hostess—who had not once taken her eyes off the shimmering miniature parasol—could no longer contain her curiosity and asked the purpose behind carrying a sunshade after dark.

"It is quite sad, really, ma'am," Samantha responded earnestly, with a twinkling glance towards Zachary that told him to keep his mouth shut and enjoy the fun. "Approximately two centuries into the past one of my ancestors ran afoul of a gypsy curse—a curse that has survived to this day." A crowd began to gather at the head of the stairs, and all was quiet while Samantha recounted in suitably eerie tones, "It was a dark, moonless night when the old gypsy first placed the terrible Ardsley Curse:

" *'Forevermore shall the name of Ardsley be shadowed by the bane of light from the sky. Each generation shall one of your family be cursed to keep his head forever hidden from the rays of heavenly light—or suffer the consequences.'*

"In other words, ladies and gentlemen, the cursed Ardsley from each generation has to keep his head shaded day and night, else the curse overtake him," she finished with a deep sigh.

"But why, and what, and *who?*" breathed Samantha's audience.

"As to that," she shrugged, "the *why* of it hardly seems important two centuries later—though I have heard it whispered that it had something to do with my ancestor and the chieftain's young daughter. But who am I to lend credence to a mere rumor. The *who* for this generation is, of course, *me*—or so I believe. And the *what*—or the effect of the curse, you might say—has only been witnessed once, as we Ardsleys are a cautious lot. But Uncle Simon, my father's cousin you understand," she whispered in awestruck tones, "was said to have once flouted the curse and it was impossible to restrain him, as he went dashing out into the night to bay at the moon!"

Amidst the *oohs* and *aahs* Zachary growled, "What a bag of *moonshine*, Samantha—pardon my little pun."

"You mean, then," his hostess asked, crestfallen, "it is all a hum?"

Zachary nodded. "Could it be else? Samantha, you are incorrigible!"

His wife grinned impishly up at him and twirled her parasol. "I but try, my lord. I but try."

Within minutes the story had circulated among the assembled guests, who in the capricious way of the *ton* decided it was a great piece of fun, and soon Samantha was surrounded by a swarm of young bucks all eager to bask in the reflected glow of the newest sensation.

St. John was content to stand back and watch his wife as she gave every sign of becoming the life and soul of the ball, while mentally recording all the provocative glances she threw his way in preparation for making her pay for them later that night—once they were alone.

When at last she spied out her sister and aunt, she demanded they be brought to her, then summarily dismissed her court of admirers and shooed them all away. Within moments of settling themselves beside her on the satin sofa, Aunt Loretta had unburdened herself of a half-hearted sermon on the folly of making an exhibition of oneself.

"Oh, Aunt, you'd throw a damper on anything," Samantha pouted prettily, before launching into a spirited discourse on her plans for Isabella's future. As a Countess, she promised blithely, she would herself launch Isabella into the upper strata of Society and have her bracketed to a title within a twelvemonth. Aunt Loretta, Samantha assured the woman, would not long have to lug Izzy around with her once the Countess of Royston took her under her wing.

"After all," she went on happily, "it is not as if Izzy were not top of the trees, being an extremely delicately-nurtured female. I was, too, in matter of fact, but with me it just didn't all quite take. Isn't that so, Aunt Loretta?" Before her aunt could answer, Samantha was off again, this time musing about the ball she would give in her sister's honor and the turban she, now a stately matron, would deign to wear.

In her fervor, Samantha saw—but refused to acknowledge—her sister's visible lack of enthusiasm over the project, and put down Isabella's reaction to a maidenly restraint that would have been most becoming had it not been accompanied by several irritatingly deep heartfelt sighs that quite disrupted Samantha's monologue.

"There is Lady Foxx," Isabella broke in, longing for a change of subject, and Samantha—diverted from her debate as to the proper decoration of the Royston ballroom in either greenery or bunting or both—pushed a small button on the stem of her parasol, activating a mechanism that extended a gilt quizzing glass from the base of the handle. This glass was raised to one emerald-green eye as Samantha openly inspected the woman in question.

"A ravishing creature," Aunt Loretta commented, "if a bit *outré* in her dress."

"Quite pretty," Isabella agreed quietly, watching her sister for any reaction.

Samantha's extended assessment was most unnerving. At the end of it she lowered her glass, snapped it back into its hidey-hole, and said contemptuously, "Nonsense, Izzy. The woman has a squint. In time to come she will resemble nothing more than a wizened old crow. About the middle of next week, I would imagine—as she is already at *least* five-and-thirty, the poor doddering old thing."

Isabella giggled at this nonsense. "Oh, Samantha, you are too naughty to be borne. You are just out of countenance because of the way she is always toadying up to St. John."

"I am not!" Samantha pouted. "Besides, somebody has

to toady up to him and his overweening ego, as there can be no hope of *my* ever drooling all over his consequence."

The time for private conversation was soon past, once it became evident that the buzzing swarm of admirers was no longer to be denied. Soon both sisters were claimed for the set then forming, leaving Aunt Loretta to gaze sleepily into the middle distance with an inane smile upon her cherubic face.

While Samantha was busily engaged in becoming the first rage of the Season, Lady Lorinda Foxx—finding herself in the unaccustomed position of looker-on—was rapidly recalculating the forces of her enemy. It was never a pleasant experience for an older woman to be cast, as it were, in the shade by a wet-behind-the-ears young chit. For Lady Foxx it was tantamount to a living death and—as she was unhappily a poisonous sort of female at heart (not to mention hedonistic and ambitious)—she was hard-pressed to expose Samantha for the upstart that she was and re-establish herself as the reigning "toast" of this and any other Season.

"Ignorant chippy," she muttered under her breath, and smiled blazingly at Samantha as she whirled by in the arms of a brilliantly uniformed young Hussar. "Totally lacking in polish, too. I see it as my duty to depress her pretensions." With the martial light of battle in her eyes, Lady Foxx went off to seek out Miss Isabella Ardsley.

She ran her to ground in the supper room some time later, sitting with her Aunt Loretta after firmly refusing numerous offers from young gentlemen who wished to fix her a plate (thereby gaining her company for an hour).

Aunt Loretta eyed Lady Foxx owlishly, dredging in her mind for her brother's conclusions as to the character of the woman and coming up with the words "rapacious female." Nevertheless, the woman was still accepted in Society, so Aunt Loretta welcomed her—if stiffly—and the three fell into a conversation that was conducted at a fever-pitch of civility.

After a few minutes, Lady Foxx concluded Isabella to be a harmless young miss, and her aunt to be the sort who could not locate her brains with the help of a lantern.

So thinking, her conversation was heavy-laden with concerned cluckings over the misfortunes of making a spectacle of oneself in company, the pitfalls that so often accompanied sudden wealth and popularity, and the inadvisability of setting oneself at odds with one's husband by means of indiscriminate flirting and hoydenish carryings-on that could be of disgust to anyone with any feelings for decorum and family standing.

Out of the corner of her eye Aunt Loretta espied Samantha, who had come up behind Lady Foxx some moments before to hear most of what was being said. The old woman, feeling one of her migraines coming on, cravenly longed to slip quietly off into a restoring snooze.

Once more the parasol's retractable quizzing glass was put into use as Samantha ran one grossly enlarged, cool green eye up and down Lady Foxx and then up again before turning to speak to her mortally embarrassed sister. "What say you, Izzy? Corralled in the supper room and forced to listen to all the tongue-bangers expound on the lessons learned by their own folly?" she questioned loudly.

Zachary, who had been standing nearby and who had hastened to Samantha's side—in an attempt to prevent just such a confrontation as the one which now seemed destined to not only prove unsettling but capable of mushrooming into a sordid scene—arrived too late to do more than pinch the tender skin above Samantha's kid glove and scold under his breath: "You imp of the devil, Samantha, can you not win gracefully?"

Lady Foxx, drawing herself up to her full height, pronounced in injured tones, "She all but cut me dead, Zachary, this child bride of yours. And you assured me just today that she would show me proper respect upon meeting me, after that sad display of ill-breeding when first we met," she finished triumphantly, seeing St. John's involuntary flinch at the mention of their rendezvous at the Bartholomew Fair.

"Um, er, *harrumph,*" interposed Aunt Loretta hastily. "Samantha, love, do behave, please. It would not do to, er, *display* your feelings in public so. It could only serve to be a vulgar titillation to those assembled."

Samantha folded away her quizzing glass reluctantly, muttering, "If it livens their dull little existences, then I am but happy to be of service to my fellow man."

Whilst Zachary was struggling to find a suitable riposte, Lady Foxx interrupted to repeat, "She all but cut me dead, Zachary. Are you going to allow that? Never—I repeat, *never*—have I been so insulted by such as she. That you could wed such a hurly-burly girl of no background is incomprehensible to your friends."

"And you are an expert on the subject of backgrounds—or at least *backs*, Lady Foxx, being as you are on yours so much!" Samantha found herself saying, before she could stop to think. She had not planned what form her vengeance would take, but as the opportunity had presented itself she was powerless to do more than swim with the tide of events.

While Isabella looked ready to sink and Aunt Loretta furrowed her brow in an attempt to appear a trifle puzzled by such plain speech (while in reality she was totally asea), Zachary bit out a pungent oath that had little to do with polite Society conversation.

Surprisingly (and much to Samantha's chagrin), it was Lady Foxx who recovered first. "Oh, my, Zachary, you have landed yourself with a real termagent, haven't you? No wonder you are looking so woefully *harassed* these days. Poor thing, the trials you men must endure to secure your nurseries. Ah, well," she conceded, as she waved her fan beneath her patrician nose, "at least you can school wife and child at the cost of only *one* governess."

Things were not going well, as the nearby eavesdroppers were quick to hear. Their snickers and giggles at Lady Foxx's quick rebuttal showed their pleasure at Devil Royston's discomfiture. "You overreach yourself, madam," was his only near-whispered reply to his widely acknowledged light-o-love's cutting remarks—that, and a searing look directed upon nearby spectators that would have prompted anyone not so entirely caught up in the deliciousness of the scene to take to her (or *his*) heels in fright.

Samantha was still standing mutely, her bosom heaving

in her agitation, unable as yet to form a set-down sufficient to shut Lady Foxx's face once and for all.

The older woman, relishing her victory, smiled condescendingly and leaned just a bit closer to Samantha to simper sweetly, "You agree then, child, that you are out of your depth, trying me on like some cock-a-hoop adolescent vying for the attention of her betters?"

St. John cut in hurriedly, knowing at once that Lady Foxx had gone too far. "I'd not be so cock-a-hoop myself if I were you Lorinda, m'dear. When dealing with Samantha, such confidence ain't —"

His words died as—more quickly than he could move to avoid what was to happen—Samantha's vision of the leering face of her rival crowding in on her set up a hum in her ears and caused her to reach out and clutch at the first thing to come to hand. That "thing" was an enormous strawberry tart, oozing juice and topped with a large dollop of finely whipped cream, that had lately reposed on a plate in front of her Aunt Loretta. Once the pastry was, at it were, *in hand,* it was almost a foregone conclusion as to where to *dispose* of the thing. Before (as the lower classes might say) the cat could lick her ear, Samantha had shoved the tart smack into the grinning mouth of one Lady Lorinda Foxx.

Zachary stood for a moment, looking as if he had been stuffed, before he could find his voice. *"Samantha!"* he bellowed. "What do you have to say for yourself?"

His young wife, busy licking cream from the tips of her gloved fingers and seemingly unperturbed by the positively deafening silence that had descended all about her, looked, shrugged, and at last offered hopefully, *"Bon appetit?"*

The entire room erupted in grins, giggles, and loud guffaws. Isabella was forced to retain consciousness in order to minister to her swooning aunt. The host and hostess of the ball, while outwardly showing all the signs of affronted dignity, secretly rejoiced at the stroke of luck that had made their humble establishment the site of the Season's latest *coup.* Lady Lorinda Foxx, tears and black mascara streaming down her cheeks, raced from the scene of her embarrassment, with berry juice dribbling from her chin and a thick mustache of cream giving her the appearance of—as one daring young buck alluded in a loud voice—a rabid dog.

Last, but by no stretch of the imagination least, Zachary St. John, Earl of Royston, grabbed his wife's wrist and trod determinedly toward the door of the supper room, his icy stare daring anyone to stand in his way. He dragged her straight across the ballroom, heedless of the mess he was making of the orderly dance in progress. Down the wide marble staircase he went, Samantha skipping behind, her parasol still unfurled and bumping along in the breeze, past the stony-faced footman holding open his wife's cape, and out into the *flambeaux*-lit street.

To the delight of the throng of ordinary citizens who normally line the flagway to observe the *ton* at one of its august gatherings, St. John paused, looked distractedly up and down the street, and then—putting the tips of two fingers to his lips—whistled shrilly for his carriage. Amid the rude calls and crude suggestions of their audience of sweeps, crossing-links boys, and cits, Zachary and Samantha (the former in the lead, the latter being hauled along like a sack of goods) made to enter the carriage. In a final burst of bravado Samantha paused on the carriage step to acknowledge the crowd. "Toodle-loo," she called out, and waggled her fingers at her admiring audience just before Zachary's well-placed boost in the region of her *derrière* catapulted her inside.

The ride back to Portman Square was achieved in half the time and ten times the silence of the trip out. As they rode, Samantha mourned the cracked sticks in her parasol in one corner of the seat and Zachary busily muttered dark imprecations in another.

Chapter Twelve

SAMANTHA—still somewhat out of breath, having been hauled out of the carriage at Portman Square, dragged willy-nilly up the wide staircase (past a snickering Carstairs and two bemused footmen), and thrust unceremoniously inside the main bedchamber—could only sit and goggle wide-eyed as her husband prowled back and forth across the carpet like a near-to-charging lion.

"Do you—*do you,*" he bellowed at last, finally coming to a halt in front of her, "have the slightest idea of the enormity of what you have done?" He ran a hand distractedly through his hair. "Oh, God, why do I ask such obvious questions? Of course you don't, do you, Samantha? How else could you sit there, looking just like a cat stretched at its ease next to an empty bird cage, with—with *feathers* sticking out of its mouth?"

He whirled away from Samantha and then whirled back again. "This is all just a lark to you, isn't it? Well, let me tell you," he leered, waving a finger in her face, "this little episode of yours tonight won't just blow over in a puff of smoke. Lorinda Foxx is very well thought of in some quarters, and there will be many to take her side in this shabby business. Don't you care about your good name?"

Samantha's attention was at first centered on that wagging forefinger, and her head bobbed up and down as she followed its movements. But at the Earl's words her head jerked up and a contemptuous sneer curled about her full lips. "Well thought of, is it, Zachary? In *some quarters,* you say? Whose, pray tell, that of the Fifth Foot? And as to my good name, husband, my name is St. John—so don't try to tell me your concern is for *me!*" she retaliated swiftly, sticking out her chin and daring him to take another stab at browbeating her. Go on, her expression screamed, just you try it!

This sudden turnabout, with Samantha suddenly going on the offensive, disconcerted St. John for a moment, cutting in as it did on his righteous anger. He could only mutter darkly, "How is it, madam, with *your* behavior so obviously at fault, that *I* have suddenly become the villain of the piece?"

To Samantha's reasoning the answer was so apparent she almost threw up her hands in mute disgust. But silence (especially when anyone of any sense could see silence was called for) was a stranger to Samantha's personality. She unhesitatingly counted off on her fingers: "One: you are the reason I—a mere nursling, if that titled vixen is to be believed—am in Society at all, cradle robbing lecher that you are. Two: and I dare you not to flinch at this home truth: it is your involvement with that same dubious *lady* that has made me the target of her viperous tongue. Three: —"

St. John reached out and grabbed his wife's hands, pleading mockingly, "Enough, enough, hellcat! You have made your point. My actions do have some bearing on the unfolding of tonight's events, but this admission does not totally absolve you of blame, you know. I *was* present throughout your exhibition tonight, and you did have a major part in pushing matters past a typical feminine exchange of insults. Lady Foxx was spoiling for a fight—anyone could see that—but it was you who cut her, just as if you were the one looking to make trouble." He squeezed both her trapped hands between his in the beginnings of husbandly forgiveness and said, "And that was *before* Lorinda so cunningly worked her meeting today with me into the conversation." Once the words were out, St. John knew he had made a tactical blunder, opening a subject best left closed. His wife wouldn't understand; wives never understood the good intentions of their husbands.

While Zachary was making pretty speeches (ending with his one damning remark) and fondling Samantha's hands, she herself was busily searching her brain for a way or ways to soften him even further before his anger had a chance to rekindle and his mind fell to the phaeton he had promised her the day before. He might just think putting paid to any hope of setting up her own stable to be a suitable punishment for his scandalous mate. Never let it be said Samantha St. John would whistle such a fine equipage down the wind over a woman such as Lady Foxx!

So, just as Samantha was about to swallow her pride and agree that she had been a naughty puss, kicking up in public just for the thrill of it, Zachary's ill-timed reminder of his recent *tête-à-tête* with "Lorinda" jarred her back to reality—and smack into a different sort of argument.

"Lorinda," Samantha sneered, "did not serve me with any surprise tonight, Royston, as I saw you both this afternoon at Bartholomew Fair—her hanging all over you like a wilting flower and you a pot of fresh water!"

She was sure she could hear the bones of her fingers cracking under the strain of Zachary's steely grasp. "You were *there*, Samantha?" he asked. His voice sounded strangely strangled.

Wriggling her fingers free she flexed them experimentally before folding them discreetly in her lap. In for a penny, in for a pound, she sighed inwardly, mentally waving her very own yellow-wheeled phaeton farewell. "I was," she replied, in a voice that trembled only a very little bit. "What has that to do with anything? It is *your* indiscretion, not mine, that brought on this evening's scene at the ball."

The pieces of the puzzle at last all fell into place for Royston. His wife, who had not been very convincing at playing the innocent anyway, had not only taken an active part tonight: she had gone to the ball *anticipating* making such a scene. Lady Foxx had merely been cooperative (and foolhardy) enough to play into her hands, giving Samantha the opening she craved. Innocent! St. John scoffed with an audible sniff. My wife is about as innocent as a parlor maid in a whorehouse. St. John's eyes narrowed as his lips pursed, and as he took several deep breaths through his nose Samantha imagined she saw puffs of smoke coming from his nostrils.

She began to mount a prudent retreat. "N-n-ow, Zachary," she stammered, and moved to hide behind her chair, "don't do anything in the first heat of anger. It doesn't pay. Isn't my example from tonight proof enough for you?"

"How," St. John barked, making Samantha flinch. "Just *how* were you able to see me this afternoon? Were you escorted, or has Mr. Samuel Smythe-Wright taken up residence here in Portman Square?"

Samantha squeezed her eyes shut, wincing as her husband's ice-cold anger froze the air around her. "It was Mr. Smythe-Wright, sir," she answered quietly, as if her low tone would lessen the degree of his anger.

She had gone abroad alone—alone and easy prey to a score or more different evils, all too sordid to contemplate. "You have no more sense than a newborn babe, Samantha. Have you no feelings for your own self-preservation?"

Slowly Samantha edged out from behind her chair, allowing the firelight to turn her hair to flame and her gown to starlight, and ventured, "You mean, because I ventured abroad alone in London, Zachary?"

"No!" he ejaculated fiercely. "Because *you allowed me to know* you ventured abroad alone in London, you headstrong madcap. How dare you gad about town unescorted, rubbing shoulders with the sweepings of Piccadilly?"

With a returning show of spirit, Samantha corrected: "I was not within six blocks of Piccadilly, Zachary."

St. John's head felt as if it would burst. "That is nothing to the point, burn it, and you know it. You could have been killed—or worse!"

That stopped him in his tracks as his blood ran cold. Samantha could have come to grief today. Suddenly his anger dissipated, to be replaced with a fierce need for this girl-woman who had so unsettled his serene (or was it boring?) existence. With one quick movement he crushed her to his chest, holding her there with one hand on her back and the other in her hair, and rasped, "I could have lost you, imp. I could have lost you."

From her vantage point scant inches from his chin she asked, "Would you have missed me, Zachary? I am really abominably slow, but until a few moments ago I would have thought my continued presence in your life to be the very *last* of your wishes. You were cross as two sticks with me. Admit it."

As she spoke she raised her head to look into St. John's eyes. He returned her teasing gaze for a few moments, trying to still the unaccustomed nervous tumult in his heart. Then he sighed, shaking his head in wordless resignation to his fate, and groaned, "Oh, Samantha," and ground his lips against hers.

Like a match to a flame, this sudden contact sent sparks flying between them that flared so fiercely and burned so wildly, that the following conflagration threatened to consume them totally. Their differences for the moment forgotten, they clung together as they sank first to their knees, then slid bonelessly onto the carpet before the hearth, their bodies striving for closer, ever closer contact. In this one area of their relationship, at least, they were enormously compatible.

"I love you," Samantha whispered ingenuously a short time later, as she lay snuggled up against her husband's side.

St. John's black eyes twinkled as he tucked an errant curl behind Samantha's ear. "Naturally, puss," he smiled down at her, "how could you resist me?"

"Oh-h-h!" she shrieked, pulling herself out of his arms. "How like you to be so odiously smug when I have just bared my soul to you. You have no finer feelings at all you, you *libertine!* You were supposed to say that you love me, too—nay, that you *adore* me, would kiss the ground I walk on. But trust you to lap up my confession like a tomcat lapping up cream without a word of thanks or—or—*anything!*"

The unrepentant-looking Earl raised himself upon one elbow and drank in the bewitching sight of his wife, her red hair cascading about her shoulders, her bared body rosy in the firelight, and felt more than a slight pang as he tried to make her see reason. It would not be fair to take advantage of her admission, given as it was in a moment of passion, by pledging an undying love of his own that would tie this beautiful woman-child to him, if only by her belated feelings of guilt, if her mood were to change in the cold light of day.

"Samantha, my pet, do not mistake lust for love. The two are, I assure you, vastly different emotions. When you can greet my bleary-eyed, unshaven face at the breakfast table—after I have spent a night carousing with some friends in an assortment of low-life taverns—and say 'I love you,' I shall be more than happy to enter into a discussion of our feelings for each other. Well, perhaps not at that very moment, but surely as soon as I were feeling more the thing."

Samantha checked her anger to consider his words, blushed deeply (much to the Earl's delight) and mutely nodded her head in agreement.

"For the moment though, Zachary, may I say that I am tolerably pleased with my husband? Because I am, you know," she ended defiantly, "even if you are a contradictory sort of fellow."

He chuckled. "You may. And I may say—although it seems terribly immodest of me—that my first impressions of your ability to brighten my existence have been more than amply proven to be correct?" His banter eased the last of Samantha's discomfiture.

Later, after a lighthearted exchange of personal services, as St. John took on the role of lady's-maid to Samantha's comical imitation of the Complete Gentleman's Gentleman, the pair was tucked up cosily in bed, the Earl's broad shoulder proving itself to be a quite comfortable pillow.

"About Lady Foxx—" Samantha began reluctantly, only to have St. John silence her by placing his forefinger over her lips—a move that earned that finger both a sweet kiss and gentle teasing nip.

"Lorinda Foxx can be sent to the Antipodes tomorrow for all I care a fig for that tedious female," Zachary told her. "I have not been alone with the woman since I met you, m'dear, and only agreed to meet her today to put an end to her passionate requests to talk to me—requests that were as much of a nuisance as they were embarrassing to hear."

"It must be such a sad trial to you, you poor man, to be so beset by lovesick females wherever you go," Samantha goaded him. "I was a fool to nearly become another broken hearted ninny for you to trample upon. You were right earlier when you said I should reserve judgment on my feelings for such a black-hearted rogue—or at your age, is it *roué?*"

Zachary's heavy-lidded eyes scanned her laughing face and he drawled amicably, "Are you quite through, madam? Or, in order to continue, must I first turn you across my knee and give you the spanking you seem to crave?"

"Do you then deny that you are a heart-breaker?"

"I did once have that reputation, I fear. But, now that I am so firmly leg-shackled, it is a title doomed to become a relic of an unlamented past," St. John told her. "Didn't you know that reformed rakes make the most steadfast husbands? Here now, woman, stop that," he reprimanded as Samantha pulled a face at him.

"What a rapper!" she exclaimed. "I suggest we put a halt to these ego-building transports of yours and get back to the subject at hand: the dear Lady Foxx. And, pattern-card of virtue husband-of-mine, if I have a shred of pity in my body for anyone connected with Lady Foxx, it would be for her husband, not one of her paramours—past, present, or future."

"Lord, yes," the Earl agreed, "poor old Foxx has quite a rare handful in his wife." He twisted in the bed and put a finger under Samantha's chin to raise her eyes to his. "Speaking of husbandly problems, and consigning Lady Foxx evermore to perdition, may I remark for a moment that I too am in need of consolation for the rare handful I seem to have been landed with myself? Your behavior is far from unexceptionable itself, infant."

"Oh, piffle," Samantha scoffed. "I must somehow occupy my time, and even you must admit I came to no harm today. If you don't count the loss of my purse," she trailed off a bit weakly.

A rather heated discussion covering Samantha's activities of that day consumed a goodly amount of time until at last, in exasperation, Zachary commented, "It would seem my earlier warnings have gone entirely unheeded. It would, in fact, appear that I have pointed out the pitfalls only so that you can be sure to tumble into them headfirst. Samantha, you are a sad trial to me."

His wife commiserated with him. "Poor, poor Zachary,

made to suffer so in your extreme old age, teetering as you are on the brink of the grave. You should have thought and thought again before wedding such a scapegrace as me."

"With bated breath, may I dare to inquire whether your new-found remorse, superficial as it is, is sufficient for you to promise to mend your hoydenish ways?"

"It could be, Zachary," she replied pensively, then brightened. "But I seriously doubt it!" She poked him playfully in the chest and made to turn over and go to sleep.

"Oh, no you don't, I'm not *that* old," St. John growled, diving after her, his fingers grabbing at her belly and tickling her mercilously. Within moments their play turned to passion, and as they sank blissfully down into the satin sheets, Samantha's hair splayed out across the pillows and Zachary moaned, "Fool that I am, I cannot resist you, Samantha my pet."

Her arms, marble-white in the darkness, slid up his chest to link behind his head. "Then we are a pair of fools, my lord," she whispered, her voice deepened by emotion.

Moments before his lips claimed hers, St. John—mindful of his own strictures—reminded her, "We must do our utmost to strive not to let our passions overcome us."

"Yes, my lord. As you say, my lord." Samantha breathed. "But for the moment, dear, sweet my lord, could you stop talking and kiss me?"

"Just one kiss, my lady?" he countered, his voice hoarse in his agitation. "It would seem a great waste to stop at just one kiss."

"Criminal," his young wife agreed, "absolutely criminal." St. John lowered his head for a slow, searching kiss before raising up slightly to look into Samantha's emotion-darkened emerald eyes.

"Say it," he rasped before he would allow himself to claim her eager lips again. "Tell me once more about this foolish notion you have. Just for now. Just for tonight."

A slow smile lit Samantha's face like a beacon. She breathed on a sigh, "I love you, Zachary. Just for tonight."

St. John's face—for once not the impassive mask he showed in company—suffused with triumph. "Sam!" he whooped loudly into the quiet chamber, then swooped down to capture his wife in his embrace.

Chapter Thirteen

THE NEXT FEW WEEKS—whirlwind days that made up the centermost chunk of London Society's annual Silly Season—passed in a hazy blur before Samantha's slightly bemused eyes. Her days all ran together to become a rose-colored fantasyland of fun and excitement, and the heady thrill of finding herself—overnight, as it were—the rage of the Season. And her nights? Ah, those glorious nights!

Added to all this splendor was the news that Lord and Lady Foxx had been unexpectedly summoned to their country estate on "urgent family business" (*that* obvious farradiddle immediately became the punchline for many a sly joke in and out of the clubs along St. James's) and would probably not return to the City until the Little Season in the fall.

Having so successfully routed her enemy (and having overheard St. John telling a friend he had given the woman her *congé* weeks earlier without suffering a flicker of regret) could very easily have gone to some young girls' heads, making them just the slightest bit cocksure of themselves and perhaps even a teeny bit giddy with their own power. Samantha, however—being quite used to getting her own way for all of her headstrong young life—did not allow her pretty head to be turned by any such illusions of omnipotence. At least, not so that anyone would notice.

Wise beyond her years in the fickleness of the two-edged sword of victory, she refused to follow up on her triumph by sharing publicly the *ton*'s amusement at Lady Foxx's expense. People invariably search to seek out flaws in their heroes eventually, she reasoned, and all the sooner if that champion begins to look too satisfied with the elevated status to which his admirers have raised him. So Samantha simply ignored the jokes and the gossip, and airily dismissed her encounter with Lady Foxx as having not even the slightest thing to do with that Lady's precipitant departure for the wilds of Cumbria, before pointedly changing the subject. If, once safe in the privacy of her own chambers, she indulged herself for a moment or two—congratulating herself for routing Lady Foxx so handily, or quietly preening over her subsequent meteoric rise to such great heights of popularity—it was only because, of all the many adjectives that could be applied to Samantha, *angelic* was not one of them.

The Earl's days were mainly filled with government business that left him a few idle hours each afternoon to seek out male companionship at one or another of his usual haunts. Except for their never-missed early morning rides together (St. John looking magnificent mounted on his coal-black Arabian, and Samantha acquitting herself admirably on the bay gelding the Earl had cleverly dubbed Jester), the newlyweds were not in the habit of meeting during the day much before the dinner hour.

Samantha filled these hours with many of the customary feminine pursuits: shopping, visiting acquaintances, and attending tame ladies-only functions. Her purpose in all this was primarily to take advantage of any opportunity to show off her sister, Isabella, in Society. Aunt Loretta could not (although she was overheard to say she "would not," even before she was asked) keep up the mad pace normally set by a debutante bent on capturing a husband in a single Season, thus Samantha saw it as her duty to take up Aunt Loretta's slack. And take it up she did, bear-leading poor Isabella about Mayfair from morn till night, on the lookout for some likely specimen to present Isabella to, in hopes they would hit it off.

All this frantic matchmaking did not mean that Samantha had resigned herself to the role of dowager, not by a long chalk. The threatened turbans did not make their appearance, but a seemingly endless progression of one-of-a-kind parasols did.

Each day found Samantha dressed in yet another startlingly magnificent creation. Be it her green and black riding habit, her morning gown of palest pink *mousseline d'Inde* (so very striking with her red hair), her brown-and-gold matched walking *ensemble* that had every female who saw her grinding her teeth in despair, or her deliciously outrageous, diaphanous silver-spangled Zephyr cloak that caused such a stir at Almack's, Samantha had a matching parasol for every outfit, every occasion.

She flirted from over top of her lowered parasol, or peeked impishly out from behind it, or twirled it either to the music in the room or the variation of her mood. When one of her throng of admirers dared to be impudent she used her closed parasol to rap his knuckles. And if a gentleman was very, *very* lucky, when she was feeling fatigued she allowed him to stand behind her and hold the confection over her indulgent head.

Sonnets were written to Samantha's parasols, odes penned to their praises and hers, and soon, wherever one looked, one saw a multitude of parasols—multiplying and spreading like mushrooms until it became perilous to one's eyesight to become lax in the lookout for projecting parasol spines.

Alas, only Samantha thus far had the power to commission one young swain to hold her parasol (and looking perfectly ridiculous in evening dress and lace parasol in the process) while she joined in the dance with a second admirer. The rest of the ladies were forced either to abandon their precious creations to whatever fate usually befell unprotected parasols, or fold them and slip the ribbons over their wrists while they danced. As the gentlemen twirled their partners round and round the floor the parasols would swing in ever-rising arcs, until the musicians were nearly drowned out by the sounds of splintering wood and ungentlemanly grunts of pain. It wasn't sack-cloth and ashes, but Samantha was well satisfied with her first excursion into the art of style-setting.

Evening entertainments were always spent in the company of her husband. The two of them graced with their presence at least two or three functions per night, but it was the nights spent at the theatre that most pleased Samantha.

"Ah, my pet," observed St. John, just as they were settling in their box in Drury Lane Theatre, "it seems we are to be graced with the royal presence this evening. Pudgy Prinney himself is just coming into the royal box."

As Samantha strained to seek out the Regent's party, Zachary gave out with a short crack of laughter and added irrepressibly, "Do hurry, if you wish to spot him. It's the third box down from Lord Worcester's party. You can't miss Lady Worcester, my dear: she's wearing so many diamonds it looks like she's dressed all in mirrors. Ah, good, you've spied him out. What think you now of our Regent?"

Samantha surveyed the royal personage intently. Closer to him now than she had ever been at any of the crowded balls he infrequently blessed with his august presence (St. John not being one of the Carlton House set), she told the Earl truthfully, "He is just about the most *enormous* man I have ever seen. He—he's *bigger than life!*"

Just then the Prince was called upon to rise, turning his back to his audience in order to lean over to retrieve his mistress's shawl and drape it around her plump, matronly shoulders. While Samantha hid her giggles behind her gloves Zachary intoned heavily, "Observe: the Royal Behind, truly one of the sights of London!" As they rose for the customary musical salute to the Regent, Zachary was busily occupied thumping Samantha's back as she choked and coughed in a fit of suppressed mirth and, in the end, gained for herself an annoying attack of the hiccups.

Even as the first act wound down, Samantha's hiccups showed no signs of abating, so St. John—making excuses for himself and Samantha to Isabella and her escort of the evening (they felt no need to wake Aunt Loretta)—guided his wife out into the hallway and the two went in search of a restorative glass of lemonade.

Once the drink was acquired, Samantha—her sides tender from the incessant spasms around her rib cage—longed only for a comfortable seat out of the way of the other playgoers until the lemonade could turn the trick and rid her of those awful hiccups. She trailed over to a curtained alcove and the narrow flight of stairs hidden to the rear of it. Then, heedless of her gown, she plunked herself down on the second step and crossed her arms about her ribs.

"Oh-h-h, this is all your fault, Za-*hic*-Zachary St. John. How cou-*hic*-could you so malign our Re-*hic*-Regent? It's not like you to—*hic*—be pet-*hic*-petty-minded," Samantha rasped, looking up at the Earl with fiercely narrowed eyes that were betrayed by her smiling mouth.

St. John commiserated with his suffering bride (although in truth his condolences seemed a trifle tongue-in-cheek) and then informed her that those who served in the Peninsula were, as a rule, not too kindly disposed towards a man who lived a life of expensive indulgence in the safety of London while English soldiers were short-rationed and under-equipped in Portugal and Spain.

Samantha could see the dark shadow of remembered pain in his face—memories of hardship, brutality, and long-dead comrades-in-arms—and quickly searched for a way to lighten St. John's mood. She turned her head to peer up the dark, narrow staircase that was so obviously not for general use. "What's up these steps, do you suppose, Zachary?" Before he could answer she was on her feet, her hiccups finally routed, and climbing rapidly she called over her shoulder, "Come on, Oh-aged-one. Perhaps this is the stairway to adventure!"

"Samantha, you come down here this instant," St. John called after her, his tone not to be denied by anyone less courageous (or foolhardy) than his young wife. "The gallery lies up there, and it's full to the rafters with unsavory characters who'd think you were a gift sent early from Father Christmas!" As he spoke he grabbed the rickety newel and swung around to climb after his wife, two risers at a time, catching up with her before she had taken more than a half dozen steps down the darkened hallway.

The play was once more in progress and, luckily, the actors were a bit of a sad lot. Thus, the patrons in the gallery were intent on loudly venting their displeasure by means of catcalls, foot-stompings, and the shouting out of lewd suggestions as to the hero's off-stage activities with the female lead.

St. John grabbed Samantha by the upper arm and hissed into her ear, "Let's get you out of here before one of those idiots spots you, or there'll be the devil to pay. I'm too old for drunken brawling—at least when I'm outnumbered twenty to one." The Earl had mellowed since his marriage, but he had not become senile!

Samantha, however, was in the mood for a little excitement. She perversely stood her ground as she cast her eyes about in the gloom to see all she could of the greasy hallway before Zachary picked her up bodily and lugged her down the stairs, back to the stuffiness of Society manners.

"Wait just a moment, please, dear, *dear* Zachary," she pleaded in a whisper. "I just want to read that sign over there on the wall. No one has seen us."

St. John could have argued the point. Many a man (most particularly those who possessed less self-confidence than the Earl of Royston, who everyone knew had the devil's own arrogance) would have felt justified in hauling Samantha up over his shoulder like a sack of meal and beating a hasty retreat. But St. John merely gave the men in the gallery one more look, shrugged his shoulders, and accompanied Samantha over to the dimly-lit sign.

At first her shoulders shook only slightly above the emerald-green silk of her gown. Then a few repressed sniffs and a single choked snort escaped her. But as her lips, acting against her will, opened to let out her delighted laughter, Zachary clapped his hand across her mouth and propelled her down the stairway in much the same way as a gaming hell bouncer rousting a card-sharper.

Once safely back on the lower level, Samantha and the Earl were free to unleash their mirth, which they did—clinging to each other and chortling until tears appeared in their eyes. Not since his salad days had he felt so alive, so free.

"There you are!" Isabella called. Now that the butchered two-act play was done and the farce was about to begin, Isabella and her escort had been searching for their missing host and hostess. "What on earth has set you two off like that?" she questioned, chuckling a little herself at their obvious good humor.

"Whatever it is," Sir Edward, Isabella's escort for the evening, said sadly, "I'll bet we missed it." Then he looked about and noticed that no one else in the vicinity seemed to be in on the joke. "You know what it is: they're castaway, that's what," he offered as explanation. "Porter's out of lemonade, and they was forced to drink what they could get. Poor bas—er, blokes, we'd best get them off home."

Zachary was back in full command of his senses by now, but Sir Edward's remark had set Samantha off into another paroxysm of giggles. Pushing his wife down on the stairs, the Earl endeavored to explain. He told them of their exploration of the gallery, and then recited the message on the sign they had read—the message that had so unhinged even the sophisticated Earl.

"Attention!" it pleaded. "Gentlemen are respectfully entreated not to throw stone bottles over the rail, as this practice has been found to cause inconvenience to those in the pit."

As he finished, Samantha went off into fresh gales of laughter. Zachary, presented with Isabella's plainly uncomprehending features and Sir Edward's patently disbelieving face, sat down next to his wife and chuckled along with her. It was not everyone whose imagination could appreciate the ridiculous.

"Oh, Samantha, my most incorrigible sweetheart, you make me laugh as I haven't laughed since I was a boy. But come now," he admonished, rising to his feet and pulling her up with him, "if we are discovered here, Isabella and her solemn swain won't be the only ones thinking we're deep in our cups—along with those that would call us Bedlamites. Let us return to our seats and see if the farce measures up to our standards for successful comedy."

It didn't. And when those in the pit—the lords and the porters and the shop boys and the half-pay soldiers—began to make their dissatisfaction known, the rest of the theatre-goers were treated to rare fine displays of street manners: the versatility of week-old garbage in the hands of marksmen; samplings of the sounds produced by assorted rattles, horns, and whistles; and, inevitably, the speed with which those with disparate tastes in theatre can allow their arguments to degenerate into an every-man-for-himself *mêleé.*

While pickpockets in the crowd did a whopping business, a few enterprising fellows commandeered the wares of the many orange girls in the crowd and began pelting the actors—with remarkable accuracy.

In the boxes, fine ladies shrieked and fainted into the arms of their escorts, and more than one outburst of strong feminine hysterics added to the general din. The royal party was long gone, the Regent leaving quietly at the first hint of trouble (and before the crowd recalled that he was not one of their favorites), but the crowd in the gallery were still present to a man. They stomped their feet and called encouragement to the combatants in the pit. Bits of food, wads of paper, and one or two wooden benches sailed past as they crashed into the pit—as did several of those "inconvenient" stone bottles.

Zachary, believing his party to be secure in their box, had decided to wait out the crush of people, who were all trying to escape at once. Thus was Samantha able to look her fill at London theatre in one of its less than shining hours.

She loved every minute of it—until her hiccups returned that is, whereupon she turned to Zachary and politely inquired if he was ready to—*hic*—leave.

All in all, an enjoyable evening.

The following day St. John received a message from the steward of his estate in Kent, requesting his presence as soon as possible to discuss some problems of drainage and other pressing estate business concerning some of the tenants.

St. John was a model landowner—knowledgeable about his holdings and a conscientious landlord—so there was not a moment's indecision as to whether or not he would travel to Kent the following day. The only problem he could foresee was Samantha's reaction when he told her he wanted to travel alone, although he honestly doubted she would wish to miss a single day of her exciting Season.

He was wrong. "But what will I do with you miles away in Kent, Zachary?" Samantha argued, as soon as she heard his news. When he seemed unimpressed by the possibility of her being bored while surrounded by her adoring admirers, she (in her usual forthright fashion) went on doggedly, "If I appear happy in town, it is because I know you are here too—to talk with me and, and everything. If you are in Kent, then I'll be happy in Kent. Now do you understand?" she challenged him. He might pooh-pooh her declarations of love, but he should understand the appeal of close friendship.

The Earl would have been inhuman not to have been pleased with her flattering disclosure, but he saw this short separation as a good chance for Samantha to be alone with her feelings—to see if she would, in reality, be as lost without him as she professed she would be.

Before he left the next morning he and Samantha shared the breakfast table, he pretending to read the newspaper and she absently shredding a slice of toast as she stared off into space.

St. John had done his best to arrange to have Samantha amply occupied while he was gone, hoping she could be kept much too busy to indulge that nose for mischief that twitched so dangerously whenever she found herself at loose ends.

To this end he began a recital as to which of the invitations now reposing on his desk he felt suitable entertainments for Samantha, her sister, and Aunt Loretta, who would act as chaperon. "Not that I put much faith in your aunt's abilities in that direction. I never met such a somnolent creature in my life. Every time I try to hold a conversation with her, she falls asleep in my face."

Samantha, carefully keeping her face expressionless, replied, "Perhaps you should take steps to endeavor not to be such a dead bore."

"Minx," Zachary smiled, and—reaching out to smite her playfully on the side of her nose with one long finger—continued, "In all seriousness, Sam, you owe it to Isabella to keep her out and about in Society more than your aunt is willing to do. Left to herself, Isabella would never venture anywhere. I begin to think she is a victim of unrequited love."

"Isabella?" Samantha scoffed. "Don't be silly. She has yet to meet a single man fit to clean her boots. It is so vexing," she added candidly. "Now that Society has somehow decided that I am all the crack, the dratted bucks and dandies are always hanging about me like flies. I felt sure at first that Isabella could not help but benefit from being constantly in my company, with so many scores of eligible bachelors, but of the few that have paid her any attention, none have impressed her. There are times I think I made a mistake when I wished to be an *original.* It really is more tedious than enjoyable, especially if Isabella refuses to gain from it."

Tipping back negligently in his chair, St. John admonished her, "I wouldn't be so offhand about my popularity if I were you, m'dear. One swallow does not make a summer, so they say, and Society can just as abruptly drop you as it picked you up in the first place."

At once Samantha bristled. "You know I was not bragging, Zachary. I was merely making a comment. I do not, as you think, have such a swelled-up head that I believe myself to be the finest thing to come along since the discovery of fire." At St. John's snicker of amusement she warned him, "Don't laugh. Except to be seen with the 'parasol lady,' I can see no reason for all this attention I am receiving."

"Is that right, Samantha?" said Zachary, mocking her agitated tone. "Do you think part of the reason could be that you are an incorrigible flirt?"

Because it is extremely difficult to carry on a two-person conversation when one of the persons has slammed down her napkin, stuck out her tongue in fury, and stomped heavily from the room, St. John returned to his newspaper until it was time to leave.

Samantha's temper cooled sufficiently (when her irrepressible sense of humor surfaced) for her to descend to the foyer, just in time to be thoroughly kissed farewell by her devastatingly handsome husband.

"I'll miss you, puss," he whispered hoarsely in her ear, holding her close in his embrace while Carstairs stood patiently by, holding his hat, gloves, and silver-handled whip.

"Pooh!" Samantha scoffed, in a curiously trembling voice. "You will do nothing of the sort. Once closeted with your steward you'll be so involved in plans for draining off bogs and re-thatching laborers' cottages, you'll not give your poor, lonely wife another thought."

St. John reached behind his back to disengage Samantha's clinging arms and, retaining his firm grasp on her hands, he lifted them together to his lips to press a kiss in each of her palms. "There is no need for you to miss more than those few engagements I would rather you did not attend without my escort. There is plenty to keep you and Isabella occupied until I return. All I ask, Samantha, is that you be good."

Samantha was having a mighty struggle within herself to keep from breaking down and bawling like a puling infant. Taking a shuddering great breath, she pinned a comically pained expression on her face as she complained, "Ho-hum, Zachary. What else could I be, with that deadly dull itinerary you have laid out for me?"

Zachary looked at her for a long moment, then muttered darkly under his breath, "I cannot imagine. But if there's a way, I am sure you will find it." Before she could begin to argue the point, he planted a hard, swift kiss on her parted lips and went out through the open doorway to mount his curricle and spring his team, without once looking back at the figure staring after him from the doorway.

Samantha watched until he drove out of the Square before turning to slowly mount the stairs that led to their chambers. In Zachary's dressing room, she located the dressing gown he had worn that morning and—clutching it to her breast so that she could smell that special mixture of tobacco and cologne that was peculiar to her husband—climbed upon his wide bed to curl herself into a tight little bundle of confusion and pain.

Zachary refused to take her declarations of love seriously. Now he was going off by himself, when he could so easily have taken her along. Perhaps she was becoming a bore; an immature girl had scant chance of holding the interest of a man with the experience of a Zachary St. John.

Or perhaps she embarrassed him, what with her impulsive actions and bizarre—yes, she told herself, *bizarre*—affectations, like those idiotic parasols. Good lord, even *she* doubted she could take such a zany creature seriously!

Lying on the bed all the rest of that morning, Samantha decided it was time she grew up and took on a more sober outlook on life. Once she had proved herself to be worthy of his regard, Zachary might come to return her love. It wasn't an easy task she set herself, but she felt the prize of Zachary's love to be worth any cost.

At the same time Samantha was vowing to take steps to "civilize" herself, St. John was bowling happily along the roadway, a smile hovering about his lips as he thought of his enchanting child bride. "Never change, infant. Just promise to go on forever being my very own silly, sweet Sam, and I'll be the most envied man in the world. And the luckiest." He shook his head slightly and allowed himself a rueful grin. "I must be demented, talking to people who aren't here, and—worse yet—talking to myself." He shook his head again and spoke aloud one more time. "And they say marriage has a stabilizing influence on a man! Obviously anyone who believes *that* has never met my Sam!"

Chapter Fourteen

FOR THREE DAYS, Samantha's behavior was a model of circumspection. For three days she kept her social engagements limited to At Homes, tea parties, and musicales during the daytime, and only the tamest, the most innocuous of amusements were graced by her presence after dark. For three days. Three endless, boring, insipid days.

And two nights. The fateful third evening was devoted to Lady Mallory's premiere musical evening. The gathering was masterfully designed by that distinguished lady to serve as a fitting showcase for her daughter Sybil's extraordinary expertise on both the spinet and the harp. Also—since the dear child would not dream of disappointing her audience—Miss Sybil might also be persuaded to render a few songs whilst some other willing debutante (no doubt hand-picked by Lady Mallory for her unprepossessing appearance) accompanied her on the keyboard (since Miss Sybil's short and somewhat pudgy figure appeared taller and less plump when standing before an object even more squat and wide than herself).

Samantha, who had not been informed that Miss Sybil was to be the sole (and interminable) performer, had promptly taken up a seat near the front of the room, and was perforce unable to make a discreet withdrawal for the eternity it took Miss Sybil to painfully plod through her mundane *répertoire* on the spinet.

The girl's assault on the harp was just as determined, just as lengthy, and—as if it were possible—twice as painful to the listener. Somewhere in the house, Samantha smiled to herself, there is a kitchen cat writhing in extreme ear pain, and if the dogs outside on the street do not soon set up a howling chorus, it won't be for lack of inducement.

When at long last Miss Sybil's rendition of "Greensleeves" wound down (not before Samantha's lifelong affection for the ancient song was, alas, blighted forevermore), Samantha breathed a sigh of relief and turned in her seat to observe Miss Sybil's effect on the rest of the politely applauding audience. She winked across the room at Isabella, who was just then wearing the wide-eyed, blankly-staring face of an infantryman who has stood in close proximity to one too many cannons.

Aunt Loretta, who could conceivably have napped through the sacking of Rome, was at last located—stuck on a Sheraton sofa, partially tucked behind an unsightly clump of hothouse greenery that was wilting nearly as fast as the gentlemen's starched collars in the stifling atmosphere of stale air and overheated bodies. With her head tilted attentively toward the cleared area of the room where Miss Sybil had lately paraded her talents, Aunt Loretta looked the picture of attentiveness—that is, until one peeked under her childish fringe of curled bang and saw that the woman was, as a boxing enthusiast might say, out for the count.

Samantha watched the gentlemen as, one by one or in pairs, they made overly dramatic protestations of pressing engagements elsewhere and bowed themselves from the room, lying through their aristocratic teeth as they praised Miss Sybil and congratulated her mater on her talented daughter before escaping to the street—nearly leaving behind their evening capes in their haste to be away—or skulked off to join the equally bored Lord Mallory in his private study for a few hands of whist, doubtless to send up fervent prayers that no one would succeed in smoking them out of their masculine hidey-hole.

A satin slipper tapped the parquet floor while an apricot-and-ivory striped-silk parasol that matched an apricot-and-ivory striped gown twirled absently. Samantha debated whether to plead a headache or stick out the evening as a sort of endurance test that would prove once and for all that she could play the game of social graces with the best of them.

Having made a decision to hold firm until the last yawn, she settled back in her seat with a cup of punch—brought to her by one of her dutiful admirers—ready to suffer all to prove herself worthy to be Royston's Countess. To be fair, she probably would have lasted out the night with nary a hint of a blot in her copybook had it not been for the singlemindedness of her hostess.

So what, thought Lady Mallory contemptuously, if more than half the gentlemen had faded off into oblivion during the short intermission. What did a man know about things artistic anyway? After all, wasn't it a man who invented those cursed howling bagpipes, of which the Prince was so odiously fond? And then there were those distasteful, raucous standing ovations they all gave nightly to that new singer at Covent Garden (who couldn't carry a tune in a pail)—which certainly settled the case.

Well! Just wait until they heard her little Sibbie sing. Then the few that were left within earshot would fight each other for the privilege of sitting at the girl's feet in adoration of her glorious voice. So long as young Lord Lampson was still in the room (it had not occurred to the hostess that he was too bovine in temperament as well as body to have shifted himself in time), there was hope yet for the evening.

Clutching the reluctant Sibbie by the elbow (girlish modesty being so *very* affecting), Lady Mallory marched up to the piano, gesturing to the very compliant (and very plain) Miss Bradwell to seat herself at the keyboard and cleared her throat before reintroducing her daughter.

"Oh, no, you don't!" Samantha hissed under her breath, snatching up her reticule. Holding a scented lace handkerchief delicately to her lips, she hastily excused herself as having been suddenly taken ill.

Isabella saw Samantha's precipitant departure and, being above all else a good sister, followed after her to lend assistance—only to find Samantha leaning against the wall outside the music room, giggling into the scented bit of lace.

"Lord, Izzy, have you ever seen such a dense woman? Half the gentlemen near trampled the other half, so in a quiver were they to make their exit, and still she persists.

Mother Love overlooks a multitude of faults in her offspring, but if Sybil's voice ranks anywhere near the quality of her ham-fisted plucking at the harp, one wonders how even Mother Love does not feel duty-bound to strap a muzzle on the chit."

Isabella, recognizing the gleam in Samantha's dancing green eyes, hastily suggested they rouse Aunt Loretta and make an early night of it. Her sister didn't answer, but continued to cast her eyes about the wide hallway, her head cocked to one side as if listening for some sound.

"Well, then," Isabella persisted, "if you don't wish to leave we'd best make our way back inside. Sybil has begun her first rendition, but I'm certain there are seats in the back, where we can slip in without distracting her."

Samantha harrumphed in amusement. "Heaven forbid! If the looby should be jostled out of her deadly concentration, she would probably be so befuddled she'd have to go back and start over at the beginning of her piece—and that would be unforgivable! Besides," she continued quickly, "I have no intention of subjecting myself to another off-key note. Right now I'm searching for the whereabouts of the disappearing gentlemen. What do you suppose they are about? Whatever it is, it's a sure thing it's a hundred times more enjoyable than the ear-beating they've cravenly left their women to suffer alone."

Samantha set off down the hallway, following a footman carrying a tray of glasses and a full decanter, with her sister skipping along behind and begging her to reconsider.

"Oh, do stop whining, Izzy," Samantha scolded. "Can't you ever comment on *anything* I do, other than to point out the possible pitfalls? Don't you ever—even if just for a fleeting moment—consider the enjoyment to be had in life if one does not opt for the safety of dull propriety?"

Isabella was indignant. Out of breath from trying to match her sister's longer strides, yes—but indignant just the same, much in the way of an enraged kitten. "If I don't choose to risk my good name and peace of mind on a spur-of-the-moment lark that would most likely prove to be not half so diverting as I had hoped, that is my concern—and you have no right to poke fun at me!" Isabella protested, her lower lip trembling in her agitation.

Her sister was immediately contrite and put a reassuring arm about Isabella's slim shoulders. "I'm a beast, aren't I, Izzy?" she apologized sincerely. Then, assuming herself forgiven, she went on, "If you'll stay with me for just an hour, to lend me the respectability Society requires—though I can't imagine why, for I doubt the gentlemen here tonight would take it into their heads to attack me *en masse*—I promise not to do anything to place myself beyond the pale. Agreed?"

Isabella did *not* agree, but—as Samantha had not bothered to wait for an answer to her question and was already pushing open the door to the study—Isabella had no choice but to follow her.

Several hours later, buried up to her chin under her satin coverlet alone in Royston's huge bed, Samantha giggled deliciously as she relived her evening at Lord Mallory's gaming table.

After the gentlemen's initial reluctance to allow two females to invade their sacred territory was overcome by Samantha's witty tongue and dazzling appearance, Isabella had been escorted to a comfortable chair while Samantha reintroduced the players to the childhood card game called My Son's Pigged.

Watch-It-And-Catch-It was another crowd-pleaser, with more than one peer ending the evening feigning chagrin when he had lost all his blunt—the matchsticks Samantha insisted as using as the only stakes.

"Better than the money I dropped at Watiers the other night, playing blind-hookey," one gentleman was heard to comment as he watched the last of his stakes being swept into the massive pile in front of Samantha, whose luck had been quite in all night.

Lady Mallory, it must be noted, was not best pleased. As one by one they went off in search of the sound of laughter filtering into the music room, poor Sybil lost all the remaining souls in her audience but two: the comatose Aunt Loretta, and the hapless Lord Lampson, who Lady Mallory kept pinioned to his chair with her menacing gaze.

Still chuckling, and hugging St. John's bolster pillow tightly to her breast, Samantha fell into a sound sleep undisturbed by any repercussions the night's activities might bring. She awoke amazingly refreshed, until she realized that she was facing yet another endless day full of singularly dull and uninteresting social pursuits.

As she paced her own chamber after her bath, clad only in her dressing gown, she paraphrased a line from *Hamlet* in her mind: To be good (and dull) or naughty (and happy)—*that* is the question.

"Oh, stuff!" she at last admitted aloud to herself. "I am fated to be a sad trial to Zachary for the remainder of my unnatural life, and—and he may as well become accustomed to that fact!"

So saying, she, with Daisy's help, made short work of donning Wally's trusty breeches. Then, tucking up a lunch in her coat pocket, Samantha tiptoed out through the kitchens while Carstairs's condemning eyes were turned discreetly towards the pantry door.

There followed a glorious day of adventure as Samantha rubbed shoulders with the people in the city: passing the time of day with a friendly apple woman; tipping her hat to a bandbox man as he struggled to guide a long pole, hung heavily with bandboxes, through the crowded streets; watching as a chair mender did repairs while blocking the flagway; and clutching at her sides with glee while a bear ward and his beast stopped traffic and terrified horses as they made their way through the streets.

She might have gotten through her day of truancy without incident had it not been for her sighting of the train of vast, hooded wagons, with their wheels as big as rollers, all drawn by magnificent horses—beasts, Samantha was certain, the size of elephants.

She followed them awhile, marvelling at their size, which seemed to her to be on a par with that of the famed straw statues she had read about—Gog and Magog—before they disappeared into the yard of a large brewery.

Just as she was turning away to retrace her steps, a young gentleman detached himself from his party and invited the obviously interested young man to join them in their tour of the establishment. Samantha accepted eagerly.

She walked through the building with her mouth agape and her eyes round as saucers. This suitably impressed the proud brewer; a peach-fuzzed gent marvelling at the sight of storage vessels as large as ships that towered over the group on either side.

During the customary partaking of the brewer's hospitality at the end of the tour—a meal that consisted of a gigantic steak cooked on a shovel—the host plied his most appreciative guest with several complimentary pints of his "best entire."

"Good for washin' it down," the brewer winked playfully, as the reputed potency of his brew made itself evident in the flushed cheeks and sparkling and faintly glazed eyes of his young customer.

Dusk found Samantha striding purposefully, if crookedly, down the street, reveling in the freedom of the huge strides allowed by the cut of her breeches. She wore a vacant grin, her curly-brimmed beaver tilted to a rakish angle, and would have been fair game for any footpad or cut-purse if not for the menacing presence of the brawny Irish laborer who followed three paces behind, obviously acting the bodyguard.

The reason for this unsolicited but providential protection was explained by the two heavy purses now clutched in the Irishman's beefy fist. Samantha, feeling in charity with all the world, had spied the man standing beside his wife and ten children just as she weaved her way from the brewery door. Their woebegone appearance touched her gentle heart (which right now ruled her muddled head), and she promptly gifted the man with all the money in her possession (a goodly sum, as Daisy had made sure there would be no chance of Miss Sammy's coming home again in a penniless state).

The Irishman, while thinking the young gentleman fair daft as well as bosky, promptly committed himself to the protection of the fellow and followed along behind him like a ragtag guardian angel until his charge at last disappeared through the kitchen door of a large mansion in Portman Square.

"And may the sainted Virgin herself protect ye," he intoned gravely, as he tipped his greasy cap and bowed himself out through the mews.

Once Samantha got upstairs, Daisy had the devil's own

time containing her mistress's flailing limbs and loud, raucous bursts of song while she tried to divest her of her incriminating costume.

"Miss Sammy, Miss Sammy," she pleaded *sotto voce,* "Yer gots ta quiet yerself. Hiz lordship's back and in hiz chamber dressin' fer dinner. Iffen he hears ya, it's the devil to pay for sure!"

This sobering fact served to quiet Samantha, but unfortunately it could not make her limbs cooperate sufficiently to make an easy job of stripping herself of the skintight buckskins.

At last Samantha gave up the fight and had Daisy help her struggle into a gown that would hide the incriminating breeches.

They had only just discovered that the cut of the gown did little to camouflage the outline of the dratted things when St. John's footsteps could be heard approaching the connecting door between the chambers.

"Oh, hang him!" Samantha wailed, and promptly hid herself behind Daisy's ample form.

"Stay with me, Daisy!" Samantha pleaded. "My buttons aren't even done up yet. Oh, what a rare bumblebath this is!" she then giggled. The spirits she'd imbibed earlier were showing their staying power, even in a situation frought with danger.

The Earl had cut short his visit to his estate when he came to the realization that a small, pert face and a pair of laughing green eyes were making a mockery of all his attempts at rational thought. He now entered his wife's chamber eagerly, as a happy smile curved his lips and stripped a dozen years from his features.

That smile only broadened when he spied out Samantha, cowering behind her maid, her hair piled atop her head (looking sadly crushed, but no matter), and her gown more off than on.

"Ho! What's this?" he queried jovially. "Modesty at this late date, my infant? Come here and greet your husband properly. After dismissing your woman, if you mislike demonstrations of, er, *affection* in front of servants."

Samantha's fingers only gripped Daisy's shoulders the tighter, making the woman wince, and it was left to the maid to try to make some sense of the situation—not an easy job, as her mistress just then let out with a rather low-class hiccup.

Royston lifted one expressive eyebrow, and Daisy launched into a muddled explanation of Samantha's unfortunate history of "queer-like takings," only to be silenced by one of the Earl's piercing looks.

Then, by means of slight head shakes and with his face softening only slightly, he induced Samantha to step out from behind her flustered protector.

Once within the circle of light shining from the brace of candles nearby, Samantha's bizarre attire gave the Earl a distressingly clear outline of the proof of Samantha's guilt—of just what crime was for the moment unimportant.

"Pernicious brat," he said under his breath, as Samantha ducked behind Daisy once more.

Taking a deep, steadying breath, St. John crossed to a chair, disposed himself in it with magnificent grace (as Prinney said, you could tell if a man was or was not a gentleman by the way he arranged his coattails when he sat down), crossed one muscular leg over the other and said amiably, "Samantha. Dearest, *dearest*, Samantha, as I do so abominate scenes, I believe it would be prudent of you to dismiss your maid." He smiled, bowed his head a moment, then raised it to show a face chiseled in ice. "*Now!*"

Daisy scurried from the room without a backward look for her mistress, and Samantha—who had remained mumchance until now, for the hiccup hardly counted as speech—squared her shoulders and turned bravely, if a bit tipsily, toward her husband. "You frightened poor Daisy," she accused, feeling an attack to be the most prudent defense. "That was a shabby thing to do—too shabby by half, for an Earl. Bullying servants lends nothing to your consequence, Royston."

St. John ignored this obvious attempt at dissemblance, and waved a hand languidly to point out the obvious failure of her thin cambric gown (the one she was just now clumsily attempting to secure about her shoulders) to hide the existence of breeches under its folds.

"It requires no great flight of the imagination to suppose

you have been indulging yourself with one of your, er, 'queer-like takings,' " the Earl purred smoothly.

Samantha's chin came up and she retorted, "Don't you dare rattle me off in that high-nosed tone, Zachary. If you had but given me a moment I would have explained—eventually."

"Once you had thought up in that devious brain of yours some outrageous farradiddle that you, with your own ridiculous brand of logic, believed I would swallow whole, you mean," countered the Earl.

"It's no such thing!" Samantha lied swiftly. "There are times, dear husband, when you are nothing but a horrid prig." Her chin jutting out pugnaciously, she told him, "I was moped to death here, acting the proper lady while you shoveled manure or whatever in Kent—although I was quite odiously circumspect until today, I might add. So what if I rewarded myself by taking a small tour of the city?" Samantha was still slightly unsteady on her feet, but she was recovering rapidly.

"Oh? If I may be so bold, madam, where did this 'small tour' take you?" St. John asked, his smile making a slight reappearance.

"I traveled fairly widely, but I suppose you are most interested in my guided tour of a brewery this afternoon," she answered in a lower tone.

St. John's smile faded as he said stiffly, "At least you don't plague a man with a pack of humbug. However, your honesty would be more refreshing were it less incriminating."

"Is that so?" Samantha huffed back at him. "Well, it seems to me that you are behaving in a devilishly strait-laced way for a rakehell. Is this in aid of your new status as a husband, or are you just repenting in a hope of Heaven—now that you are aged and tottering on the brink of the grave?"

The Earl shook his head wearily as he heard his wife attack his age yet again. "Samantha, your constant reminders of my years are becoming redundant as well as being patently untrue. I believe it would be in your best interests to fortify yourself to the likelihood that I shall live forever."

Samantha—not down and by no stretch of credulity out—sneered back, "You may not be as ancient as I say but you are certainly behaving in a most Gothic way. Yes, that's what you are: Gothic, utterly Gothic!"

St. John laced his hands together and recrossed his legs. "And what would a Gothic husband consider appropriate punishment for a wife who flaunts propriety—and, by the by, her own safety—by junketing about the city, touring breweries and committing all sorts of other equally depressing indiscretions, all while being more than a little bit on the go—or drunk, if you're unfamiliar with the expression?" After further infuriating his wife by taking his time to mull over this question at his leisure, he snapped his fingers and announced, "I have it! What you need, gel," he pronounced, his face taking on the narrow-eyed semblance of a leer, "is a good spanking!"

"Oh, no, you don't!" Samantha shrieked, and turned to flee, her dress slipping from her shoulders and the skirt tripping up her feet so that she was caught easily and hauled, protesting loudly, across Royston's knees.

What followed were five hearty smacks on Samantha's tightly-encased buttocks before St. John dumped her unceremoniously onto the rug, stood up, brushed his hands together in satisfaction, and made to leave the room.

Samantha rose up in a flaming fury and flung at him, "You blackhearted whelp of a she-hound, you'll rue the day you dared touch me! Never, I say, *never,* do that again!"

St. John halted, turned, and grinned, "All right, pet, I'll answer in the way you so obviously wish. I will not touch you again—*or* . . ."

"Or face the consequences," Samantha was so enraged as to reply. "My revenge may well terrify you. In fact," she told him menacingly, tears quivering on her lashes, "if I were you I would be afraid to put my head on my pillow tonight."

With that she turned smartly and plunked herself down in the chair just vacated by her husband, her unwilling wince of pain clearly observed by St. John. He stormed to the entrance to his room, muttered, "Welcome home!" between clenched teeth, and slammed the door behind him.

After he had gone, Samantha rose gingerly from the chair, moaned quietly, and ruefully rubbed at her bruised posterior. She paced the room for some time, experiencing a strong desire to murder St. John and indulging in wild fantasies that would suit her purpose. Mad as a baited bear was Samantha, and as she entertained thoughts of boiling oil and thumbscrews, the clock ticked on until a goodly time had passed.

As the hour struck, an evil smile curled about Samantha's lips and she went to the connecting door and listened for the even breathing that would tell her St. John was asleep. Once satisfied that he was, she tiptoed over to her washstand, ascertained that the pitcher was full to the brim with ice-cold water, and moved stealthily until she stood beside Royston's slumbering form.

She raised the pitcher—a lovely porcelain thing—and, with just a twist of her wrist, dumped the contents over St. John's head.

He yelped, spluttered, and sat upright shaking his wet head before he exploded in a round of curses that made Samantha's ears burn. When he had cleared one eye with a corner of the coverlet, he peered up at her and offered, "Your trick, I fancy, madam," and then—unbelievably—he smiled.

Samantha, her anger spent, relapsed into the ways of the female of the species, and began to murmur contrite apologies while she dabbed at the Earl's wet shoulders with the hem of her bedraggled gown.

"Where did you learn that particular piece of nastiness?" Zachary asked, as he slipped from the bed and began stripping off his sodden silk pajamas.

"Wally and I once did it to Izzy. She had snitched to Father that it was us who drew a rather revealing picture of the vicar on the outhouse door," she confessed, without a blush.

"Izzy, Wally, Sammy. Gad, what ridiculous names. Sound like nursery names for pet turtles or frogs or some other creatures good only for giving off bad odors and manufacturing slime."

Samantha flung a towel at him. "Oh, really?" she returned, not overly offended. "Did you never have a pet, then, that you so disparage the probable inhabitants of the Ardsley menagerie?"

"Of course I had pets: dogs and other normal animals. Except, that is," he admitted sheepishly, "for my pet pig."

As Samantha giggled he defended, "He was the runt of the litter, poor thing. I secreted him in my bedroom so he wouldn't be slaughtered. It would have worked, too," he reminisced, "if that damned chambermaid hadn't left the door ajar."

"What happened?" Samantha asked, her former animosity forgotten.

Zachary chuckled softly. "He escaped, naturally. Made his social debut at my grandmother's dinner party for Lord Clerwick, he did. Caused quite a stir with the local gentry, not to mention Grandmother."

Once she had stopped laughing, Samantha prompted, "And this pig's civilized name, Zachary?"

St. John averted his head and muttered sheepishly, "Pinky," whereupon Samantha shrieked, "*Pinky Piglet!*" and threw herself on her husband's damp neck.

He hoisted her into his arms, pressing her against his bare chest, and whirled her around once before moving in the direction of the bed.

"No, Zachary, it's all wet," Samantha protested to no avail, as the Earl plunked her unceremoniously on the center of the mattress and—with a war whoop that would have done a red Indian proud—joined her on the bed.

Much later they discussed Samantha's adventures, and she fetched him a packet of monogrammed, Irish linen handkerchiefs. She had found them to be such a bargain that she could not resist purchasing them from the rosy-faced woman hawking them on some street corner or other.

"How do you know they are truly Irish linen?" he gibed, knowing full well she had been taken in like any greenhorn.

Poking him in the ribs she answered, "It was easy. See the embroidered R? It's in green thread. It has to be Irish."

So diverted was St. John by his artless wife that he even relented so far as to say, when she belatedly promised (yet again) to strive to be better behaved in the future, "Don't let the niceties of manners discommode you from your fondest desires, if you're really set on them."

Instead of accepting this offering, Samantha bristled and shot back: "Niceties of manners, is it, Zachary? If I were a man, my actions would be considered nothing out of the ordinary."

Sitting up, the Earl replied testily, "But you are *not* a man."

"So what? I can do anything a man can do, or at least I could in a free society."

St. John clucked in mock sympathy. "Poor Sam! And would you also like to fight in wars and serve in Parliament and even smoke cigars?"

"I would!" she concurred vehemently, ready to do battle again until she caught sight of Wally's rumpled breeches at the foot of the bed. "Oh, Zachary," she wailed, reaching for him, "I never want to be a man. It is too altogether wonderful being a female. It's just my wretched, wretched tongue."

Gathering her into his arms (after deciding this discussion could be carried on more comfortably in Samantha's chambers and her dry bed), he moved towards the door, correcting her, "Not your wretched tongue, pet, but my tiresome temper."

It was the start of a friendly argument that was destined to last most of the night.

Chapter Fifteen

SAMANTHA was happily ensconced in the sunny morning room, blissfully jamming flowers into a variety of vases—without once considering the color schemes of the rooms for which they were destined, or taking care to choose blooms that complimented each other in size and shade, or even arranging them in any semblance of symmetry or proportion. Instead, she was humming snatches of several tunes under her breath, stopping her work entirely more than once to stare off into space while an inane grin decorated her face, and otherwise generally making a fine muddle of a simple task she had once been able to accomplish with remarkable speed and pleasing results.

But this day was the morning after St. John's return to London, and for that reason Samantha's lapse was understandable (if not forgivable, at least not by the bruised and battered hot-house blooms that now resembled nothing more than Thomas Moore's pathetic "last rose of summer").

Just as Samantha was about to butcher yet another carnation by leaving it only a three-inch stem, Carstairs scratched discreetly at the door, entered, and announced—with barely-veiled distaste—that my lady's sister and aunt awaited her in the small salon.

Samantha wiped her hands on a towel and asked Carstairs to have "someone see to this mess I have made" (which he did gladly, affording a zealous housemaid a chance to display her artistic expertise and saving at least two dozen prize blooms from the dustbin). "Have tea sent in fifteen minutes, if you please, Carstairs," she tossed over her shoulder, as she tidied her mint-green striped morning gown and went off to join her relatives.

The first thing she noticed upon entering the room was that her aunt had come to nap, not to chat, for she was seated in a chair that could not be considered to be in the best position for conversation. If further proof was needed it could be found by watching her head, which was already beginning to nod towards her chest.

Due to Aunt Loretta's behavior—being neither unexpected nor unwelcome—Samantha chose not to disturb the woman by saying hello. Instead she went directly to her sister, holding out her hands in greeting.

Isabella's response owed more to the conditioned response of years of training than it did to joy at the sight of her so extraordinarily (if not perhaps even a wee bit nauseatingly) cheerful and happily married sister.

"Isabella?" Samantha puzzled, looking closely at her sister's pale cheeks and rather pinched mouth. "You're looking a little downpin, if you don't mind a bit of sisterly candor—born of concern, I assure you." Sitting herself down next to Isabella without relinquishing her grip on the icy hands, she went on, "Do you have a problem? Tell me what it is and I'll be more than happy to help you solve it."

"No one can help me," Isabella whispered, so quietly Samantha had to strain her ears to hear.

"I know what it is," Samantha guessed obligingly. "You've overspent your allowance. Well, that's no problem, now that your sister the Countess can advance you any amount you wish until quarterday."

Isabella's china-blue eyes filled with tears and her full lower lip started in to trembling.

"No?" her sister marvelled. "Forget a loan; I'll make the funds a gift. There, now will you dry those silly tears?" Honestly, there were times when it was hard to remember that Isabella was the elder by almost eighteen months.

Samantha screwed up her face in thought for a moment and then declared triumphantly, "A man! It's something to do with a man, isn't it, Izzy? Oh, dear," she recalled suddenly, "say it isn't that scapegrace Lord Clarion who's been hanging at your skirts these weeks past."

With a vehement shake of her golden curls, Isabella denied it was Lord Clarion who had so upset her. "Besides," she explained ingenuously, "however amusing he may sometimes be, he owes much of his humor to a bottle and is at times prone to become more oppressive than entertaining in his antics. No," she told her sister solemnly, "I cannot like Lord Clarion."

"My, my, how deftly you sugarcoat your censure, dear Izzy," gibed Samantha. "But, in this case, I fear you are right. St. John told me once that Lord Clarion downs at least five to eight bottles a night, and would sip ink if nothing else were to hand.

"But if your problem doesn't concern money or men, just what is the matter?" Samantha pursued doggedly. "Anyone can see you are under some great stress. Have you discussed it with Aunt Loretta?"

At last Isabella showed some little sign of animation when she sniffed and said, "Aunt Loretta is of no help to me. She has a mind filled with—with *feathers!*"

Looking down the room at the somnolent woman, Samantha remarked impishly, "Her mind filled with feathers, you say. That explains then why she *pillows* her head at every opportunity." Samantha laughed gaily at her joke until she noticed that, instead of joining in with a chuckle of her own (which would after all have only been polite, even if it was a rather weak joke), her sister was instead indulging herself in one or two irritatingly unreadable, long, heart-felt sighs.

All at once Samantha had had it up to her back teeth with Isabella's histrionics. "You are fair bidding to become a genuine tragedy queen, Izzy, what with all those secret sighs and that die-away air you're sporting."

Isabella lifted speaking eyes to her sister and declared, "I have allowed myself to sink to irreclaimable depths of depravity."

"Oh, good grief," Samantha spat, totally disgusted now. "I'm sure you are indeed past all salvation—if your hopes were to tread the boards at Covent Garden, that is. As to your ever committing any sin more dastardly than the time when you were ten and you fibbed to Aunt Loretta about having a bellyache, when in truth you were too embarrassed to go to church the day after Freddie Symons caught and kissed you in the spinney and then ran through the village shouting to everyone what he'd done—well, I'll not believe it until I hear it."

Isabella lifted her face to her sister, her expression so woebegone that for a moment Samantha's heart was truly touched. But then Isabella vowed again that her secret was just "too awful" to share, not even with her beloved sister. Samantha's ire rose tenfold.

She made a move toward Isabella, her hands reaching out in a sudden urge to throttle the girl, before common sense told her (to borrow a phrase from Zachary's crew on the yacht) to try another tack. "Very well, Isabella," she agreed, her smile amicable although her tone was a trifle terse. "You don't have to knock me down with a brick before I can take a hint."

She moved to a chair directly across from Isabella's and sat down decorously. "Your problem is not to be a topic for discussion. So," she queried airily, "what shall we talk about?" She hesitated a moment, as if in thought, and then said brightly, "The weather. Yes. That's a capital idea. We shall discuss the weather."

But no sooner than she had begun to wax poetic over the unusually sunshiny days they had been experiencing than her sister interrupted, saying, "Aunt Loretta's as dead as a house, Samantha, did you know that?"

Samantha, cutting off her speech in mid-rapture, frowned, and then agreed with her sister.

"It's there, you know, right in front of her, just as plain as the nose on her face," Isabella complained. (Samantha stole a peek at Aunt Loretta's quivering nostrils, tucked beneath her aristocratically humped nose, and thought, "and nothing can be any plainer than *that!*") "And yet she failed to see it."

Samantha also felt herself to be a dismal failure, for she also had not a glimmer of whatever "it" was. But nonetheless she sat back, comfortable in the knowledge that her sister, once started on one of her rare tangents, would soon satisfy her curiosity on all points.

"Anyway, since Aunt Loretta wouldn't help me, and there was no one else to turn to, I decided to come to you."

Samantha allowed herself a small smile. "That was very common-sensible of you, dearest. But perhaps if you looked upon me more as a confessor than as a soothsayer who can divine your problem by, say, examining the entrails of a freshly-butchered chicken, I could be of more help to you."

Yes, Samantha thought wearily, Izzy will tell me all sooner or later. But a person could grow old in the waiting!

Isabella looked down at her hands and reluctantly agreed with her tactless sister. She had decided that Aunt Loretta couldn't help her, she had decided to be guided by Fate, and she did acknowledge that, in this instance, Dame Fate had a mighty resemblance to her sister.

Nothing was left now but the presentation of the problem. This Isabella would do clearly, concisely, and truthfully, no matter how strong the resultant emotions tore at her sensibilities. And if, once she had stripped her soul virtually naked before her sister's eyes, if that infuriating girl chose to laugh at her—*she'd murder her!*

"I'm in love!" Isabella blurted out at last, totally dumbfounding Samantha—who all but had her sister guilty of committing high treason or worse.

"Is *that* all?" Samantha fairly sneered, and relaxed her taut muscles in relief. "Who is he? Do I know him?"

Isabella sighed. "I doubt it, dear. His name is Robert—that's all, just Robert, that's all I know—and he works for a glover in Conduit Street. *There,*" she ended daringly. "Now you have the whole of it, do you see what a bad person I am?"

"*Bad,* Izzy? I'm not sure you're a *bad* person," Samantha drawled slowly. "I do admit that you have filled me with dismay, however, as I can see no happy ending in sight for you and—what's his name?—your glover. It certainly is a good thing you didn't confide in Aunt Loretta, for she most probably would have been immediately convulsed in strong hysterics, throwing her right off her schedule. And you know how out-of-sorts she gets when she hasn't gotten her quota of naps for the day: why, she becomes as cranky as a baby for days on end."

Bobbing her head furiously in agreement, Isabella added, "Even worse, she'd fly straight to Father with the story, and—as we all know she hasn't gotten the straight of anything in her life—she'd garble it beyond recognition."

Samantha took up the conjecturing from there. "Then

Father would call down a lecture upon your head that would leave your ears still blistered as you marched down the aisle with the first eligible man Father saw looking in your direction," she prophesied, with unwarranted gaiety. "Gad, Izzy, for a girl I roasted as having no adventure in her soul, you certainly went to great lengths to prove me wrong."

That sobered Isabella. "I have about as much chance of marrying Robert as I do of being wed to Napoleon Bonaparte," she murmured miserably.

Lifting her eyebrows in rueful agreement, Samantha concurred, "You have two chances, Izzy, as I see it: slim and none. But before we give up all hope, you must tell me more of this Robert," she encouraged.

Before Isabella could speak, the tea tray arrived. It was a half-hour late and pushed by none other than Carstairs himself, his supercilious expression plainly showing his distaste at performing such a menial task. But the footmen were all helping out in the stable with a half dozen new cattle the Earl had just purchased, and the housemaid had been so overcome by sneezes after working with the flowers that the housekeeper had sent her to her cot. That left only the haughty butler to man the tea trolley.

After he had set out the cups, bowed ever so slightly, and marched out of the room, Samantha remarked, "Be careful to taste the cream before adding it to your tea, Izzy. I've often thought old Carstairs's puss could turn it."

"Why do you put up with him?" Isabella asked, adding an extra sugar in lieu of the cream she was now reluctant to touch. "Can't you turn him off or retire him or something?"

"He was an inheritance from Zachary's father, I was made to understand, and is almost a fixture in the household," she replied. "I must admit, though, that the man fair makes my flesh crawl sometimes. He only tolerates me so that he can eavesdrop on my conversations and carry tales to Zachary after my every misstep. But enough talk of snoopy-snooty old Carstairs. Tell me more about your Robert."

So Isabella told Samantha of her trips to the Conduit

Street Glovers and her meetings with Robert. She began by expounding on the intricacies of proper glove-fitting (Samantha hid a yawn) and went on to explain that a proper fitting could easily take two hours or more.

"First, you see, they have to measure each finger. Robert measured my fingers," she admitted, a rosy blush stealing into her cheeks.

"Please, Izzy," Samantha cut in rudely, "all this measuring and fitting is just too much. I readily acknowledge the giddy adventures you had, having your hands held by this Robert for over two hours, but please, spare me my blushes and let us not drag out your story by going over all these lurid details."

Isabella pouted. After all, this was as close as she had ever come to romantic intrigue, and besides, it was *her* story. But she firmly suppressed her newborn flair for the dramatic, and was about to proceed, when Samantha interjected—for no good reason—that she had been bored to flinders at her first and only glove fitting, and had commissioned plaster models of her hands to be made and delivered to her own glover's for future reference.

"Sam," her sister said, in complete disgust, "you have no romance in your heart. Not a single drop."

"Never mind about me. Tell me more of this Robert," Samantha countered, dismissing a statement so ludicrous (especially after the decidedly romantic events of the previous evening) it was not worthy of rebuttal.

Sam learned that Robert (no known last name, an omission that bothered Samantha no end) lived above the glover shop with the owner, Jack Bratting, and Bratting's wife. The two men had served in the army together, and Jack offered Robert employment after their muster home to England. About his past, admitted Isabella, Robert was strangely reticent.

All that Samantha really knew, she had discovered almost immediately: that Isabella was in love with this Robert person and—if her sparkling eyes and heightened color were any indication—that she was ready to toss her bonnet over the windmill and marry the man.

A plan began to form in her mind.

There was nothing else for it and Samantha said so. "I shall have to meet this Robert for myself. As Mr. Smythe-Wright, I should have no problem striking up a conversation with the man at his place of business or the tavern he undoubtedly frequents after hours!"

"Oh, no," Isabella wailed, "not another one of your harum-scarum ideas. I forbid it! What if Royston were to get wind of it?"

Samantha shrugged unconcernedly. "So what, if Zachary finds out I wore breeches again? What of it? He's aware I've done it before, heaven knows. I'm not saying he'll *like* it above half, but he'll not kick up about it."

Isabella—not privileged to see the fingers Samantha had prudently crossed behind her back, said doubtfully, "I don't know, Sam. The Earl seems a bit—just a bit, mind you—*stuffy* to me."

Smiling at some secret reminiscences, Samantha blithely replied, "Zachary is *never* stuffy. On the contrary, he is the most easygoing, pleasant-natured man of my acquaintance. He is also forward-thinking and—and emancipated in his views. Oh, no, Izzy," she purred, "my Zachary is *never* stuffy."

"But going abroad in breeches is dangerous," persisted Isabella, to which Samantha replied succinctly, "Twaddle!"

Then Samantha had another thought. Her eyes narrowed as she asked pointedly, "Are you ashamed of Robert, Izzy? I hope he's not some dull stick, or knocker-faced, or such an effeminate twiddlepoop that you're afraid to let me meet him. Or," she pressed on, "is he some pretty-faced, smooth-talking fortune-hunter who's leading you on, bamming you with false stories and taking you royally to the fair with promises of marriage—but only *after* living with him for the weeks it would take to travel to Gretna?"

Isabella could not listen to another word. She jumped out of her chair and drew herself up in her most formidable, aggressive posture: shoulders back, chin high, chest out. "How *dare* you!" she shouted, incensed. "You do not wish for me to speak ill of the Earl, though all I said was that he seemed a bit stuffy. I did not cruelly malign him, as you did my Robert. In return I must ask you not to say another word—not another word—against my Robert. Is that clear, Samantha?"

Isabella was furious. Samantha was impressed sufficient to rise, cross to Isabella, and put her arms around the livid young woman. "What you're saying, sister, in plain language, is that I'm to shut up about your Robert. I agree: I was overstepping the bounds of sisterly candor." She stepped back a pace, lifted Isabella's drooping chin with her fingers, and said what she knew she had to say, "But he isn't *your* Robert yet, is he, sweets? Let me work on it, will you?"

Smiling through a haze of tears, Isabella launched herself at her sister and exclaimed, "I'm such a gudgeon, Sammy. Please forgive me!"

The bell rang then, signaling time to dress for dinner. The sisters roused Aunt Loretta and steered her towards the Ardsley carriage.

Isabella was eager to get home herself—as her appetite was back at last now that all her problems had been dumped in her sister's (she hoped) capable lap.

Of the three women, only Samantha (for nothing was known to have ever dulled Aunt Loretta's appetite) picked at her food that evening. Her mind was too preoccupied with other things to register any pangs of hunger.

Only later, in her husband's arms, was Samantha able to banish the vision of her sad-eyed sister from her mind. But once in those arms, it was a simple matter for Samantha to postpone further thoughts of Robert and Izzy until the morning.

She didn't get quite as early a start as she had hoped the next day—not because she had any difficulty getting out of the mansion, but simply because the "ancient" man she had married had reserves of stamina at which she could only marvel. He had kept her pleasantly (and almost constantly) occupied the night before until she was at last forced to plead fatigue. She had, shamefully, overslept.

Samantha thus felt more than a twinge or two of guilt as she let herself out into the mews and trotted off down the alley to hail a hackney to take her the scant mile to Conduit Street. Chary of confiding in anyone her whole life long (as most of the confidences she had to share were self-incriminating), she hesitated about telling Zachary of Isabella's dilemma and her own part in the situation, for fear he would disapprove—and for fear he would throw a rub in her way, thus letting Isabella down and depriving herself of an investigative lark that made her feel like a Bow Street runner on the trail of a case.

Soon she would get her first glimpse of the encroaching toad who dared to play fast and loose with her sister's affections.

The glove shop impressed her as soon as she saw it. A smallish establishment, tucked away as it was down one of the less favored (but still fashionable) streets near New Bond Street, it had an air of respectability about it that was echoed in its clean flagway, sparkling bow window, and tasteful display of wares.

She entered the shop and was stopped in her tracks by the sight of the young gentleman who had come to her aid at the Bartholomew Fair. He was standing now behind the counter, obviously waiting on customers.

Robert? She searched her memory. Yes, he *had* given his name as Robert when they exchanged introductions. Samantha had called herself Smythe-Wright on that occasion, so her scheme was still operable.

Robert saw Samantha at much the same time. He quickly smiled his recognition and waved a greeting before a rather large female and her two companions (daughters if their near-identical rotundness could be used as a guide) rudely called him back to attention.

In all it took a most tediously long and tension-filled hour before Madam's sausage-like fingers could be stuffed inside the fragile pigskin gloves she insisted were "just her size." As she waddled majestically out of the shop, with her daughters in tow, Samantha noticed that the woman's forearms were already becoming mottled as a result of her pigskin-restricted circulation.

Samantha approached Robert just as he was wiping the perspiration from his brow. He grinned and commented, "There she goes at long last: the sow and her two piglets, heading back to the trough. It's a pity, isn't it, how the need to be fashionable pushes people into wearing on their hands the hides of their own relatives. Ugh!"

What an odd fellow to be an assistant glover, Samantha thought. Not only is he too handsome by half—with that coal black hair and those magnificent, yet strangely sad, grey eyes—to be stuck away behind this counter, but he's got the arrogance of a lord, though he wisely keeps it hidden. He's too thin, and he could use a few weeks in the country to put the color back in his face, but nothing can take away from the fact that he is an extremely well-set-up young man.

"Robert," she ventured, as the young glover returned his stock to the shelf behind the counter, "I sought you out purposely to thank you again for your assistance when first we met. Now that my pockets have been, shall we say, *re-lined*, I would be honored if you'd be my guest at some local tavern of your choice, where we can share a bird and bottle and get to know one another better."

This improvisation on her plan—thought up, as it were, on the spot—proved believable, and when Jack Bratting came downstairs a few minutes later and heard the plan, he was quick to shoo Robert away, saying it was high time the young lad had a bit of relaxation.

Two plump birds and three bottles (largely consumed by Robert) later, Samantha had learned no more about her companion's background than she had known before. But she had, by way of observation and a quick ear, learned that Robert ate, drank, spoke, and thought like a gentleman—not a glover.

It was only when Samantha brought Isabella's name into the conversation—neatly done by saying he was staying with the Ardsleys, as they were old family friends—that Robert's composure suffered a shock.

From then on until she could shut him up over an hour later, Samantha was subjected to a nonstop recital of Isabella's saintly qualities and declarations of her unrivaled beauty. This brought on first a desire to giggle, and eventually made Samantha want to gag. Greater love hath no sister than that she be forced to listen to such a cataloguing of her sibling's virtues—while refraining from sharing a few choice reminiscences of some of that same sister's less than shining hours.

"So it sits serious with you, does it, Robert?" she broke in at last, forestalling yet another maudlin antidote highlighting Isabella's angelic character.

Robert slumped in his chair, all the stuffing having suddenly gone out of him. "Isabella is worthy of only my highest regard," he intoned heavily. "She is quite above my touch, you know, but I would not feel it hopeless if I could but believe she felt even the smallest *tendre* towards me."

Samantha was quick to pick up on Robert's casual use of French, and she was more confused than ever about this paradox of a man who was half gentleman, half clerk.

Robert had been silently inspecting the tabletop, as if for flaws, for some minutes. Samantha waited patiently for him to go on before he suddenly slammed his fist down on the wood—scattering the cutlery and rocking their half-empty bottles—and declared vehemently, "There is nothing else for it. I cannot ask her father for her hand. I shall have to give her up. There can be no future for a poor glover and a delicately-nurtured female deserving of nothing less than the best life has to offer." He hung his head and muttered dramatically, "I have said it all. I cannot trust myself to say more."

My gracious, Samantha thought—perhaps meanly—either all hot-blooded young men become perfect fools when they fall in love, or Robert's manners and airs come from a background in the theatre. Aloud she only said, "Robert, I beg you not to be such an ape. Giving Isabella up would be gallant to the point of idiocy. You'd be heartbroken and Izzy—I mean, Isabella—would probably take it into her head to go into a sad decline. No," she concluded firmly, "your answer lies elsewhere. As an opener, I suggest you be more forthcoming about your past, or the gel's father won't even give you the time of day."

"I'm nobody, from nowhere, and that's all there is to that," Robert groaned fatalistically. "It's hopeless."

Three hours and another bottle later (her companion still doing the imbibing, as Samantha had learned her lesson and was not one to make the same mistake twice), Robert had agreed to the loan of ten pounds—enough to buy himself a suit of clothes and the other necessaries he would need if he were to present himself to Sir Stephen with any hope of being heard.

Just as they were parting, Robert asked if Sam had any "special feelings" for Isabella himself, having had the privilege of knowing her almost since the cradle. "How could you know her and not love her?" he reasoned, with all the blindness of a man deep under Cupid's spell.

"Isabella and I grew up together—almost as brother and sister, you could say. I love her, of course I do, but I love her as a sister," Samantha said, tongue-in-cheek.

"Ah," smiled Robert, "like a sister. And that is why you are helping us. I understand perfectly now."

Samantha patted Robert on the shoulder, rose to leave, and—as she gave her hat a securing tap—retorted smoothly, "Robert, old sport, you don't perceive the half of it!"

They agreed to meet the following week to talk again, and Samantha stepped out into the waning sunlight and flagged down a hackney. She did not see Carstairs as he watched from the flagway in front of the chandler's shop, where he had just completed an errand for the housekeeper.

Instead, Samantha was concentrating on what she had learned that afternoon. One: Jack Bratting treated his employee like a friend. No, more than a friend: he acted as if he were slightly in awe of Robert. Two: Robert was honestly and sincerely in love with Isabella, as she was certain Isabella was in love with him. Three: much as she liked him, Samantha would feel uneasy about lending herself to their purpose unless Robert revealed more of his past. And Four: the pair had about as much chance of gaining Sir Stephen's blessing as did the hulking Prince Regent of ever again looking down to see what color stockings he had on!

She sobered then, and pondered once more the advisability of sharing her problem with Zachary. After a short tussle with her conscience, she decided to postpone her decision for a few days. Perhaps longer.

It can't be but wondered if she would have changed her mind had she seen the smirking face of Carstairs as he hurried back to Portman Square—there to seek an immediate audience with his employer.

Chapter Sixteen

ZACHARY ST. JOHN was just splashing some of the Royston cellar's best wine into a crystal-stemmed glass, in anticipation of spending a pleasant hour before his fire reflecting on his new-found domestic happiness, when the study door opened and Carstairs—hat still in hand—asked permission to enter and have a few words with his lordship "on a matter of some delicacy."

St. John nodded his head in the affirmative, without even attempting to hide his displeasure at being disturbed. Dreadful pest of a man, he thought idly: I cannot fathom why I continue to tolerate his presence in the household.

As the butler postured and cleared his throat, the Earl stared up at him impassively. When the silence became intolerable, he at last prompted, "Well, man, get on with it. You have something of great import to say to me, else why would you dare to disturb me in the privacy of my study. If you have had second thoughts, just say so, and ask my permission to retire. Shortly I must go and dress, as her ladyship will soon be returning."

Mention of the Countess seemed to bring Carstairs to life (if the slight smile and the raising of two thin eyebrows could be said to be animating) and, sneering condescension and malicious pity evident in his voice, he told his sordid little story.

"It was in Conduit Street that I observed her, my lord, your wife (he seemed to have an aversion to connecting Samantha with her new title) and the young man. I am sure it was she. Having seen her parading about in breeches before, there can be no doubt in my mind of her identity, and she and the gentleman were—I wish I could spare you this, my lord—they were coming out of a public tavern, *arm in arm!*"

Zachary was all attention now, although he took pains to hide this from his smug servant. "Proceed," he intoned placidly, as Carstairs paused, most probably for effect.

"Yes, my lord," the butler said, slightly taken aback by St. John's seeming unconcern.

"I could not see her companion's face, as they separated and the man went off in the other direction—away from where I was standing, for if you understand my position was somewhat up the block and across the street."

St. John rolled his eyes. "Yes, Carstairs, I think you can be assured that I have sufficient imagination as to picture the scene you describe. Continue."

But Carstairs was slowly coming to the realization that, instead of taking this information in the spirit in which it was offered—the disclosure of the tawdry activities of the Earl's wife as related to him by a reluctant but loyal servant, who felt it to be in his lordship's best interests to have the lady's indiscretions brought to his notice—the Earl was looking at him with more than faint distaste.

His lordship must understand that he was not tattletelling for any hope of personal gain. Well, perhaps that was stretching the point a little. Carstairs did not, it was true, entertain any thought of personal reward—in a monetary sense, that is. However, if his lordship was moved to discipline his outlandish wife—or even, in time perhaps, to shed himself of the dratted woman entirely—the servant would not be able to find it in his heart to be saddened.

But the Earl must be made to realize the enormity of his wife's crimes. To this end, the servant went on to expound at some length on the unacceptable behavior of Lady Royston, starting with her first footstep across the threshold on their return from their honeymoon. He went on, in his audacity, to conjecture that Samantha's meeting with the shabbily-dressed young man that day was in the nature of continuing a clandestine romance that had been the cause of all of Samantha's deplorable excursions in masculine dress. When at last his impassioned speech trailed off in mutterings about the Royston good name and warnings of what the dowager might think, the Earl rose from his chair and, with his hands clasped behind his back, proceeded to pace about the room.

Eventually he halted in front of the butler and said, "Is it not strange, Carstairs, that for the last ten minutes I have listened as you unburdened yourself of your dislike of my wife? Don't try to deny it, sir," he shot, as the butler began to protest. "As you were speaking, I tried racking my brain to come up with a single instance when my wife—*her ladyship* to you, my man—ever spoke an ill word of you. I could not do so. Not a one."

Carstairs wanted to say something—it was clear by the way he opened his mouth—but then he seemed to think better of it and shut it again.

It made no matter in any event, as Royston had already made up his mind. "You are dismissed, Carstairs," he told the man.

"You mean, my lord, I may return to my duties?" Carstairs offered hopefully.

"Meaning you are *dismissed*, sir! See my secretary about your wages and a reference," the Earl returned wearily, before turning his back on the servant and taking up his wineglass.

"Well, that's that," he told himself, as he raised his glass in a mock salute. "Any hope I harbored that Samantha would heed any of my lectures on tramping about London on her own have been thoroughly scotched. I may as well have saved my breath."

He settled himself in his armchair and gave himself over to contemplation of his wife's behavior. True, she was a hoyden—but a harmless hoyden. Or at least, she had been until now. The introduction of a young man to her travels put, if he chose to lend credence to his former butler's opinion, a sinister light on her activities.

Had she sought out a younger man—a man more open in his manner, who would give his heart unstintingly instead of only taking what was offered him while still holding a part of himself back from a relationship that could prove personally painful?

Ah, pride! It was his besetting sin. Silently he acknowledged that there had been, even in their passion, a certain want of openness on his part. Mayhap it was time he bared his soul to his young wife: admitted once and for all that he was her slave unto eternity. Hadn't she done as much when she told him she loved him?

But she was so young, so inexperienced. How could she, a child actually, know for certain that what she felt for her husband was the very real, lasting love that he so craved from her?

He couldn't bear it if he confessed his love, only to have her repudiate it for some younger man who better fitted her immature image of true love. He banged his fist down on the table. Pride! His own damn fool pride. He was too afraid of losing face to give voice to his feelings.

"Oh, Sam," he moaned aloud. "You are an imp sent specially to torment me. When first we met I saw you as a diversion, a plaything. Who is whose puppet now, eh? Damn it!" he exploded, coming to himself with a start. "I was never any woman's tame cat, and I'll not start now."

Regardless of this show of independence, Zachary was lost in a brown study when Samantha entered the room some time later. She had shed her breeches and donned a fetching blue shot-silk gown whose daring neckline showed the Royston diamonds to great advantage.

She knew she was in looks tonight, her flushed cheeks the result of guilt at her deceit of the afternoon. But Royston wasn't to know that, was he, so she could not understand her uneasiness in his presence. Covering her nervousness with a show of bravado, she called out, "What ho, husband? Why are you hiding away in here alone? I had the devil's own time finding you, with the halls full of wandering footmen and Carstairs nowhere in sight."

The Earl roused himself sufficiently to appreciate his wife's dazzling appearance, and rose to kiss her outstretched fingertips. "Carstairs is gone, pet. I dismissed him," he told her, quite without emotion.

Samantha frowned for a moment, then said the very last thing the Earl expected. "Old Carstairs has been rousted, has he? I wonder if he took the mice with him."

"Mice? What mice, dearest?" the Earl asked, his mind finally registering that Samantha had never been very enchanted with the Royston family butler.

Instantly regretting her verbal slip, Samantha threaded

her arm through Zachary's and deftly changed the subject. "Look at my discovery, Zachary," she exclaimed, shoving a tiny enameled-gold box in his face. "I have decided to set a new style. I am going to start taking *snuff!* Yes, yes," she nodded, as St. John began to speak, "I know ladies have been taking snuff since before I was born. But only *some* women, Zachary. The practice has never become that widespread. By the time I am done—my collection of boxes and I and my dyed-and-scented snuff, that is—there shan't be a female in town not sniffing and sneezing in imitation of me."

St. John allowed his doubts of the afternoon to recede to the back of his mind, and decided to enjoy his wife while he yet had the right. "And you really think you wield that much control over Society? Your arrogance, my sweet, near overwhelms me—not to mention that your manners, if you really intend to go public with this distasteful habit, are deplorable."

Samantha made a face. "Oh, really, sir? And you, on the other hand, are the complete nobleman?" With a swish of her skirts, she turned and seated herself with a flourish to sit glaring up at him.

Seeing the militant gleam in her eye, Zachary decided that—after his travails of the afternoon, brought on by his wife's misbehavior—he was to be excused if he had himself a little sport at her expense and teased, "Has London's *première* Original and style-setter *extraordinaire* then, in her capriciousness, discarded parasols?"

Samantha arranged her skirts with some care. "La, yes, my lord," she cooed, playing her role of society queen to the hilt. "I have, in fact, become quite bored with the contraptions. All that putting up and taking down—quite fatiguing, I vow," she sighed, only to spoil her performance by ending with a giggle, "Can you just picture all the ladies' maids parading mornings in Green Park, with their mistresses' discarded lace parasols shading their self-satisfied noses!"

St. John could not keep a straight face at this thought, and as he laughed, Samantha quipped, "There, Master Grump! I have lightened your mood. Now," she prodded, patting the space beside her, "since I have once again performed the task for which I was hired—that of entertaining you—I demand you show your appreciation by sitting with me and giving me some little instruction in the proper taking of snuff."

There followed a lesson on the proper grip (one-handed, as per Beau Brummel's own technique), pinching, and sniffing of snuff. After observing her husband for some minutes, Samantha felt herself ready to give it a try—an attempt that ended with her face turning beet-red, her eyes watering profusely, and her nose twitching uncontrollably until she gave out with a resounding sneeze that shook the ostrich plumes atop her head.

A prudent man would have refrained from laughter at his wife's discomfiture. Zachary St. John, however, threw back his head and roared, a tactical error he paid for immediately as Samantha held up the open snuffbox and, with one breath, succeeded in blowing up a huge cloud of the stuff that settled all over Zachary's head and shoulders.

One look at him—sitting there, looking like a real-to-life snowman—was enough to instill Samantha with a belated sense of self-preservation, and she quickly ran from the room, sure Zachary was hard on her heels. He would have been, too, had he not been otherwise occupied—doubled up as he was in a paroxysm of sneezing.

Samantha studiously avoided being alone with St. John that evening at the dinner party they attended with Isabella and Aunt Loretta. But she knew his revenge, when it came, would not be too unpleasant. He had, after all, been winking at her across the table all evening—as she strove unsuccessfully to keep a suitably solemn expression on her face while Lord Holland recited his agonies with the gout in great detail.

It was only after the ladies retired, leaving the gentlemen to their port and cigars, that Isabella could pigeonhole Samantha and pump her about her meeting with Robert.

Her sister's first impulse—to roast Isabella a bit about her glover swain—was stifled by the pair of wide-blue eyes gazing at her, full of trust and hope. "Marry him," Samantha found herself blurting out. "Elope with Robert just as soon as you are able and leave the consequences to me."

"Marry him!" Isabella squeaked loudly, causing Aunt Loretta to look over at her nieces and lament yet again Samantha's regrettable influence on her elder sister. Really, raising her voice so shrilly while in company! What had the girl said? Marry? Who was to be married? Aunt Loretta drew her shawl more securely about her shoulders and shrugged carelessly. Her meal had left her too comfortably drowsy to encourage heavy thinking, which was not an easy task for her at the best of times.

Isabella, hand clasped to her mouth, nervously cast her eyes about the room to see if anyone else had heard her and, satisfied they had not, whispered hoarsely to Samantha, "*Marry him,* Sammy? How can you be so cruel? You know it is impossible."

Samantha took our her snuffbox and sniffed a prudently dainty pinch before answering blightingly, "Don't be so missish, Izzy. By the time I left Robert today, he had all but screwed himself up to the sticking point. But on rethinking the matter, I believe it best we bypass asking Papa's blessing and present him with an accomplished fact. Robert does really love you, you know. He's quite soppy about you, as a matter of fact. I could hardly keep a straight face at some of his outrageous avowals of your perfection."

Isabella blushed furiously. "Th-that is all very well, Sammy. But to *elope*! My head whirls at the thought."

The snuffbox snapped closed with a click. "Izzy," her sister warned, "if you are sincere, you must prove it to Robert. If you cannot make the least push—show you are willing to dare all for love, as it were—I may as well put an end to this foolishness and tell Papa what you are about. After all, it will save Robert further hurt if you are merely toying with his affections, with no real intention of marrying him."

As was to be expected, Isabella began to sniffle as Samantha's bluntness overset her fragile sensibilities. "I don't know if I am on my head or on my heels. I love Robert, but to *elope*—it is all so frightening. It is not that I am so hen-hearted that I hesitate. It is Robert I am worried about. How happy will he be if Papa refuses to know him?"

Unbeknownst to either of the earnestly conversing plotters, the men had entered the room. Zachary was even then moving to within earshot.

"Never fear for that," he heard Samantha aver confidently. "As a Countess, I wield no inconsiderable weight in Society. Once he is seen with me, he will be accepted. And if the thought of money worries you, Royston is so deep in the pocket that he'll never miss any funds I may choose to grant Robert until he can set himself up in some enterprise of his own."

What the deuce is the chit talking about? St. John wondered to himself. And who the hell was Robert? He edged closer and Samantha obligingly enlightened him.

"Robert may only be an assistant glover in a small shop on Conduit Street, but he is handsome enough to be a by-blow of a prince of the blood. With those haunting grey eyes and that coal-black hair, I vow Isabella, I can see why . . ." The rest of Samantha's words were drowned out by Lady Harold's shriek of alarm as her trailing shawl fell victim to a hot ember from the fire, and the entire company laughed uproariously as Lord Harold stomped the blaze down with all the fervor of St. Patrick trampling down snakes.

But Royston had heard enough to put him in a deep melancholy for the rest of the evening—indeed, for the remainder of the week.

Samantha, in her turn, was at first angered, then dismayed by Zachary's seeming withdrawal of his affections. Not that he turned her from his bed. On the contrary, his lovemaking became even more intense, almost desperate, in fact. It was in their daytime relationship that she sensed him watching her covertly. Yet when she spoke to him, he did not always respond, as if his mind were miles away and concentrating on some weighty dilemma.

Now Samantha had two problems: Zachary's odd mood and Isabella's elopement, for she had finally seen things Samantha's way. Not to be mistaken for a person who readily succumbed to difficulty, she decided to get this business of Isabella's and Robert behind her, leaving her mind free to devote all her energies to improving St. John's humor.

So thinking, she made several forays to Ardsley House and Conduit Street in the next week, gradually becoming aware that she was being followed each time she set foot outside Portman Square in the guise of Samuel Smythe-Wright. Perhaps Zachary was still nervous about her "little adventures" and—knowing it to be the height of folly to believe she had foregone her excursions at his request—he had decided to lend her the protection of one of his servants.

She was partially correct. St. John did have Samantha's well-being in mind, but he had an ulterior motive as well. He wanted to ascertain the identity of the unknown Robert who had somehow placed his wife in his debt, to the point that she would set up clandestine meetings with the man.

On the day Isabella and Robert had chosen for the elopement, Samantha left Portman Square as quietly as possible and then, fighting down serious qualms as to her actions, proceeded to lead Zachary's man a merry chase until at last she was sure she had lost him. She then doubled back to meet Isabella and her abigail in the park.

Once the young maid was sent off on some trumped-up errand, the two conspirators hailed a hackney that deposited them in Conduit Street.

Within moments of entering the glove shop, Robert whisked the pair of them up the stairs and was even then sitting close beside Isabella on the small threadbare Bratting settee—fondling her hand as she gazed adoringly up into his face, her eyes shining like carriage lamps.

Tearing his gaze reluctantly away from his beloved, he exclaimed, "Samuel, you are a genius!" to which Samantha waved a hand dismissively and returned modestly, "Pooh! I'm nothing of the sort."

"Too right," came a voice from the other room, before Jack Bratting joined the little group.

"Robert, old friend, your Miss Isabella may be a fine lady, and your Mr. Smythe-Wright a great gun, but I see naught but disaster comin' from this day's work." Robert's friend and employer, a right dapper-looking older man, then shook his head sorrowfully and added, "And you not even sure you are free to wed the lass at all."

Isabella gasped and looked fearfully at Robert, who quickly protested, "I would know that, Jack. I would *sense* it, I'm sure of it!" and then set himself to comforting his suddenly tearful sweetheart.

Samantha looked about the room, taking in its shabby furnishings: the cooing lovebirds on the settee, and the glover—who was just now glowering at her—and could not help but feel uneasy. Perhaps she should have talked to Zachary before she took the action so firmly into her own hands.

While Samantha was pacing the small room, nervously chewing her lower lip, Zachary St. John was closeted with his spy, Rooker—a maggoty-looking fellow but (to St. John's mind) a necessary evil, employed as he was to keep the Earl abreast of Samantha's activities and to protect her from herself, if need be.

"Tried to gimme the slip, her did, yer worship, but Oi weren't buying it, ya ken," said the redoubtable Rooker with a gape-mouthed grin. "Oi jist doubled back to Conduit nice and tight, figgerin' her'd show up there by the by. Her always do, and sure 'nough, Oi seen 'em—her and that sis of hers a-sneakin' in the glover's shop." Rooker laughed. "Rumbled their lay proper, Oi did, them bein' amateurs an' all. Then Oi hot-footed it back 'ere, 'cause sure as check they's up ta somethin'. Wot do Oi do now, yer worship?"

Indeed, Royston thought. What do we do now? "I've not the foggiest idea, my good man," he drawled, as he tossed a coin in Rooker's direction. "But whatever it is, I'll take it from here myself. Good job, man. I thank you."

Rooker bit the coin—from habit only, for he knew he could trust this gentry cove—and hinted helpfully, "Best keep yer peepers open and yer fives at the ready, guv'nor. Her's a slippery piece of goods, beggin' yer worship's pardon."

Once Rooker was shown out (the servants' entrance of course, the successor to Carstairs being no less high in the instep when it came to matters of protocol), Royston sat himself down in order to do some serious thinking.

He trusted Samantha. Deep down inside, he knew she would never go behind his back with another man. No, if she were to fall in love with someone else she would come to Zachary directly and confront him with her dilemma. She would trust him to help her seek a suitable solution. Wouldn't she?

Yet her recent wanderings about town, if Rooker was to be believed, were not the aimless rambles she had indulged in during the past. These outings all had the same destination—the Conduit Street glover's shop or the tavern two doors down the street. Rooker said the customers in the shop varied, and Samantha hadn't been seen speaking to anyone in particular. So who was she meeting in the glover's shop?

Just a minute! Royston sat bolt upright as he remembered an old joke he had heard at his club. It seemed there was this laborer working at a building site, or so the story went. Each night the man was seen leaving his job, pushing a wheelbarrow full of debris before him. The foreman checked through the debris to see if the laborer was concealing stolen building materials or tools, but never found any evidence of the laborer's guilt. It took the foreman two weeks to realize that the laborer was stealing *wheelbarrows.*

Of course! Samantha was not meeting someone at the glover's shop. Her business was with the glover himself. Royston already knew Samantha had struck up an acquaintance with Robert, the assistant at the shop, but he had thought she had done so only to secure the fellow's help in arranging her secret meetings.

St. John gave himself a punishing slap on the forehead. How could he have been so dense? Talk about not seeing the forest for the trees! The unknown Lothario was none other than the assistant glover himself!

He jumped up, ready to dash out to meet with the slimy creature who dared toy with his wife's tender heart—for he was certain the man had also enlisted Samantha's sympathies and aid in some wild scheme or other by dint of a sad tale of woe—before sitting back down with a thump when he remembered Isabella had accompanied Samantha to the shop.

What on earth did Izzy (he did not for the moment realize he had slipped into Samantha's deplorable habit of gifting all and sundry with less than edifying nicknames) have to do with anything? Could *she* be the reason behind all this intrigue?

St. John sniffed at that thought disdainfully. Isabella guilty of deception? It was too ridiculous to believe. The girl hadn't the wit, not to mention the bottom, for it. No, it had to be something concerning Samantha.

In the end, Royston found himself astride his horse and heading purposefully toward Conduit Street, with full intentions of putting an end to Samantha's loose-screw adventure, shadowy notions of blowing a hole in the assistant glover, or—since he had neglected to bring a firearm with him—hitting him on and about the head and shoulders repeatedly. Belatedly, it occurred to him that he still, for all his serious thinking, had not the haziest notion of what he was about to discover.

When the flimsy door at the head of the stairs above the glover's shop burst in noisily, the reactions of the people already in the room were as diverse as the people themselves.

"Heyday! What's this?" shouted a startled Jack Bratting as his wife shrieked in alarm.

Samantha, who had expected to see her father (if she had been expecting anyone at all, which in truth, she had not), could only stare at her redfaced husband in stupefaction.

Meanwhile, Isabella—who had a healthy respect for her brother-in-law's consequence already—wailed, "Oh, Gemini," before burying her head in Robert's shoulder.

Robert—who had felt uneasy about the whole enterprise from the beginning, but had beaten down his doubts in his desire to marry the woman he loved—jumped up stiffly to place himself between Isabella and her would-be rescuer. He struck a "you'll have to go through me to get to her" pose, and closed his eyes so as not to flinch when his attacker took the first swing at his defiantly stuck-out chin.

The expected blow did not come. After stopping to take in the scene before him and seek out the likeliest target for his assault, St. John's eyes seemed to start from his head as the blood drained quickly from his face.

Staggering over to grab at the back of a nearby chair—his heart at first shocked into missing a beat, only to start in pounding as if it would burst within his chest—St. John rasped hoarsely, "Oh, my God! *Robin!*"

Chapter Seventeen

AS A DRAMATIC ENTRANCE, Zachary's arrival lacked nothing but a fanfare of trumpets to herald his advent into the room. But from that point on, the action degenerated into a comic farce.

While Jack Bratting blustered and his wife shrieked in alarm, Robert opened his eyes and stared blankly at St. John for a moment, then brought both hands to his head as if he were in some sort of pain. That done, he succeeded in unnerving everyone in the room by sinking quietly to the floor. Isabella immediately dropped to her knees beside him, calling to her sister hysterically, "Sammy, help me! I think he's dead!"

But Samantha was otherwise occupied just then, her concern for Zachary being uppermost on her list of priorities. She allowed herself only a moment to judge Robert to be in no great danger before deftly removing some wilting flowers from a nearby vase, dumping its liquid contents full down over the unfortunate youth's inert form (all the while admonishing Isabella to stop carrying on like a "brainless ninny"), and then racing hotfoot across the room to her husband's side.

"Zachary, my dearest," she begged fearfully. "Speak to me, please. Tell me you are all right!"

Indeed, Royston was fast recovering his composure. The shock of seeing his supposedly dead brother, Robin, had almost been too much even for him. But he was definitely too overjoyed at his discovery to indulge his astonishment overlong. Rising from the chair his suddenly weak knees had required him to seek, he hauled Samantha into his arms and gave her a resounding kiss on the lips—having seemingly decided to give her credit for finding Robin—

and she wisely refrained from disabusng him of the idea just yet.

"My own sweet angel, how ever did you manage this miracle? I never dreamed, when I heard you were seeing some young man, that you were—but never mind, that is all beside the point. To give me back my brother—why, it's like, it's like giving me back a part of myself that I thought to be forever denied me." After whirling his wife about in a circle until they both were in danger of falling, he gave vent to a ear-splitting shout of unbridled joy and then stopped in his tracks to reward Samantha with yet another impassioned kiss.

It was probably a combination of both the dousing he had suffered at Samantha's hands and the noise of Zachary's warlike cry (that could no more be blocked out than could be the thundering roar of charging cavalry) that roused Robert. But the sight that greeted his bemused eyes nearly sent him posthaste into another faint.

The amnesia that had plagued his mind for over a year, only to be suddenly stripped away like so many cobwebs by the shock of seeing his brother again, was replaced by a confusion of another sort—brought on by the sight of this same brother soundly, and very conspicuously, *kissing* Mr. Samuel Smythe-Wright.

The strength of character that had seen Robert—now once again Robin—through the rigors of a terrible war remained undaunted, allowing him to deal calmly (for the moment, at least) with his elation at finally discovering his true identity. He merely patted Isabella's hand soothingly before drawling in amusement from his place on the floor. "I say, brother mine, have the manners of the *ton* so changed in my absence that a hearty handshake is no longer the accepted method of showing thanks to a man for favors rendered?"

Brought back to his senses by the sound of his brother's voice, Zachary abruptly released Samantha, nearly sending the girl sprawling as he deserted her and put out an eager hand to Robin to pull him to his feet. The brothers looked at each other for a long moment, and then—grinning widely like two mindless idiots—they fell to embracing each other with great emotion and much enthusiastic back-slapping.

Samantha rushed over to Isabella and, in her exuberance, hugged her sister fiercely to her chest. "Isn't it above all things wonderful, Izzy? Robert isn't a nobody without a name or background. He is *Robin*, Zachary's brother, who was lost in the war!" She then stepped back a pace, retaining a hold on her sister's shoulders and giving her an inquiring shake. "Izzy? Don't you think it's wonderful? *Say something* for goodness sake! You look like a statue!"

Isabella looked up into her sister's dancing green eyes and, plainly bewildered, asked timidly, "Does this mean he is not married?"

Samantha shouted with laughter, "Oh, you poor, poor puss. You come with me." So saying, she grabbed her sister's hand and pulled her over to Robin, who was only just then disengaging himself from Zachary's affectionate grasp. Bowing deeply from the waist, Samantha addressed the young man. "Please, my lord, if I might intrude a moment on your reunion. I would like, you see, to present to you a most eligible young lady. Miss Isabella Marie Ardsley, may I introduce to you Robin St. John, Viscount Royston, a fine young man of impeccable reputation. Doubtless I have overlooked his several prestigious middle names and sundry lesser titles, but no matter, for these are but trifling things, don't you agree, Miss Ardsley?" Her facetious observance of the proprieties completed to her satisfaction, Samantha gave Isabella a discreet shove in Robin's direction and retreated to watch—grinning like the village idiot—as the pair fell into each other's arms.

Just how long Zachary and Samantha may have been privileged to view unnoticed the personal exchange of affection they were witnessing was not to be discovered, as Jack Bratting—thoroughly confused by all the rare goings-on in his front parlor—had at last regained his voice, if not his former bluster.

"Pardon me, my lord," he began meekly, tugging timidly on St. John's coat sleeve, "but am I to believe you know our Robert?" As a question it was not indicative of any great mental profundity, but it served to divert the

Earl's attention from his heretofore near-to-cannibalistic devouring of his brother by means of his sparkling black eyes.

Turning to grab up the glover's hand and pump it to within an inch of breaking all the poor man's fingers with his fervant two-handed grip, Royston delivered himself of a speech of thanks that left no doubt in Jack Bratting's mind that indeed Robert had at long last found his family.

A scant half-hour later, the little group was back in Portman Square, leaving behind a dazed Jack Bratting and his happily tearful wife, still overwhelmed by Royston's promise of a grand new glover shop of their very own—and in Bond Street, no less. Had the man been the grasping sort, he could conceivably have demanded and received half the Royston fortune, what with Zachary being so beside himself with gratitude. But then, if the man had been of a mercenary bent, he would never have had befriended the injured, penniless Robert in the first place, would he?

While Zachary was in his study—hastily scribbling off a note telling his grandmother of Robin's miraculous reappearance, to be dispatched immediately to her in Richmond—Samantha, Isabella, and Robin were getting reacquainted in the main salon. They had at last exhausted the subject of Samantha's alter ego, Samuel, and had moved on to other subjects.

"You know," Robin was saying, gazing about the familiar room with a look of some awe on his face, "I have been troubled with vague remembrances of silly things like platters of pork chops for breakfast and the feel of silken sheets on my bed. But the reality of what my life was before last year fair bids to overwhelm me. I always knew I was *somebody*, perhaps even a person of some means, but this—" He spread his arms wide to encompass the tastefully decorated room. "This is almost *too much!*"

He turned in his place beside Isabella on the satin sofa, and lifting her hand to his lips—told her, "When we are married you shall set a new style by never, *ever* being seen in any of those blasted gloves I have been forced to fit this last three months and more, since Jack agreed I was well enough to help out in the shop. What a painful penance those fittings are, for both customer and glover."

"But only think on it a moment, my dear," Isabella replied, feeling at ease again with her beloved. "If I were to succeed in turning the ladies of London against gloves, your friend Mr. Bratting would suffer greatly by their desertion. That would be a fine way of thanking him for all he has done for us."

Robin took possession of Isabella's other hand and pressed kisses in both her palms before bowing to this feminine logic. "Then I shall have to content myself with being the only husband of the *ton* to personally fit his wife with each and every pair of gloves she owns. No one else, my pet, must be allowed such intimacy with these beautiful fingers."

Watching this interchange from her position in a nearby armchair, seated as she was at her ease and still dressed in her inappropriate attire—with her comfortably relaxed posture and sprawling lower limbs showing a picture that could be titled "The Young Buck At His Leisure"—Samantha quipped to Zachary as he rejoined them, "Do come and sit down, dearest. This is as good as a play. Such a delighful pair of cockleheads you are apt never to see again."

"Stow it, brat," Zachary admonished her cordially. "Robin," he then went on in a more serious tone, "I have just now sent off a message to our grandmother, apprising her of the return of the prodigal and requesting she meet us at my estate in Kent in two day's time. If we are to beat the dear dragon to the country—as this place, despite its size, is not nearly large enough to house both her and me without war breaking out—I suggest we make ourselves ready to travel by tomorrow morning, if you feel yourself up to the journey."

As Robin nodded his agreement to this plan, without bothering to disclaim Zachary's allusion to the less than wonderful relationship between his brother and the dowager, Zachary went on, "Naturally, we will ask Sir Stephen's permission to take Isabella with us to the country, as I can see by that death-grip you now have on her hands that you are not likely to let her out of your sight any time soon."

"Time has not dulled your intelligence, brother," Robin agreed happily, as Isabella flushed to the roots of her hair—an occurrence that caused Samantha no end of amusement.

"Do strive to control yourself, Samantha," her husband warned, as her laughter brought her back to his attention. He could not help but frown at her outrageous attire, even if it did mean admitting to himself just how greatly he resented anyone else (including his own brother) being privileged to glimpse his wife's long, shapely limbs parading about in skin-tight breeches. "And sit up straight, if you please," he almost growled, in his agitation. "At times I believe you to be ramshackle past reclaim. Parading about town as Samuel Smythe-Wright was bad enough, but to instigate an elopement—well, it is at times inconceivable to me to understand the workings of your mind." Adding that last little bit was merely a ploy to keep Robin from guessing the true, if petty, reason for his brother's outburst.

Yet it was Isabella who was moved to protest. "I was also part of the plot, Zachary," she was emboldened to say.

St. John readily accepted that this was true, but added that she never would have contemplated it if not for the urgings of her sister and that, by and large, he had found Isabella to be a "most sensible puss."

Neither was this statement to be left unchallenged. "Meaning," interpolated Samantha, "in your backhanded way, that I am not?"

St. John turned to face his wife and favored her with a bow. "If you wish, m'dear," he returned affably.

Isabella, feeling brave as long as Robert—she still could not think of him as Robin—was close by, was again moved to speech. "I think that is excessivly shabby of you, seeing as how it has all worked out so famously." She clapped her hands to her mouth as she belatedly realized she had just dared to challenge "the Devil" himself—and in his own house! "Oh, dear me!" she exclaimed. "I'm so dreadfully sorry, my lord."

"In a pig's eye you are, Isabella," Robin laughed. "Don't

try to wrap it up in clean linen. The man's behavior is indeed—excessively shabby, did you say? How mild that sounds! A royal pain is what he's being, that's more like it. Though I must say," he added reflectively, "I doubt if I myself could be brought to find enjoyment in the thought of *my* wife traipsing about, kicking up all sorts of larks while dressed as Samuel—I mean, Samantha—is now."

Isabella, her sisterly loyalty having flown in the face of wishing to be known as a woman who agreed with her man in everything he said—be it that the moon was made of green cheese or that her sister's behavior was indeed reprehensible—voiced her agreement with Robin.

Seeing that Isabella's defection had raised Samantha's hackles, Zachary—his mood again on the upswing—decided to have himself a bit of fun at her expense. "Quite so," he sighed with the air of one sorely used. "In fact, dear friends, my wife is the embodiment of far and away too many ills for me to contemplate them all without risk of my becoming emotionally overset."

Robin took a sip from his glass before saying, "I really must confess to being abominably slow, brother. Please enlighten me a bit if you will on a few, um, *minor* points. You speak as if Samantha's mode of dress and behavior both are no recent news to you, certainly not as recent as they are to me. If you are so disapproving, why have you not simply put a stop to her little escapades? You know, I believe that your wife—in the guise of one Samuel Smythe-Wright—and I have met fairly frequently in recent days. In the space of that time, she has at times spoken to me of her travels in London. Please, dear brother," he pleaded, in patently feigned worried tones, "*Please* tell me she has only conjured up these stories in her head. As I cannot imagine her actually doing all the things she told me she has done, I must inform you of another of your enchanting-but-naughty wife's failings: she tells some shocking rappers!"

One side of St. John's full mouth shot up in a rueful grin. "Unfortunately, my dear, *concerned* little brother, I can only plead guilty to your supposition that I, in my indulgence, have turned a blind eye toward Samantha's truancy until only recently. But I must disabuse you of harboring any doubts as to my wife's credibility. All that she has told you—and most probably much more that she has *not* mentioned, too alarming to contemplate—is all so lamentably true. I have been," he ended, with a splendid imitation of deep sorrow, "sorely, sorely used by this woman I have married. Pity me, brother—moderate, temperate man that you know me to be—for I am bewildered by such irresponsible actions as hers." His outrageous speech concluded entirely to his satisfaction, St. John repaired to the Adam fireplace to rest one arm negligently against the mantel and wait for Samantha's inevitable explosion of fury.

It would have come too, had not Robin intervened. "I do believe my head to be sufficiently free of concealing fog to recall a few less than laudable exploits committed by you in *your* grasstime, Zachary, old fellow. Let's see. There was that time when I was about ten, and you were sent down from school for firing blank cartridges at one of the proctors. Oh, yes, I remember that incident well. It was also while you were at home that you and some of your ragtag friends from the village went about changing all the inn signs, causing no end of confusion, as I recall."

Zachary stood away from the mantel. "Enough, Robin, enough," he cut in hastily, not liking at all the militant gleam that had come into Samantha's eyes.

But his protest fell on deaf ears, as Robin was not finished. "When you grew older and went up to town, you were still known to kick up a lark or two—or so Grandmama's cronies wrote her in their tattlemonging letters. I also remember hearing how you bought out some baker's entire stock and paraded down St. James' Street in broad daylight, pushing this huge cart before you and calling out, 'Buy my fresh loaves' at the top of your lungs. Oh, Grandmama squirmed for days after she heard about that one. And there was the year you took to wearing a nosegay of gilded oak-leaves on your lapel—oak-apples you had saved from the previous fall, I recollect, taking care not to wear them until they were out of season and nearly impossible to come by. As a gentleman known to be an arbiter of fashion, it was not long before half the young bucks in London were sporting oak-apple clusters—though to what lengths they went to procure them I shudder to contemplate. And what did you do then, my fine, conservative, temperate brother? You immediately stopped wearing your nosegays and made snide jokes about anyone who would wish to wear such an emblem on any day other than Oak-apple Day!"

It was plain to see that Robin was enjoying himself mightily now, basking in Isabella's open admiration and thrilled with Samantha's eager attention. "Tell me, Zachary: was it before or after the gilded oak-leaf incident that you and your fellows had that punch-up with the Charleys, the one that landed you all in the local guardhouse overnight?"

"Blister it, Robin!" St. John succeeded in breaking in at last. "Must you throw my past in my teeth?"

"Certainly not," Robin answered, seemingly much affronted. "My memory, total as it may again be, is really most adaptable—if that is what you wish. But first, Zachary, may I tell of the time you and three friends were tossed out of that brothel near Covent Garden for—"

"*Pas devant la enfant!*" Zachary warned—not in front of the child—meaning Samantha, of course, who would, were she ever to hear of them, no doubt fling the details of such an incident in his face at every opportunity.

St. John's plea came too late however—about five sins too late as a matter of fact.

Samantha having had time for a bit of reflection, was just then feeling more than a little out of countenance with her husband. Rising from her chair to stand at her full height, she confronted the Earl, her legs spread defiantly wide and her hands clenched into fists jammed down on her hips. "Not quite the perfect paragon of propriety yourself, eh, husband? Though I admit sins committed in your youth are only to be regarded as ancient history. And yet, after indulging in adventures of your own—far and away adventures more scandalous than my worst departures from the accepted feminine pursuits—you would deny me the very excitement you so obviously once craved yourself! Oh, that is very poor spirited of you, Royston."

Zachary, with Samantha's scowling face and dramatic stance totally wasted on him, smiled unrepentantly back at her.

This served only to make Samantha truly angry. "And worse—yes, everyone, the worst is yet to come—you did not even trust me to be discreet, or even honorable for that matter, if I read your interpretation of my visits to Conduit Street correctly. *You,*" and she said the word with magnificent contempt, "hired some lowly Benedict to dog my every step each time I set foot outside Portman Square. Oh, yes," she told him heatedly. "I saw your man following me. I allowed it for a time, I admit, but today I led him on a merry chase. I really believed I had lost him, but he was a tenacious little monster wasn't he, this man you set on me like a jailhouse guard."

Robin and Isabella were silent as their eyes shifted back and forth between Zachary and Samantha, like spectators following a batted shuttlecock. Robin was still prone to believe Samantha was feigning her anger, but Isabella knew better. She reached for Robin's hand and squeezed it hard.

Advancing on her husband and wagging her finger in his face, she accused, "Like some deity judging a lowly sinner, that's what you were as you came bursting through Jack Bratting's parlor door. Confess, Zachary. What wild scenes of debauchery did you have pictured in that great hoary head of yours? How low did you think I had sunk, husband? Speak to me, Zachary! Have you lost your tongue?"

Samantha was full to bursting with pent-up wrath, soon to explode completely, and St. John saw no choice but to reluctantly recognize that fact. More to the point, he had to agree she had a few valid arguments—not to mean she was *entirely* in the right of things—and his attempts at a bit of playful teasing *had* run afoul of Samantha's acutely probing mind.

Seemingly without wasting time on any detours along the way, she had gone straight to the heart of the matter: Zachary had not trusted her. It was lamentable, but there was nothing else for it. He would now have to take his punishment like a man; that is to say, he would feel inwardly guilty while outwardly admitting to nothing.

He looked to Isabella and Robin, cravenly seeking a clever way out of this hole he had so neatly dug for himself. But Isabella was nervously worrying her lower lip, and

Robin—the coward—was busily engaged in smoothing away a nonexistent crease on his coat-sleeve. No help was forthcoming from that timid pair, Royston told himself.

He looked again to Samantha, who now stood tapping one booted foot, her accusing finger still aimed at his nose. He searched his brain for a way to mollify her. Thinking it best to get over the heavy ground as lightly as he could, he smiled, chucked his wife playfully under her belligerently thrust-out chin, and whispered meaningfully, "Couldn't we settle this little misunderstanding later, pet? Perhaps in my chambers, *um*?"

Samantha bid Isabella a pleasant, well-mannered *adieu*, and bowed before Robin in her best Samuel Smythe-Wright way before quitting the room with a flourish—leaving in her wake a goggle-eyed sister, an openly amused brother-in-law, and a sadder-but-wiser husband still gingerly touching the livid red handprint blazoned on his left check.

"Pity I missed the ceremony, Zachary. Would that I could have known this Samantha of yours before she could be so mellowed by marital bliss," Robin remarked, his ready smile hovering about his lips. "What first drew you to her? Her beauty? Her dainty footwork on the dance floor? Surely not her dowry—you would not be so mercenary, not to mention blind to her more obvious attributes.

"Confess, brother, what was it about my sweet new sister—soon to be my sister twice over, if Isabella chooses to bestow her hand on this humble servant—that caused London's premiere bachelor to stick his head in parson's mousetrap?"

St. John sniffed. "It all seems so ridiculous now, but, with you gone—or so I supposed—I felt obliged to beget myself an heir. As Samantha's antics (I first saw her dressed as Mr. Smythe-Wright, you see) also served to amuse me, I felt I would get both an heir and a diverting companion who could banish some of my depressingly ever-present *ennui* by the simple expediency of marrying the child."

"That was a bit cold-blooded, even for you, Zachary," Robin admonished.

St. John's only answer was an acknowledging grimace, an admission of fault that, coming from him, was on a par with anyone else donning sackcloth and ashes and parading through the streets ringing a bell in repentance. That made it twice in one day that St. John had admitted to being fallible: once only to himself, and now publicly to his brother (if a grimace can be called a public admission). Even more damning, both his lapses from perfection could be attributed to his less than tactful handling of the same infuriating red-headed minx.

In retrospect, it all did seem somewhat shoddy. But he also knew that his feelings now—indeed, almost since the beginning if he just agreed to face facts—were above all things honorable. Not one to beat his breast crying *mea culpa* over unalterable facts, he told his brother (and, incidentally, Isabella, who had not been successful in her bid to blend in with the upholstery), "There is nothing I can say to that, Robin. In any case, my initial reasons no longer apply. You—my heir, should I choose to cock up my toes any time soon—would make an estimable Earl, not to mention being the cause of such transports as to which such an event would send dear Grandmama, so I need have no fears on that head. As for the ability to amuse mine own self, I do believe that the natural melancholy of a bereaved brother somewhat distorted my view of life for a time, and I would have recovered eventually in any event—Samantha or no Samantha.

"So you see, Robin," he continued, striving to exonerate himself of any hint of having married only to serve his own selfish interests, "if I am to be judged guilty of using Samantha to my own advantage, then it must be acknowledged that I have been neatly trumped by your return. Thus, the reasons for my marriage, most happily, no longer apply. I now have my brother, a renewed interest in living and, for good or ill, an impetuous, headstrong, unorthodox bride—who is little more than a baby herself. Surely I have been paid out for my folly," he ended, with a broad wink at Robin.

The young Viscount hadn't lived all his young life with his brother without learning to recognize when Zachary was poking fun at himself. Why, it was as plain as the nose on his face that Zachary was totally besotted with that scapegrace wife of his, and more than apparent that he would gladly let her lead him along in a merry dance for the remainder of their lives.

Zachary, in his turn, knew that Robin had instinctively understood that he was being facetious. He flashed his famed, devilish grin as he reveled in that rare communion of minds he and Robin were fortunate enough to share.

Watching that faintly satanic grin grace a face that had so recently borne the proof of the depth of Samantha's outrage, Isabella admitted to herself that she was living dangerously indeed—contemplating marriage into a family that already boasted a positive demon of a dowager and (as it seemed to her now) had the Devil incarnate for its head. Poor Samantha! For all her beauty and fine spirit, she had not escaped becoming nothing more than a temporary convenience for this enigmatic Earl.

But Robert—Robin, that is—is different, she told herself. He is nothing like the rest of his family.

She peeked up at Robin through her lashes and surreptitiously inspected him for any hidden flaws. Her love-blinded eyes could find nary a one, although even a likable young man such as Robin St. John must have at least a single blemish. But then, love was never known to be an emotion conducive to objective thinking.

Comforting herself with the sure knowledge that in Robin she had found herself a jewel beyond price, Isabella again turned her mind to the plight of—she thought, affectionately—her dear baby sister. She looked over at Royston, engaged now in a deep conversation with Robin, and vowed never to breathe a word to Samantha of what the Earl had said. She must be oh-so-careful never to let anything slip out inadvertently. The poor girl would be totally crushed, as Isabella was well-nigh convinced her sister had a decided tenderness for her supercilious husband.

Isabella might as well not have worried her pretty head about somehow spilling the soup to her sister. Zachary—whose meaningful sniffs, winks, and other miscellaneous clues to his brother would have served to inform Samantha (who was beginning to know her husband's ways at least a little bit) that Zachary's tongue had been firmly stuck in his cheek throughout his entire speech—might conceivably have given up his hope of Heaven to have had Samantha as a witness to his facial histrionics.

For while Isabella was weighing the pros and cons of aligning herself with the Royston family and Zachary was earnestly discussing Napoleon's disastrous retreat from Moscow, they were unaware that Samantha's withdrawal from their company had taken her no farther than the other side of the salon doors, which were slightly ajar.

She had heard every word that had been exchanged after her exit—with only Zachary's vital gestures missing—and had quickly learned to respect Aunt Loretta's recitation of the axiom that eavesdroppers seldom hear good of themselves.

She stood rooted to the floor in the hallway, unable to run even though her every instinct cried out for flight and the preservation of blessed ignorance. By the time Zachary had done with his tongue-in-cheek disclosure (which, in reality, seemed more like a foot-in-mouth disaster), Samantha felt sorely tempted to shove open the salon doors, cry "Aha!" and confront Zachary with what she had heard. She did not succumb to the urge.

She did not because she could not in good conscience dispute what he had told Robin. St. John had been quite above-board with her as to his reasons for wanting the marriage, and it was equally true that those reasons no longer applied.

Now Zachary was stuck with a "baby" of a wife, whose usefulness was a thing of the past.

What a pickle! Wally would probably have said "damn and blast" if he were confronted with a problem of this magnitude.

"Damn, damn, and blast!" Samantha muttered grimly, once in the privacy of her chamber. The words provided her with only a limited amount of relief. Swearing wasn't after all as grand as Wally had it trumped up to be. It was merely another invention designed by men to impress each other with their masculinity and to hold over the heads of the female gender as proof of their more relaxed code of behavior. Frankly, as an aid to relieving her frustrations, it left Samantha totally cold.

Daisy came in to assist her mistress in wriggling out of her breeches and into a nice hot tub, as Samantha—so clearly subdued that Daisy worried that the child might be sickening for something—submitted to the maid's ministrations with an air of resignation most unlike her usual self. When Daisy suggested a supper tray in her chambers and an early night, Samantha meekly agreed, thereby convincing Daisy that she indeed was ailing—and so she informed the Earl when he rapped at the door, only to be denied admittance.

St. John was concerned, but he was not unduly upset. He knew Samantha was incapable of maintaining her anger for any great length of time. By morning she should be mellowed sufficiently for the two of them to cry friends (for St. John really did consider his wife to be his friend, as well as the custodian of his heart), and all would be well all around.

Robin was home; Isabella would make him an admirable wife; and he and Samantha would be free to enjoy London Society until such time as she conceived and they retired for a space to Kent and they began to raise a brace of little St. Johns.

Ah, the Earl mused to himself as his valet helped him into his dressing gown in preparation for an informal meal with Robin in the study—at last I feel free to confess my love to Samantha. With Robin back, and my original motives no longer of any import, she will have to believe I am sincere in my feelings for her. He felt confident he could change her infatuation for him into a love as strong as his for her. Yes, he smiled to himself complacently, suddenly life was very, very good.

So much for the reliability of that sixth sense called the power of perception when it is exercised by the male of the species.

Chapter Eighteen

THEY HAD BEEN three days in Kent, and at last the excitement of Robin's return had begun to abate. Everyone was slowly returning to a more normal existence.

Robin's reunion with his grandmother had been an emotionally fraught scene, with the proud old dame near overcome with joy. After a lengthy session spent weeping into Robin's cravat, she was so mellowed as to embrace Samantha, thanking her profusely for having taken Robin under her wing and only once making reference to the fact that she was even willing to forgive the more bizarre details of that little escapade—details she'd rather forget.

Robin's tenure as an assistant glover was only mentioned as being a "lamentable episode," and then—carrying her new benevolence to quite astonishing lengths—she even embraced Zachary and gifted him by pressing her rouged cheek to his in a gesture of affection.

After settling herself close beside Robin, the dowager snatched up a small dish of comfits from a nearby table, and—keeping her eyes riveted on her younger grandson in a look of slavish adoration—she announced herself ready to be formally introduced to Robin's intended bride.

Oh, yes, she admitted freely, she *had* clapped eyes on the chit once before. She had not, however, taken time to thoroughly inspect her, as she had no idea *both* her grandsons would be picking their brides from the same nest. Isabella, flushing and stammering as she made her curtsy, was cooed over by the dowager as an excellent choice (by that meaning she looked biddable, and no match for a managing grandmother) and the woman even commiserated with the poor child, comparing her to a "pigeon thrown in amongst the hawks."

Patting Isabella's cheek condescendingly, she congratulated the girl for having the good sense to leave her flutterbudget aunt back in London, and promised her own presence as chaperon would strike just the correct moral tone as her sister Samantha—though a Countess in her own right—could not be supposed be exercise any restraining influence if her past behavior was to be used as a guide.

On their second day together, the subject of Robin's trials in the war was at last broached and Robin—ignored in his protest that the tale was no more than a "dull hash"—was forced to explain the events that had led him to Conduit Street.

After Napoleon's dismissal to his island prison, Robin's regiment was sent to Gibraltar to await transportation back to England. In the heat of the summer months, yellow fever broke out among the troops, and the physicians in charge of the small overcrowded hospital—having been given permission to accept fees for treating the affluent Jews and Moors on the Rock—deserted their charges, leaving their care in the hands of drunken orderlies.

Soldiers who had arrived on Gibraltar already weak from wounds received in battle were the first to succumb to the fever, and Robin—sickened at the sight of the sad waste of so many brave young lives—spent all his free time at the hopital tending to his mates.

As corpses began to pile up in the corridors outside the wards, tempers inside the wards ran as high as did the fear of death. One sultry night these fears erupted in a small crowd made up of rioting foot soldiers, all bent on escaping what they felt to be certain death by the simple means of leaving the hospital in a group and commandeering some civilian household for their barracks. Crawling or leaning on crutches, the more badly wounded trailed after their comrades as Robin and a handful of fellow officers tried in vain to stop them.

Robin was talking to a group of the men from his position at the head of some stone steps, frantically appealing to the men to reconsider their plans and not subject innocent townspeople to the chance of infection. He need not have bothered. Just as he held up his hands in one more appeal, a soldier in the crowd hacked at him with his rude crutch, calling for the officer to stand aside, and Robin—unbalanced by the blow—tumbled backwards down the stairs to land heavily on the stone floor below.

When he woke, he was in a side ward, his whole body battered and bruised, having been nearly trampled by the panicky soldiers. His uniform was in tatters, his head ached abominably, and without the ministrations of a fellow calling himself Jack Bratting he might have been in a sad state indeed.

It was the whim of fickle Fate that Robin should become a victim of the fever and Jack Bratting his nurse. During the days of Robin's delirium, Bratting found a letter in Robin's pocket (a letter from Zachary, it was later discovered), the script rendered almost unintelligible by dirt and bloodstains. All that Bratting could decipher was that the letter was addressed to "Dear Ro—" and ended with the words "Your loving brother."

In the mad rush to take passage on the troop ships that had belatedly sailed into the harbor, Bratting was unable to find anyone who knew his young patient. He decided to wait for a later transport, as he was convinced the young soldier would die for sure if he were taken aboard ship.

It was only when Robin regained consciousness that Bratting discovered that amnesia had been brought on by the blow to the young man's head. Months passed as Robin—now Robert, in Bratting's mind—regained his strength, and the pair was able to take ship to London. By then, Napoleon had broken free from his prison and was arriving in Paris, even as Jack Bratting and Robin were sailing into Dover harbor.

Once installed in a small room above the glover shop, Robin was able to regain enough strength to eventually assume a helpful role as Bratting's assistant. In this way, he could at least hope to begin repaying his friend for his kindness, while at the same time his very presence in the shop might lead some customer to recognize him and help him regain his identity.

Bratting was sure, said Robin, that the young man was a

gentleman, and just three months later he was proved right—by Zachary's discovery while confronting his wife's supposed paramour.

His story finally told, Robin was free to accept the ministrations of his adoring grandmother, while laughingly telling Isabella that her claim that he was a hero was "pitching it rather high." Instead, he put all claim to heroism squarely where he felt it belonged: on Jack Bratting's humanitarian shoulders.

At that, Isabella was moved to include Samantha in any list of heroes, a sentiment her sister acknowledged with only a slight inclination of her head before excusing herself to go to her chamber and lie down for a short nap before luncheon.

Isabella's sunny spirits didn't incline her towards any detailed thinking, and she remained oblivious to Samantha's unusual dampness of spirit.

Zachary, however, was painfully aware of a marked friction between his bride and himself since their argument, an argument that Samantha seemed in no great hurry to resolve.

His concern for Samantha was intensified by his sure knowledge that this new, docile Samantha who now lived beneath his roof could only be considered a temporary resident.

At long last St. John was beginning to have a better understanding of the workings of his wife's distressingly volatile mind. He made it a point to keep himself as close to Samantha's side as possible at all times, waiting for the moment when she would take to the countryside in an effort to brighten her melancholy mood.

He didn't have much longer to wait. Samantha was even then upstairs pacing her room, her thoughts a jangle of doubts and vague longings.

It wasn't due to any meanness of spirit that Robin's return had served to upset her so. Oh, no. She was much too tenderhearted a person to find fault in another's good fortune. Robin was safe; Isabella was in alt over their engagement; the dowager was so delighted she had unbent sufficiently to consider all the unhappiness of the past ancient history and had made her peace with Zachary; and

St. John himself no longer felt the lack of either his brother or his once delinquent zest for life.

It was all very well that the situations of all these people had come about so neatly. But, to Samantha's mind, all this good fortune had left her a bit of an encumbrance: a physical reminder of an indulgence of folly on St. John's part that was no longer wanted or needed. Her presence in the Royston household was become superfluous, but what does one do with a Countess who has outstayed her welcome—outlived her usefulness, so to speak?

"Confound it all anyway!" Samantha told the silent room. "He wanted me, now he's stuck with me, for good or ill. He'll just have to reconcile himself to that fact!"

Ah, but I must pity the poor man, she told herself silently—for he could not have known he was saddling himself with a sad trial of a girl who plagued him half out of his mind with hoydenish pranks and infantile mischief, such as her poking fun at Society with outlandish parasols or the daring taking of snuff. She must make him very uncomfortable at times, even though he had made pains to hide his distaste in the past. But now that Samantha was to be released from her position of resident court jester, her husband's patience was sure to diminish in proportion to the increase in his embarrassment.

Knowing she was only compounding the problem, aware that she might even be deliberately instigating a nasty confrontation—and in the end deciding that she didn't really give a tinker's damn either way—she ripped into the drawer of a highboy chest and dragged out Wally's breeches.

From his position behind some artistically clipped shrubbery in the garden, Zachary spied out Samantha's breeches-clad figure as it tiptoed stealthily out the French doors and out onto the crushed stone pathway.

So much for all my lectures on propriety, he mused, not really surprised. I may as well have tried to tame the wind. But, not exactly being a citadel of propriety himself, he mentally shrugged and forgave his bride her lapse, then set off to follow her at a discreet distance. This dogging of Samantha's footsteps was fair bidding to become an everyday occurrence, and he chuckled silently as his eyes ran appreciatively over the delectably outlined *derrière*—one of the original causes of his being brought to this pretty pass—playing Bow Street Runner to his wife's escaping felon in the first place. Ah, Sam, my sweet skipbrain, he asked her silently, could it be you *have* been placed here as punishment for my sins?

He was sorely tempted to call out to her once they had both entered the home woods, but he was curious to see just what maggot she had taken into her head now, that required her present attire to adequately indulge herself in it. His curiosity stayed him, just in time, from calling out her name.

Pushing branches out of his way and watching where he stepped—as he could not risk being spied out on the path and was forced to keep to the woods—St. John reflected yet again on his folly in compromising Samantha into marriage in the first place. He loved her (he now admitted that to himself quite freely), but he had started off their married life on the wrong foot, feeding her that Banbury Tale as he did. Oh, yes, he reminded himself ruefully: there had been more than a little truth in his arguments more's the pity—but had he left it too late for Samantha to forgive him and begin again?

She may have declared her love for him in days past, but her recent behavior had not been in the least like a lover. He could only hope she would not be so cruel as to flaunt her lovers in his face when he was a decrepit old man (as she was so fond of calling him) and she still a beautiful young woman.

Breaking out of the trees to find himself at the edge of a field dotted with the wagons and stalls that declared a country fair to be in progress, St. John came to himself with a start and called a halt to his melancholy musings.

Now where was that termagant? His eyes roamed over the booths in the field, passing by the gaily decorated gypsy-wagons and the freak shows featuring a dwarf and his physical opposite—a great giant of a man who was just then flexing his immense muscles, to the awed amazement of the crowd of farmers, laborers, and village children.

St. John threaded his way past a whirling acrobat, weaved through a small crowd watching a rope dancer displaying his special talents, and neatly dodged a dancing bear that seemed to have designs on the Earl's new curly-brimmed beaver.

"Damn and blast!" he muttered under his breath. "Where in thunder could she have disappeared to now? That girl is enough to plague a man half out of his mind."

He thought he had spied her out standing at one of the booths purchasing a "fairing"—an inexpensive trinket meant to be a remembrance of the day—but lost her again as two young lads of no more than ten fell into fighting with each other, rolling about on the grass as a crowd gathered around them. Instead of separating the boys, the crowd busied itself making a ring around them and began laying bets on the eventual winner. By the time St. John could get past, Samantha was once more out of sight.

His breath hissed audibly between his teeth as he cursed his ill luck, and he tipped his hat back on his head as he searched the blue sky above him—as if he were seeking heavenly assistance.

His wish was granted, for as he raised his eyes he could see far off at the edge of the fair, a huge red and white checked *balloon*! A smile dissolved his hitherto solemn expression as he clapped one hand to his hat, and—showing none of the dignity that should by rights have gone with his modish dress (now sadly sprinkled with leaves, twigs, and other debris)—he loped off towards the balloon and (he was sure) his own dear Samantha.

She was just then engaged in her first close inspection of a real balloon gondola, and was therefore startled into giving a slight squeal of alarm as a hand came down heavily on her shoulders. "Planning an excursion into the skies, Mr. Smythe-Wright?" Zachary's voice asked silkily, a trace of humor in his tone.

Her initial nervousness fled as she whirled from his grasp and turned to confront her tormentor. "Spying *again*, Zachary? And now you are going to read me yet another of your famous scolds, I have no doubt. Well, go on. Get it over with," she challenged him heatedly.

But Samantha's beautiful face—made even more appealing by the heightened color her indignation lent her—framed as it was now by her beaver hat and high shirt points, only served to cause Zachary to lapse even more deeply into a rollicking mood.

"Please credit me with more elegance of mind than to berate you in public, my dear," he teased her gently. "I have only approached you here so that we may at last speak together with some modicum of privacy. I may be abominably slow about some things—a side-effect of my advanced years, no doubt—but I am confused as to why you have been avoiding me these last days."

"Your mind must be failing if you cannot recall a certain blow to the cheek you received at my hand," Samantha rebutted. "Perhaps the shock of it addled your wits, but if you so wish your memory refreshed I can repeat the exercise."

St. John lifted his hand and rubbed at his cheek. "I am not such a zany as to have forgotten the incident, or so arrogant as to claim it was not deserved. But, having got your revenge, Samantha, surely you are satisfied? It is not like you to hold a grudge."

It was time and enough she told him she had overheard the conversation with Robin that had taken place after they believed her out of earshot and she did so now, not sparing herself in the recital.

"So that rankled, did it?" St. John gibed at her, and then added, "I did not mean a word of it, infant. I was merely having Robin on, as has been our custom whenever we are together. Robin didn't believe a word of it, of course, and neither would you if you could have seen as well as heard our interchange. Poor puss," he ended softly. "All this suffering for no good reason."

"I did not weep millstones, if that's any comfort to you," she returned, her chin thrust out aggressively.

Zachary was looking down at her in such a self-satisfied way—the sight of the tears shining in her eyes providing him final proof that she did care for him at least a little bit. Before Samantha's anger could cause her to say something that might take them off on another tangent, he told her sweetly, "I love you, you know, infant. Quite to distraction, actually."

Samantha's moist eyes became quite dazed with sudden bliss as she gave back an incoherent answer and launched herself at her husband.

He lifted her in his arms, and they spun crazily in a circle until he had the happy notion of dumping her into the gondola.

"Idiot!" she spluttered from her ignominious position on the floor of the basket. "You have gone stark, staring mad!"

Vaulting gracefully over the rim to join his wife inside the basket, Zachary busily began loosing the moorings holding the balloon to the ground.

When Samantha protested (quite vocally, actually), he merely turned to her and quipped, "You must have the poorest opinion of me, not to believe I can navigate this thing. Have you no desire to go sailing with me in the sky on such a glorious day?"

Samantha's ready sense of adventure (not to mention her love of the ridiculous) came to the fore, and she sprang up to help him with the ropes, telling him, "I am not such a zany as to believe the Devil incapable of anything. But we must be quick about it, dearest, as some rather large men are fast approaching, and I don't think they appreciate us, er, *borrowing* their balloon."

The men Samantha had seen—certainly the owners of the balloon—were most predictably *not* pleased at the sight of their property rising slowly out of reach. As they vainly jumped in the air to try to grab at the trailing ropes, Zachary and Samantha bid them a cheery *adieu* and waved at the gathering crowd.

The balloon soared above the treetops, and with the aid of a friendly breeze was soon sailing across the countryside as a delighted Samantha squealed and clapped her hands in delight.

"*Wheee!*" she shouted, as she threw her arms wide. "Look at me! I'm flying!"

Zachary hastily restrained her flailing arms and caught her up in his embrace. Her last barriers crumbled at his touch, and they sank together to the cushiony, woven floor of the gondola in a heated embrace.

Just as things were getting just a bit out of hand, Samantha pulled back to ask if Zachary was bothered overmuch by her penchant for setting the *ton* on its ears, via her parasols and the like. Now that she knew he loved her, she was anxious to ascertain whether or not he *liked* her as well.

He quickly denied any discomfit at her shenanigans—between playful nibbles at her ear, that is—and told her that her very unpredictability was a major part of her charm.

"That's good," she sighed, as his lips descended to wreak havoc with the pulse at the base of her throat. All her earlier thoughts of becoming a model young matron were thus summarily dashed without a smidgen of regret. "But I *am* weary of parasols, Zachary. Snuff, too, for that matter. I have all but decided to start sporting a walking stick."

"*Umm?*" Zachary returned vaguely, his mind not really on the subject. "What sort of stick, love?" he asked at last.

Samantha launched immediately into a description of various sticks she had seen, and was just telling him of one such remarkable stick that had a hidden recess for keeping money or other valuables, when Zachary was forced to interrupt her.

"Later, my pet," he whispered hoarsely. "We will talk of this later." He blazed a trail with his lips in the direction of her mouth, and just before claiming his prize said once again, "*Much* later."

As the setting sun glinted off the red and white silk of the large balloon that had mysteriously appeared in the middle of Seth Brumbley's barley field, and the gathering crowd of villagers *oohed* and *aahed* while trying to figure out just how it had got there in the first place, a pair of slightly disheveled looking gentlemen were settling into their room at a local inn. The pair had been oblivious to the curious looks and open stares of the patrons drinking ale in the common room as they mounted the stairs arm in arm.

And, indeed, what concern could it possibly be to others

as to the time and place a couple picks as the perfect spot to spend their belated honeymoon?

After all, it was only the mutual inclination of the couple involved that mattered—wasn't it?

This is the special design logo that will call your attention to new Avon authors who show exceptional promise in the romance area. Each month a new novel—either historical or contemporary—will be featured.

CAPTIVE OF THE HEART

Kate Douglas — October 1982

Set in the American Southwest in the mid-19th century, this big, romantic novel is about a courageous white girl who has chosen to live with the Comanches, and the young chieftain who falls in love with her.
81125-1/$2.75

DEFIANT DESTINY

Nancy Moulton — November 1982

While on a dangerous sea voyage to deliver secret information to the rebellious colonies a young English beauty is captured by a notorious American privateer who soon captures her heart as well.
81430-7/$2.95

LOVE'S CHOICE

Rosie Thomas — December 1982

A lovely newspaper reporter finds herself torn between her desire to remain independent, and love, when she is caught in a passion for two different men. They are rival winemakers, and as Bell tries to decide between them—a debonaire, aristocratic Frenchman and a warm, vibrant Californian—a dangerous competition for her love arises.
61713-7/$2.95

Avon Paperbacks

Available wherever paperbacks are sold, or directly from the publisher. Include 50¢ per copy for postage and handling: allow 6-8 weeks for delivery. Avon Books, Mail Order Dept., 224 West 57th St., N.Y., N.Y. 10019.

Avon Romance 10-82